Wordsmith: Th

CW01512952

The fast-paced fantasy sequel t   ng
author of the smash hit romantic co   ____ *Sides* and its
sequels *Love... And Sleepless Nights* & *Love... Under Different Skies.*

From the pages of the past, a new threat to Max Bloom rises in The Chapter Lands...

A year after his life became a lot less boring (and a lot more dangerous, if he's being honest) Max Bloom finds himself the unwanted centre of attention at the spectacular Chapter Lands Wordmeet, a magical competition laid on in his honour - whether he likes it or not. This unfortunately means having to wear an uncomfortable suit and talk politely to other people; two things that Max does not excel at.

Events take a grave turn however, when the Wordmeet is gate-crashed by a man with murder in his heart and revenge on his mind. He kills an innocent boy and threatens Merelie's life before Max manages to intervene.

Who is this interloper? What does he want? Why is he so intent on killing? Only The Cornerstone can provide the answers, and on its pages it reveals a single name... *Venhaligan.*

So begins the hunt for a murderous ghost from the past with connections to The Cornerstone, and inexplicably to Max's family.

From the strange and magical Chapter Lands, to the familiar surroundings of Farefield, Max must pursue this madman across dimensions using The Cornerstone. He must prevent more innocent people getting hurt, as well as uncover the truth about his past before it kills him.

Wordsmith... The Cornerstone Book 2 continues the thrilling story of Max Bloom's adventures in The Chapter Lands - with twists, turns and excitement throughout!

Wordsmith: The Cornerstone Book 2
Nick Spalding

Racket Publishing

Contents

Part One

- Before -

It was, without a shadow of a doubt, the perfect day to open a library.

A warm, sunny spring afternoon - it was the kind of day to put a smile on the face of the most hard hearted of men.

Ernest Brooks, the Mayor of Farefield, was not a hard hearted man, so the grin he beamed at all and sundry was broader than Norfolk.

This was a very proud moment for the portly Mayor. The opening of Farefield library was something he'd championed through the council for the past four years, and to be here on this glorious day to rub the collective noses of the naysayers in the dirt was a thing to be savoured.

He stood on a plinth (only slightly reinforced to cope with his girth), a microphone in front of him, and a large semi-circle of people all looking up to him and expecting a decent speech.

He wasn't about to let them down.

'Good afternoon, ladies and gentlemen. Thank you all for coming to the opening of this brand new library!' This was greeted with some cursory clapping. 'I am pleased to be here, along with Frank Potherington, our new head librarian,' Ernest said, putting his hand out to indicate a small, bespectacled man standing next to him, 'to officially open the new library, built to benefit all the citizens of this wonderful town.'

This brought a couple of snorts of derision from the crowd. Farefield was far too boring to be described as wonderful, unless you were either drunk or mentally unstable. You'd have to prepare yourself, and take a good long run up, just to convincingly describe it as average.

'As we head towards a new decade,' Ernest continued, 'Farefield is growing all the time, and is fast becoming a jewel of the south coast!'

The snorts got louder.

'To reflect this, our new library is chock full of the kind of brand new technology that will see us well into the nineties and beyond! It will be staffed by dedicated individuals, determined to provide a swift and efficient librarian service to all who use this modern facility.' Ernest was particularly pleased with that last sentence. He felt it was thrusting - and quite uplifting into the bargain.

'And so, without further ado... ' He held out his hand to a waspish looking woman in tweed standing to his right. She handed over a pair of gigantic scissors. Ernest turned to a large red ribbon strung across the library entrance. A couple of bored photographers stepped forward as he posed with the scissors hovering over the ribbon. The smile on his face threatened to engulf his eyeballs.

To the accompaniment of flash bulbs, the Mayor brought the scissors together, and Farefield library - a place that would remain in a largely decent condition, until the night twenty eight years later when Imelda Warrington and Merelie Carvallen would destroy it trying to defeat a Dweller – was officially open to the public.

Frank Potherington (real name Farran Witherbed, and fourth generation Wordsmith under Chapter House Carvallen) trailed along behind Ernest Brooks as he toured the new library. He was quite happy to put up with all this pointless ceremony, safe in the knowledge that he had at last found somewhere permanent to keep The Cornerstone.

He'd been its guardian on Earth for some five years now and had worked in almost every library in the area, making sure the remarkable book always had a place to rest and recharge.

He'd applied for head librarian at this new library knowing that getting the job would mean an end to being constantly shuffled around by his superiors. Head librarians tended to stay in one place for a long time, and Frank was looking forward to putting his feet up for a while and letting The Cornerstone collect some dust on a shelf somewhere quiet and out of the way.

'Where are those micky fish things, Frank?' Ernest Brooks asked as he made his way along the science fiction aisle, a gaggle of council toadies, reporters and library staff following behind.

'You mean the microfiche, sir?'

'Yes, yes, that's what I meant.'

'Over here, sir.' Frank pointed to a row of large black objects sat on sturdy desks along one wall. Frank had been hoping to get at least one Apple Mackintosh computer installed, but the bean counters had strenuously objected, given the cost of such a brand new piece of technology.

'Ah yes. They look lovely,' Ernest said and walked straight past the machines without a second glance. While he was keen on the idea of technology thrusting Farefield into the next century, he didn't actually give a tinker's cuss about the practicalities.

'I need to take a book out Frank,' he said under his breath. 'I must be the first one to do it. It'll look good for the cameras.'

'Certainly sir. What kind of thing would you like?'

Ernest waved a hand. 'Something classic. Personally I'd rather get tucked into a Freddie Forsythe, but let's find a book that's a bit more cerebral for the cameras, eh?'

'Right this way sir,' Frank replied, leading the Mayor to the classic fiction section.

Ernest made a show of looking through the collection on offer for a few minutes. It gave him time to think about what to buy Mildred for her birthday. He then randomly selected an old book that seemed to fit the bill.

Frank's eyes went wide with horror as the Mayor pulled out the dark green book from the stack and looked at the cover.

'What the hell is The Cornerstone Frank? I've never heard of the bugger. Is it something to do with the Freemasons?'

'Er... probably not your kind of thing, Mister Mayor!' Frank said, pulling the book from Ernest's chubby fingers and deftly replacing it with a copy of Bleak House. 'This should be more to your liking.'

'A ha! Dickens. That fits the bill.'

Frank breathed a deep sigh of relief and slotted The Cornerstone back into the shelf. Things could have become very awkward if Brooks had cracked the cover. The opening of this library wasn't likely to make the front pages, but the Mayor being transported to another dimension definitely would.

The rest of Farefield library's first day went off without a hitch. Ernest Brooks left safe in the knowledge his re-election campaign was off to a flying start, the press had a nice local community piece to be buried on page twelve, and several local residents had enjoyed being the first to browse the library stacks.

By closing time at 5.30pm, a total of sixty two books had been taken out (along with the Dickens, Brooks had eventually settled on A Clockwork Orange – a decision he would later come to wholeheartedly regret) and Frank was pleased with his day's work, locking the front doors with a contented smile.

The smile dropped off his face quicker than the trim on a French sports car when The Cornerstone started to scream like a pig being molested with an egg whisk.

Frank rushed over to where the book was now ricocheting from one stack to the other, sending out bright flashes of silver light across the newly painted beige library walls.

Anyone who's tried to catch a daddy long legs when it's been trapped in your bedroom would recognise Frank's frantic grasping hands and hunched posture as he gamely tried to retrieve the caterwauling book before people walking past the building noticed the light display going on inside.

Frank was only able to grab the book when it bounced its way into a section of shelving that hadn't been filled yet. He covered the whole opening with his chest, wincing a couple of times as the book hit him hard enough to leave a nasty bruise, and let out a huge sigh of relief as he took hold of it with one firm hand.

Backing down the aisle, the Wordsmith tried his hardest to stop the book's cover flying open again. It shook violently in his hands as Frank headed towards the staff room, where he could at least confine the loud wailing and lightning to one room. The Cornerstone was having none of it though, and started to heat up in his hands at an alarming rate. Frank tried his best to keep hold of the thing but it became burning hot and he had to drop it.

The second the spine hit the floor, the book flew open and blinding silver light filled the entire library.

A hand, blazing with silver fire, rose from the open Cornerstone, clutching at the air as if desperate for someone to take it. Frank stepped forward, his own hand out. As he caught hold of the other, searing fire licked its way up his arm, forcing a cry from his lips.

Frank held his burned hand close to his chest and backed away as The Cornerstone screamed its loudest, shuddered violently, and spat a shape into the world from the swirling vortex between its pages. A boy of no more than fourteen shot out of the book and into the library, narrowly avoiding a nasty concussion on a nearby heavy wooden bookshelf as he fell to the floor.

The instant he hit the thin corduroy floor tiles, The Cornerstone snapped shut again, becoming still and silent at last.

Frank looked from its smoking cover to the bedraggled boy beside it. 'What in the Writer's name is going on?' he said. 'Why have you crossed the void? Why did The Cornerstone let you through?' Frank approached the boy. '*Who are you?*'

The boy's head snapped around, looking everywhere. 'Where am I?'

'On Earth lad… and you shouldn't bloody be here!'

Frank gave the boy's face a closer look now his vision had stopped blurring. His expression darkened several degrees. 'Wait a minute. I know you. You're Xander Florren's boy, aren't you? Petren Florren?'

The boy looked at Frank gravely. 'My father is dead,' he said in a dull voice. 'All my family are dead. Please help me.'

Petren Florren's eyes rolled into his head and he collapsed in a dead faint.

-1-

When you have a dog with a cold wet nose, you don't really need an alarm clock. Max let out his customary yelp as Nugget's nose touched the back of his neck.

No matter how many times he tried to convince the Labrador that his bedroom was off limits, Nugget still entered Max's room at eight thirty every morning and woke him with either a friendly poke of his nose, or on the days when Max simply refused to get up, with a long wet lick across the cheek with his coarse tongue.

'Alright I'm awake!' Max wailed as he sat up and rubbed the sleep dust out of his eyes.

Nugget sat and regarded him with suspicion. He'd heard this line before, and had left the room, only to have to come back five minutes later to apply the cold nose of doom again when Max had buried himself back under the covers. Nugget wasn't budging until he was properly up and about.

Max's journey into wakefulness was helped by the smell of frying bacon coming from downstairs. 'Grandad's cooking bacon is he?' he asked the dog.

Nugget wagged his tail enthusiastically. Max's Grandad invariably cooked way too much bacon when he set about it – at least eight rashers per person usually – so Nugget always got an unhealthy amount of leftovers. Max got up, and with a zombie-like shuffle made his way out of his bedroom and downstairs, the smell of frying food propelling him forward to a cholesterol packed start to the day.

Max had been living with Charlie Pearce for a year now. As far as his parents were concerned this was because Charlie had been feeling lonely recently and in need of more human companionship. The real reason was so Max didn't have that far to travel when he needed to access The Cornerstone. It meant he could keep a watchful eye on it when it wasn't being used as well. Amanda Bloom had objected to the move for a couple of weeks, before her father and her husband had both convinced her it was a good idea. Max was somewhat annoyed that his opinion didn't appear to count for much in the decision, despite the fact that he'd recently turned eighteen and was now an adult in the eyes of the law.

In the eyes of the mother though he was still a little boy, and there had been tears and arguments aplenty before she eventually caved in and let him go.

'Morning Maxwell,' Charlie said as he prodded at the pound of bacon sizzling in the pan. 'Once more my faithful hound has awakened you from your slumber, I see.'

'Yeah.' Max glared at Nugget. 'I'm tempted to Wordcraft him out the door when he sticks his nose against my neck like that.'

Nugget, knowing full well this was the emptiest of threats, ignored Max and plonked himself down beside Charlie, an expectant look on his face.

'Now, now Maxwell. I would imagine Merelie and Imelda would be horrified to even hear you contemplate such a thing.'

Max groaned and bit into a piece of toast he'd liberated from the large pile on the kitchen table. 'What's the point in being a flippin' Wordsmith if you can't have some fun with it?'

Charlie pointed the fat laden spatula at Max. 'You know how much trouble it causes when you unleash your talents, young man. I still get funny looks from the local policeman every time I walk past.'

'That was a year ago, Grandad.'

'Yes, but I fear it may take longer for them to forget about exploding garages and imploding libraries than that.'

'Fair point,' Max conceded and scratched his head, disturbing the chaotic mess of bed hair.

'You really should have got that cut, Maxwell. You have a big day today and it would have behoved you to look your smartest.'

Max groaned again as he remembered what was happening later.

The Carvallen Chapter House was holding its annual magical Wordmeet competition and Max was to be the guest of honour at the grand morning ball happening in the Great Hall of the House. This would then be followed by an afternoon tournament, where Wordsmiths from all five Chapter Houses would get to show off their skills to one another, and the enormous crowd of spectators. The last Wordmeet had been cancelled, thanks to all that bother with the Dwellers, so the people of the Carvallen Chapter Lands were determined that this year's event would be a blowout of epic proportions.

This required Max to dress in a suit.

Oh, the horror.

Max Bloom had worn a suit on three occasions in his life: his grandmother's funeral, a cousin's wedding, and a particularly strange job interview for a paper round, conducted by a man who took his work far too seriously.

For the Wordmeet, he'd begged and pleaded to be allowed to wear his daily hoodie and jeans combo, but Emerelda Carvallen, the ex-librarian of Farefield library - and regular pain in the neck as far as Max was concerned - had stared at him in no uncertain terms until he went away, resigned to wearing the monkey suit.

For a second he'd considered using his ridiculously powerful Wordsmith skills to get him out of the whole thing, but decided it was probably a gross abuse of his abilities to use them to avoid a morning with an uncomfortable neckline.

His dread at the potential discomfort ahead of him was mitigated somewhat when Merelie had actually shown him the suit he was expected to wear. Tailored in the Carvallen style and deep green in colour, it featured a rather cool three quarter length coat. Max had to admit there was a definite Keanu Reeves in The Matrix vibe to the get up.

Looking sharp didn't make the prospect of being stared at by the great and the good of The Chapter Lands any less daunting though. Merelie had warned him that the Wordmeet tended to be an occasion when the rich and successful of Carvallen's upper class enjoyed showing their peers just how rich and successful they truly were. Cozying up to the most powerful Wordsmith in history would be a *fantastic* way to improve their social standing. Max didn't quite know how long he'd be able to handle a constant stream of brown nosing rich people, but he could take an educated guess of about three minutes.

It wasn't all bad though. Wordmeets were also occasions when Wordsmiths could show off their skills in battle with one another. These battles were strictly regulated of course, but they were an exciting spectator sport nevertheless. Max was rather looking forward to watching a bunch of Wordsmiths blowing each other six ways from Sunday, and was very glad he'd have a good seat thanks to his fame. The only downside was that he'd been banned from participating himself by Jacob Carvallen.

'It would be best,' Jacob had said, 'if you sat out Max. I don't think the collective egos of our Wordsmith community could take the inevitable thrashing you'd give them.'

Max had wanted to argue, but had to grudgingly concede the point. Getting into a fight – even a carefully restricted one – when you know you're going to win kind of takes the fun away.

'Here you go, young man,' Charlie said, depositing a small mountain of crispy bacon topped off with two fried eggs in front of Max. 'Eat up. You'll no doubt need your strength today, dealing with all those important people.'

'You sure you won't consider coming Grandad?'

'Oh good gracious no. I can't think of a worse way to spend one's time than hob-nobbing with the nobs, even if the shindig is in another dimension.'

'But it'd be the perfect excuse to cross over and see The Chapter Lands.'

'I told you young man, this dimension of existence is more than enough for this old man and his portly canine companion. I'll leave the jaunting across realities to younger, more excitable individuals such as yourself.'

'Fair enough,' Max said and forked a bit of bacon into his mouth. He chewed slowly and looked across the kitchen into the front room, his gaze resting on The Cornerstone where it sat on one of the bookshelves, next to Call Of The Wild. In the past year Max had used the remarkable book to traverse realities on an almost daily basis, but he hadn't felt as nervous about the trip as he did today since he had crossed the void to meet Merelie Carvallen for the first time.

Charlie caught sight of his grandson's expression. 'Fear not Maxwell, I'm sure Merelie will guide you through the day.'

The face of the beautiful girl who had dragged Max into The Chapter Lands swam through his mind, and he felt himself relax a bit. A small smile also crept across his face. This usually happened when Max thought about Merelie these days. Their relationship had developed nicely over the past several months from that first awkward kiss in the Great Library after the Dwellers had been defeated. The kisses were no longer awkward these days. In fact, Max felt himself to be something of an expert at them now, given all the practise he was getting lately. He desperately hoped to move on to other more exciting things very soon, to see how quickly he could become an expert at them too.

'You're dribbling egg yolk onto the table cloth, my boy,' Charlie remarked, one eyebrow arched.

'Sorry Grandad.'

-2-

Half an hour, and a refreshing shower later, a well scrubbed Max Bloom stood looking in the bedroom mirror at the smart eighteen year old looking back at him.

He had to admit he looked pretty sharp. Nugget, from his vantage point on Max's bed, woofed and wagged his tail in apparent agreement.

'Right then, I suppose I'd better get going,' Max said to his own reflection, but didn't budge off the spot. Nugget barked louder. 'Yeah, yeah. I know... I'm going.'

He opened the bedroom door and walked downstairs at the slowest pace he could muster. Half way down he heard his grandfather shout up to him. 'Come on Maxwell! Imelda – or whatever name she calls herself by these days – told you to be there by ten o'clock... and it's five past!'

Max made a face and sped up a bit.

In the front room Charlie was holding out The Cornerstone, which emanated its usual cheerful silver glow, indicating it was fully charged and ready to rock and roll.

Max took the book. His face crumpled. 'What if I do something embarrassing Grandad? What if someone asks me something important and I come out with a stupid answer? What if I insult someone? I'll be a sodding laughing stock.'

'Just follow Miss Carvallen's lead and think before you speak, Maxwell.' A sly grin crossed Charlie's face. 'If all else fails just flick a finger and make them disappear.'

Max gave his grandfather a withering look. 'It doesn't work like that, Grandad.'

Charlie laughed and sat himself in the ratty armchair next to the book shelf. 'Nevertheless. I wouldn't worry too much, my boy. Your reputation precedes you, so I'm sure they'll be just as nervous around you as you are with them.'

'Let's bloody hope so,' Max replied and opened The Cornerstone.

'I expect a full report on your return!' Charlie said enthusiastically. Max groaned and looked down at the open page.

Charlie laughed and sat himself in the ratty armchair next to the book shelf. 'Nevertheless. I wouldn't worry too much, my boy. Your reputation precedes you, so I'm sure they'll be just as nervous around you as you are with them.'

'Let's bloody hope so,' Max replied and opened The Cornerstone.

'I expect a full report on your return!' Charlie said enthusiastically. Max groaned and looked down at the open page.

Bright silver waves of light erupted from The Cornerstone and enveloped Max's entire body. One moment he was stood in Charlie's front room, the next he was catapulted across the void to emerge in The Chapter Lands, his surrogate home of the past year.

Max materialised in the chamber set at the heart of the Great Library that acted as home to The Cornerstone.

'You're late, Mr Bloom,' said a voice that was clipped, clear and full of barely concealed irritation.

'Had problems getting this stupid jacket on,' Max said to Emerelda Carvallen, yanking at one lapel for added emphasis.

'Really? You can rip the tops off mountains with your Wordcraft, but you can't work out how to put on a suit?' Emerelda's eyebrow arched to such a degree it looked quite painful.

'Where's Merelie?' Max said, changing the subject to something more healthy.

'Still getting ready herself.' Emerelda shook her head. 'I don't know, the two of you are as bad as one another. You're adults now, I shouldn't have to keep following you around like a nursemaid.'

Max smiled. 'You're in a good mood this morning.'

'I have a lot on my mind. Jacob's insistence I play a large part in the organisation of the Wordmeet has aged me ten years.'

Max actually thought being back here in The Chapter Lands for a year had made Emerelda look ten years younger, but he kept that one to himself. 'You shouldn't have told him what you had to do in the job back at the library in Farefield then,' he said. 'The second he knew you were good at admin you were doomed.'

'Yes, well, we live and learn don't we?' Emerelda's eyes narrowed. 'Anyway, stop changing the subject Max. You're late and I'm not happy about it.' She turned swiftly on one heel and left The Cornerstone's chamber, heading up the aisle of the Great Library.

Max heaved a rather melodramatic sigh, tipped a wink to The Cornerstone and followed Emerelda out of the chamber.

Garrowain, the head custodian of the Carvallen Great Library, was waiting for Max and Emerelda in the Codex chamber. The tiny old man beamed as he saw them both enter. 'Good morning Max. I trust you're looking forward to today's merriments?'

'Not particularly. From the sounds of things I'm going to be the main attraction. I feel like a zoo animal.'

'I'm sure it won't be that bad!'

'No? Are you coming to the ball then?'

'Oh dear me no! I can't think of anything worse than a morning spent with those people. I will be at this afternoon's tournament though. Bevens, one of my youngest custodians, has entered and I'm anxious to see how well he fares.'

'Brilliant,' Max replied in a tone of voice that indicated it was anything but.

With shoulders now in the legendary slumped position, the young Wordsmith sloped past Garrowain in reluctant pursuit of Emerelda Carvallen, who had already left the library and was on her way to the upper floors of the Chapter House.

The halls and corridors of the huge building were bustling today. Servants trotted along with food laden plates, other members of the household staff hurried with definite purpose on a variety of errands, all of them no doubt very excited to be part of the annual Wordmeet. Max also noticed a few Wordsmiths in the throng dressed in their long coats, and by the crests emblazoned on them, not all were from Carvallen. At least two wore golden Morodai coats, and he saw a third bearing the blue of household Draveli. He'd been surprised when Jacob Carvallen had agreed to let the two Houses compete in the Wordmeet, given how much trouble they'd caused last year. Both Houses had kept their noses clean recently, it had to be said, and a tight leash was being kept on their new leaders by the other three Houses. Max was still deeply suspicious of both though, and really didn't like seeing their colours in the heart of his Chapter House.

He came to an abrupt halt.

Since when did I start thinking of it as my Chapter House?

Only a year ago this place had been strange and alien to him. It felt bizarre to now think of it as somewhere familiar. He had to concede it also gave him a certain amount of pleasure to think of himself as a member of the Carvallen Chapter House. There was a sense of belonging in this world that he'd never felt on the other side of The Cornerstone in Farefield.

'Max Bloom! The guests are waiting! Shift your lazy behind!' Emerelda almost screamed at him over the heads of the passing people.

Max winced and started walking again. Having a sense of belonging was all well and good, but it did have its drawbacks.

'Are we going straight there?' he asked Emerelda as they reached the enormous staircase with the tapestry of The Chapter Lands hanging over it.

'No. We're going to gather up Merelie first. She'd be many different shades of unhappy if I didn't let the two of you go in together.'

The look of relief on Max's face was palpable.

Emerelda noticed this and tutted. 'If you two spent as much time on your Wordcraft studies as you do on thinking about one another, you'd both be the greatest Wordsmiths in history.'

'I thought I already was?'

'You're the most *powerful* Wordsmith, Max. Not the *greatest*. There's a big difference.'

Max resisted the temptation to make a face that would have got him into even more trouble, and moved ahead of Emerelda towards Merelie's chambers. For some reason his heart had started to hammer in his chest. He'd been in Merelie's private chambers many times now and their relationship had moved way past those embarrassing first few months, but today for some reason he felt unexpectedly excited about seeing the girl who had become his best friend and probably the most important person in his life.

It's the Wordmeet, he thought. *It's a big day for both of you and it's making you nervous. Chill out, you idiot. Be cool.*

He knocked on Merelie's door and waited patiently.

The door swung open and Max's jaw hit the floor.

It wasn't necessarily the outfit Merelie was wearing (though it was exceedingly pretty) it was more the way she wore it - with an absolute grace and elegance that made Max feel even more self-conscious in his stiff collar and pressed trousers.

Merelie rarely wore a dress, so the effect was multiplied.

It was a glorious jade green, a much lighter shade than the one Max wore. Like all Carvallen clothing it was simple. These weren't a demonstrative people. It was a strappy, off the shoulder number with no garish highlights, but as far as Max was concerned it was *perfect*. It clung in all the right places and showed off Merelie's figure just enough to guarantee he wouldn't be able to think straight the entire time she was in it. Her honey blonde hair was partly held up by a series of cunningly concealed hair grips, with one long tress tumbling down over her left shoulder.

'Gah,' he said.

'Do I look alright?' Merelie asked, knowing the answer already.

'Duh,' he exclaimed.

'Max?'

'Urm,' he remarked.

'You look lovely Merelie,' Emerelda said with a smile. This rapidly fell off her face when she looked up at the clock on Merelie's wall. 'And late! Really bloody late! Your mother and father will be having kittens.'

'Sorry Emmy.' Merelie ran both hands down her sides. 'Getting the line of this dress right has been a nightmare.'

At this point Max Bloom's already over stimulated brain shut down completely in an attempt at self preservation. Merelie noticed the expression on his face and allowed herself a fleeting smile. 'Morning Max,' she said and kissed him lightly on the mouth.

'Stop playing with the poor lad, girl. It's not a fair fight,' Emerelda said. 'We have to go!'

Merelie took one of Max's limp hands and led him out along the hallway, being careful not to let him bump into any of the furniture.

-3-

The Great Hall of Carvallen Chapterhouse certainly lived up to its name today.

Every inch of it had been cleaned and polished to such an extent that even the biggest germaphobe would eat their dinner off it.

The ranks of seats that usually ringed the hall had been removed to allow ball guests more room for manoeuvre, and several enormous chandeliers had been strung from the buttresses that criss-crossed the roof around the high central glass dome. The chandeliers were purely ornamental, given the amount of crisp daylight let in through the dome's clear glass panels. After the Hall had been virtually destroyed by the Dwellers, great care and expense had been taken in designing and building an even more impressive space for entertaining and matters of state.

Hundreds of people, all dressed in their finest get-up, filled the hall from one end to the other. There was a stage set up on one side, where a band played the kind of suitable background music that wouldn't interrupt anyone's conversational flow. A few of the braver guests were dancing to the music in the centre of the hall, in an area usually occupied by the emerald green Carvallen round table where Jacob conducted his public meetings.

A serried rank of bookshelves encircled the entire hall – a new addition suggested by Garrowain that ensured the power of words was always present, even in this high place.

There was a particularly dense section of crowd to the left of the stage, where Jacob Carvallen stood with his wife Halia. It was evident that the desire to remain in close proximity to the seat of power was too hard to resist for the great and the good of The Chapter Lands.

All of this was completely lost on Max Bloom, who – try as hard as he might – could not get the vision of Merelie running her hands down the silky green dress she wore out of his head.

All three of them entered through one set of giant double doors. Emerelda paused and whispered something to a gaudily dressed man stood by the door, who turned towards the crowd of people and briefly whispered under his breath.

Max felt a small surge of Wordcraft.

'Ladies and gentleman,' the man said. His voice was low, but carried across the whole hall, augmented by word power. Max thought it was a neat trick and resolved to use it himself one day. 'Ladies and gentlemen,' the man repeated, getting everyone's attention.

Max realised what was about to happen and suddenly wished he'd brought a change of underwear.

'May I first introduce Lady Emerelda of House Carvallen, honoured sister and Wordsmith.' There was a polite smattering of applause. Emerelda gave the crowd a curt smile and strode to where her brother Jacob stood.

'And secondly,' the announcer continued, 'may I introduce Lady Merelie of House Carvallen, beloved daughter and Wordsmith.' The applause was much louder this time. Merelie was highly regarded by all. She provided a heart stopping curtsey to all assembled and swished her way across the floor, fully aware that all eyes were on her, especially Max Bloom's.

The announcer cleared his throat as Merelie reached her father and gave him a kiss.

Max's heart plummeted.

'And now,' the announcer said, his voice much louder. 'It gives me the *greatest* of pleasure to introduce - '

'Don't you dare call me *Lord Max*, pal. I'll turn you into a frog.'

The announcer gave Max a look of perplexed horror. 'Er…' he hesitated, voice still carrying to everyone. Max could see Merelie trying very hard not to laugh.

'Just say my name and where I come from mate,' Max said through gritted teeth. 'Keep it nice and simple.'

'Very well sir,' the man agreed and turned back to the crowd. 'As I was saying… may I introduce, um… Max Bloom, the Wordsmith from Earth!'

The applause this time was thunderous, sparking off a tension headache in Max's forehead.

Gritting his teeth again, and not for the first time wishing he'd never clapped eyes on The Cornerstone, he walked across the hall floor, trying very hard to ignore the awe-struck looks being directed at him from several hundred party guests.

As he got closer to Merelie he could see a look of sympathy appear on her face. She'd been round Max long enough now to know that this kind of thing was torture for him. As he reached her, she took his hand in hers. 'You're doing very well,' she said.

'Thanks. I did threaten to turn the announcer bloke into a frog.'

'Understandable in the circumstances.'

'Good morning Max,' said Jacob Carvallen, nodding his head.

'Good morning sir,' Max replied. Despite having enough power to dissemble the Chapter House to its constituent parts if he wanted to, Max was still nervous around the head of the household. This was partly due to Jacob's authoritarian demeanour, and partly due to the fact Max was dating his daughter. There had been a particularly excruciating incident a couple of weeks ago when Jacob had caught them snogging in one of the picturesque Chapter House courtyards. He hadn't actually said anything to them, just walked past and frowned. That was enough to put paid to that morning's session of kissing and fumbling though.

'You look very handsome Max,' Halia beamed from her husband's side. 'I knew that suit would look good on you the second I saw it.'

Max resisted the urge to tug his collar again, which by now was feeling like some kind of hideous medieval torture device. 'So… what happens now then?' he asked.

'A mid morning buffet will be served shortly,' Jacob told him. 'And we will mix with the members of the household during it. There are many that have requested an audience with you.'

Max groaned. He felt Merelie squeeze his hand. 'Don't worry,' she said. 'I'll be with you the whole time.'

Max gave her a half hearted smile and tried to ignore the feeling of a hundred sets of eyes boring into his back.

After Charlie's massive stack of bacon this morning, Max wasn't hungry enough to partake in any of the buffet food. It was that posh canapé stuff anyway, which always looked like snot on a cracker as far as he was concerned. Everyone else seemed to be enjoying themselves though and the desire to stuff their faces gave Max a small respite from all the unwanted attention.

He slowly backed himself away into a corner near the stage out of the sight of most people, breathing a sigh of relief as he did so.

'You look like you're about to go to the gallows, boy,' a gruff voice intoned from behind him. Max turned to see Borne, Merelie's Arma, leaning up against the wall with his arms crossed. He looked about as pleased to be at the ball as Max was.

'That would be a better alternative actually,' he replied.

'For once I am in total agreement with you. I'm not even a guest of honour here today and I feel uncomfortable as all hell. These fancy parties are not the place for a soldier like me... or a Wordsmith like you it appears.'

'Yup, I'd say so. Haven't seen you around in a while, Borne. Where have you been?'

Borne's eyes clouded for a second. 'Merelie's father has had me running errands across The Chapter Lands.' He definitely didn't sound happy about it.

'Anything interesting?' Max's curiosity had been piqued.

'There's been some... trouble recently up in the north.'

'What kind of trouble?'

'Oh, nothing for you to worry about, just a few bandits causing havoc.' Borne looked up. 'Merelie looks beautiful, doesn't she?'

Max could tell a deliberate change of subject when he heard one. This wasn't the time to push it, but there was obviously more to Borne's sojourns than he was letting on. Max filed it away in his head for future consideration.

'Looks like you're being stalked.' Borne stuck out his chin to indicate a couple walking directly towards where they stood. The woman was a good six foot three and dressed in a black gown. The man was barely five foot and decked out in a sombre ash coloured suit. Both had lofty looks on their faces. Every fibre in Max's being screamed at him to run away as fast as possible.

Borne grunted. 'Halbert and Enis Gamelow. The matriarch and patriarch of one of the oldest families aligned with Carvallen,' he said by way of explanation. 'You'd struggle to find two more officious and small minded fools in the whole of The Chapter Lands.'

Max darted his head around desperately looking for Merelie. He spotted her eating a canapé over by one of the tables. The grimace on her face indicated she wasn't enjoying it much. There was no way he could get to her before the Gamelows reached him. He was trapped. He swung his head back round to plead for Borne's help... but the Arma was nowhere to be seen.

I'm not going to let him forget that, Max thought, and turned back to the oncoming twosome.

'And you would be Max Bloom,' Halbert Gamelow said, contriving to look down his nose at Max, despite the fact he was a good nine inches shorter.

His wife didn't have any trouble doing it though. She towered over them both. Max tried very hard to avoid looking up into her cavernous nostrils.

'We've been meaning to have some of your time for months now,' Enis said, sounding highly put out.

'Oh... have you? I'm sorry, I've been busy.'

'We Gamelows are close friends to the Carvallens,' Halbert said. Max stood there waiting for something more, but the little man just glared at him as if daring him to contradict the statement.

'That's nice for you,' Max said in as bland a voice as possible.

'We have lobbied Jacob for a private audience with you, but it seems you were constantly unavailable,' Enis told him, barely concealing her fury at being slighted in such a gross manner.

'Er... sorry?' Max offered again, not knowing what else to say.

'Nevertheless, we have you now!' The woman's nostrils flared, making Max feel nauseous.

Be polite, he told himself. *Merelie will kill you if you're not.*

'What can I do for you both exactly?' he asked.

'You can damn well use all that power you're supposed to have and sort things out!' Halbert roared.

'Sort what out?'

'By the Writer's hand, you know exactly what we're talking about!' The little man prodded Max in the chest.

Thus far, the conversation with these two had made Max simply confused. The prod in the chest instantly changed his mood to highly irritated. This was good in a way, as he was on more solid ground with that feeling.

'No, I bloody don't mate,' he told Halbert. 'And I would suggest not poking me like that again unless you want me to tie your larger intestines into a complicated knot.' He waggled the fingers on one hand for emphasis.

Halbert Gamelow went a pleasing shade of white.

His wife, sensing that her husband was about to become the subject of some DIY organ surgery in the middle of a party, stepped slightly between him and the increasingly irate Wordsmith. 'Please Mr Bloom, forgive my husband. He is a man prone to his passions and the recent deaths have disturbed us a great deal.'

'Deaths? What deaths?' This was news to Max. As far as he was aware the Carvallen Chapter Lands had been very peaceful recently.

Enis looked non-plussed. 'Surely you know of the awful acts being committed on our lands to the north?'

'No. I don't. Why don't you fill me in?' This was the second time in as many minutes that someone had mentioned problems in the north. Something was definitely going on here…

'Four people murdered!' spat Halbert. 'All Wordsmiths in good standing! Blown apart they were!'

'What?'

'Yes! Killed for no reason, the poor buggers!'

Enis put a hand on her husband's arm to calm him down. 'It's alright my dear, take some deep breaths.' She turned to Max. 'I'm amazed you know nothing of this. We gave Jacob a full report of what happened. I'm led to believe the other families have done likewise.'

'Other families? This is happening in other places as well?'

'Indeed. I don't know the full details, but there have been at least three incidents in the past few weeks that I know of. Acts of violence perpetrated in towns and cities across the Land.'

'Bloody terrorists!' Halbert nearly shouted, sending him off into an explosive coughing fit.

'Please forgive Halbert, Mr Bloom. One of the men killed in Gamelow was a favourite uncle of Halbert's.'

'He taught me how to fish the lakes! A genius with the lure, he was!' the little man screeched, tears welling in his eyes.

Max was dumbstruck. There were people being murdered in The Chapter Lands and he knew nothing about it. Jacob Carvallen had deliberately kept it from him.

'There you are Max!' Merelie bustled up to the three of them, an apologetic expression on her face. 'I've been looking everywhere for you.'

'Been here the whole time,' he said to her, still somewhat distracted by the conversation he'd just had.

Merelie nodded her head at the Gamelows. 'Enis and Halbert. How nice to see you here today.'

'You've grown up well, my girl,' Enis said.

'Thank you very much.'

Max looked at Merelie. 'We were just discussing the killings on the Gamelow's land,' Max said to her in pointed fashion.

Merelie's brow creased. 'What killings?'

'You don't know what they're on about either?' Max was relieved to hear this. The idea of Merelie keeping something like this from him was awful.

'No, not a thing.'

'Your father does. The Gamelows here have told him all about it.'

'We have!' Halbert said, having regained a bit of composure. 'And nothing has been done!'

'I think we need to have a chat with him,' Max said to Merelie, a dark expression on his face.

The conversation was interrupted by a short fanfare. The voice of the announcer drifted over the hall once more. 'And now ladies and gentlemen, it's time for the entertainment. This afternoon, Wordsmiths of every house will compete one on one in the Wordmeet, but now they will delight and amaze you all with their Wordcraft in a more creative manner.'

Another set of double doors opened across the hall and twenty Wordsmiths entered, all wearing the long flowing coats of their respective houses, and took up positions in a circle at the centre of the hall. The party guests moved out to form a circle of eager spectators.

The pyrotechnic display of Wordcraft that followed did indeed delight and amaze a majority of the people present. It was an expertly crafted exhibition of word shaping that demanded one's full attention. The Wordsmiths fashioned a variety of glowing figures and shapes from thin air, each taking their turn in the spotlight. One purple clad Falion Wordsmith presented an exciting battle between a fire breathing dragon and a warrior in shining armour. Another populated the air with a variety of brightly coloured fish that swam between the legs of some of the party-goers, eliciting cries of surprise and delight.

The display that garnered the most applause came from a Carvallen Wordsmith – a tall, golden haired young man with a beaming smile - who conjured up a complex battle sequence featuring thousands of tiny figures. Great, coruscating flashes of Wordcraft flew between the enemy sides and multi-coloured lightning filled the sky. The audience was rapt and awestruck by the complexity of the show the Wordsmith was putting on.

'It's the battle of Sammerhall Max!' Merelie squealed. 'One of our oldest legends, when Wordcraft was still in its rawest form!'

'Mmmm.'

Max wasn't paying a blind bit of notice to the light show going on in front of him. He was completely lost in thought.

Why the hell would no-one tell him about these killings? He was the most powerful Wordsmith in the world after all. If anyone could do something about it, it would be him. Why would Jacob – not to mention Emerelda and Borne - keep it from him?

'Oh Max! It's you!' Merelie exclaimed.

This brought him out of his disturbed reverie.

Max looked up to see that the scene being created by the fair haired Wordsmith had changed. The battle of Sammerhall had disappeared, to be replaced by a surprisingly good re-creation of Max's confrontation with Lucas Morodai in the maniac Chapter Lord's library.

There was a lot more lightning, explosions and pyrotechnic flashes than he remembered, but the figure dealing out punishment to the cowering re-creation of Morodai was definitely him, down to the black hooded top and Nike skate shoes.

Max looked at the Wordsmith responsible for the show, whose brow was furrowed in concentration as he spilled his Wordcraft out into the air above him, expertly moving his version of Max around the room.

Max had to admit a certain grudging admiration. He may have more raw Wordcraft at his disposal, but he doubted very much that he could create such an accurate and solid illusion.

'Who is he?' he asked Merelie.

'Darel Cornelius.' She said the name in a breathy way that Max didn't like the sound of one little bit. 'He's one of our best Wordsmiths. A real talent and a creative genius with Wordcraft. You should get to know him Max.'

And you should stay away from him, Max thought privately.

He looked back just in time to see the floating illusory version of himself impaling Lucas Morodai with a length of sharp metal.

'Er... that's not what happened actually. The metal just fell on him. I pulled it out.' Max's words were lost on deaf ears. Merelie was rapt once again with the performance, as was everyone else in the room it seemed. For once, not a single person was staring at Max.

Instead of feeling relieved, he was quite put out.

The rest of the ball passed quite quickly.

Max had to endure a few more conversations with the Carvallen upper classes, but none were as confusing or illuminating as the one he'd had with the Gamelows. He kept trying to get a private word with Jacob to see why he'd been kept out of the loop, but the Chapter Lord was busy schmoozing everyone in sight.

'He's trying to hold The Chapter Lands together Max,' Merelie said when he told her it was impossible to get a word in edgeways around him. 'Since what happened last year, father's taken the role of leading the Chapter Houses through this difficult period. Morodai and Draveli have to be modernised and become democratic like the other three Houses. That takes a lot of time and a lot of conversations with people he'd rather not be speaking to.'

Which was all fair enough, but Max had some burning questions of his own he wanted answering.

29

Unfortunately Emerelda was nowhere to be seen either. She was off putting the finishing touches to the tournament field in the sprawling grounds of the Chapter House.

Max knew Borne wouldn't provide any more information, so he reluctantly had to let the matter drop. For now, anyway.

The buffet food kept coming well into lunch time; something Max was grateful for as breakfast was four hours ago now. The servants continued to trot food out at regular intervals, the frivolous canapés eventually giving way to more substantial fair.

Max was contentedly munching on his fourth chicken leg when the announcer told the assembled throng to begin making their way down and out of the House to the gardens below, where the real fun was due to begin in about an hour. Slowly, the guests did as they were bid and within half an hour or so, nearly all had finished their luncheon and departed for the tournament.

Needless to say Max Bloom wasn't among them.

He'd discovered a particularly nice stack of barbecue pork ribs and was determined to finish every single one of them.

'Enjoying those are you?' Merelie said as she came up to him. Max licked his fingers and smiled broadly. 'You've got it all over your face, you big pig,' she said with a smile.

Without waiting for a response, Merelie picked up several napkins, grabbed the plate from Max's hand, and began wiping his sauce-covered chin.

'I can do that myself you know,' he told her, taking the napkins and continuing the clean up operation.

'Well hurry up. I know you'd like nothing more than to avoid the tournament, but everyone's expecting you. I hope you've thought of something suitable to say.'

This, above all else, was the moment Max had been dreading. Merelie had told him it was customary for the guest of honour to say a few words and get the tournament underway. She'd told him it didn't have to be anything fancy, but he knew a request for a speech when he heard one, and the prospect of trying to say something profound or at least witty in front of several thousand gurning members of the Carvallen populace was a heart stopping one.

Merelie took his hand once the barbecue sauce had been successfully wiped away. 'Come on you, no more putting it off.' She smiled at him in a suggestive manner. 'Besides, if you do well today I might just give you a reward.'

This promise lifted Max's spirits *magnificently*.

If the Great Hall had been busy with people, then the gardens of the Chapter House took 'busy' to a whole new level. The few hundred members of the Carvallen glitterati had been joined by the kind Max's grandfather would have joyfully referred to as the 'great unwashed'.

Hundreds had become thousands.

The tournament was invitation only, and there had been a lottery for tickets to keep the numbers manageable, but Max had still never seen this many people together in one place. The event had the feeling of a rock concert.

Max would have been having great fun at the excitement and size of it all, were it not for the fact that he was one of the main reasons so many people were attending.

A massive temporary amphitheatre had been constructed of wood and stone in the middle of a huge flat grassy expanse that led several hundred yards down to the lazy river that wound its way through Carvallen City.

Max was reminded of the coliseum in Gladiator, the one where Russell Crowe got to act all cool and tough in his little helmet.

One thing distinguished this amphitheatre from any other in history though. Much like the Great Hall, bookshelves lined the rear stadium wall above the heads of the spectators, put there to provide enough of the ephemeral word energy that would allow the contestants to word shape successfully.

The last of the spectators were streaming their way through the archway directly across from the Chapter House main gate.

'This way Max,' Merelie guided. 'Let's get ourselves up into the balcony before anyone notices you.'

She led him away from the main entrance to a smaller one some twenty feet along to the left, in front of which were stood two stoic Chapter Guards. This was patently the special entrance for VIPs. Max had never been a VIP at anything before. A small feeling of pride welled in his chest.

They passed the guards without a word, though one of them did nod deferentially in Max's direction, which further added to his fleeting sense of high self worth.

Beyond the gate, they arrived at a staircase set into the side of the wide passageway hall. The passageway terminated in a set of double doors at the other end, which Max supposed must lead to the floor of the stadium.

A rather lengthy climb up the twisting staircase led to a broad balcony, segregated from the rest of the stands by plush ropes and stern Chapter Guards. It was large enough to seat two hundred people, and every seat was full, save two at the very front next to Jacob and Halia Carvallen. Max and Merelie joined them and took their seats.

'Max...' Halia said.

'Yep?'

'You appear to have a blob of brown sauce on your earlobe.'

Max gave her an embarrassed grin and wiped the sauce off with his fingers. Having nowhere to then clean his fingers, he was grateful that the shade of green on his three quarter length coat was dark enough to hide a sauce stain.

'Shall we get on with this then?' Jacob asked no-one in particular and nodded his head in the direction of the announcer, who had now taken up position on a plinth to the right of where they sat.

The man turned and raised his head.

'Ladies and gentlemen! Welcome to the fortieth annual Wordmeet of the Carvallen Chapterhouse!'

A roar went up from the crowd.

'Today, you will see the best and brightest Wordsmiths from across the Chapter Lands challenge each other in combat, for the right to be proclaimed the Wordmeet Champion!'

The austere, restrained tones the announcer had used earlier had disappeared, and he now appeared to be channelling a boxing promoter. Max fully expected him to scream *let's get ready to rumble!* at any moment.

'I see Borthwick is having a good time,' Jacob said to his wife.

'He does love to play the crowd,' she agreed.

'Over the next two hours,' the man now identified as Borthwick continued, 'you'll see the very best... the cream of the crop... the greatest and bravest Wordsmiths from all five houses battle it out in no holds barred competition!'

Another roar came from the crowd, even louder this time.

'So get ready to cheer on your House! Whether you're Carvallen... ' A massive cheer rang out from a majority of the audience. 'Falion... ' Another cheer, still surprisingly loud. 'Wellhome... ' The same again. 'Morodai... ' A chorus of boos filled the auditorium. 'Or Draveli... ' Crickets. 'You're sure to have a fantastic time here today!'

Max suppressed a smile. Morodai and Draveli were about as popular as he'd expected them to be.

'But first,' Borthwick carried on. 'We have a very special guest of honour here today.'

Oh shit.

'Someone who needs no introduction!'

Don't bloody introduce me then.

'The young man from our very own companion Earth, who saved us all a year ago.'

Stop building me up so much, you utter git.

'I am delighted to introduce, the Wordsmith and master of The Cornerstone… Ladies and gentleman, boys and girls, to say a few words to kick things off I give you… Max Bloom!'

The applause was deafening. The cheers even more so.

Max froze as solid as an iceberg.

Merelie nudged him in the side. 'Max… *Max*! You have to get up now.'

'Muurgh.'

Jacob also leaned over. 'I'd do as my daughter says, my boy. You don't want to make your adoring audience wait, now do you?'

'Yuurrm.'

'Max Bloom!' Merelie demanded imperiously. Jacob winced ever so slightly. 'You get on your feet now and say something nice to all these people. You're the most powerful Wordsmith for a generation. Act like it!'

Even abject fear stood no chance against what Max had come to regard as 'The Princess Tone'. It was the voice Merelie used very effectively as a weapon, but only in the most exceptional of circumstances.

He stood on wobbly legs and tottered over to where Borthwick was beckoning him. As Max climbed onto the plinth the roars of the crowd grew even louder still.

'Don't worry lad,' Borthwick said. 'I'll handle the volume, you just speak.'

Max nodded a little too quickly and turned to face a scene that terrified him more than a thousand Dwellers bursting in through the roof of the Great Hall.

'Um,' he said. The noise abated as the crowd prepared themselves for what he was about to say.

'Er,'

Silence had descended now.

'How's it going?' he ventured.

A ripple of laughter passed around the stadium.

Man up, you idiot. You don't want these people thinking you're a big wuss.

'It's great to be here with you today,' he continued, still unsure. The crowd seemed to like it though, as there was another loud round of applause.

'In fact, I wouldn't want to be anywhere else!' The cheers rose again.

'Are you looking forward to seeing some heads getting busted?' Max was gaining in confidence now and took a deep breath. 'Do you wanna see Carvallen slaughter the opposition?!' he screamed at them. They screamed back with equal vigour.

'Right then! Without anymore rubbish from me…'

He had to say it.

'Let's get ready to rrrrrrrrummmbble!!'

33

Thousands of people lost their minds. Max pumped his fists and jumped up and down on the spot. He looked round to see Merelie giggling, which made him laugh his head off as well. Borthwick was chuckling, and Halia Carvallen hid a smile behind her hand.

Then Max saw the expression on Jacob's face and instantly came to a standstill. He gave one final wave to the crowd and returned to his seat.

'Well done,' Merelie told him and kissed his cheek.

A warm glow suffused Max Bloom, and for the first time that day he felt relieved and happy. Nothing more was expected from him today as far as he was concerned. He could just sit back and enjoy the tournament.

In thinking this, he was of course, one hundred percent wrong.

Max had watched his fair share of wrestling over the years, and the Wordmeet reminded him of the big, grandiose WWE events he'd watched on pay-per-view many times. Instead of a wrestling ring, there was a large circle marked out on the grass in the centre of the stadium that indicated where the battles would take place. Stepping outside for any reason once the contest had begun counted as an automatic loss.

As each contestant was announced by Borthwick, the anthem of the Wordsmith's House would blast across the arena from an unidentifiable audio source. While the five separate anthems all stayed essentially the same, variations were woven into them to provide a unique piece of entrance music for each Wordsmith. Some came down the aisle to the circle accompanied by a light, orchestral version of their House anthem, others ran to the centre of the stadium with an enormous, bass heavy rendition playing that vibrated Max in his chair.

It was a marvellous way to introduce the contestants. And if anything, the following battles were even better.

No-one was allowed to do anything that might kill or maim their opponent, but there were a lot of Wordsmiths who got battered worse than cod in a chip shop during the course of the afternoon.

Some Wordsmiths would go for the straight forward approach and bombard the other combatant with pure Wordcraft until they either capitulated or were knocked so senseless that they couldn't continue. Others were more subtle with their approach, sending out finely honed barbs of word power like an experienced prize fighter, sizing up his opponent before lashing out with a swift jab to secure victory.

Several Wordsmiths even employed distraction techniques to help them win the fight. They would conjure up waves of rainbow colour or ghostly apparitions to befuddle the Wordsmith opposite, using the confusion to land a decisive blow.

It became clear to Max that those who could combine all of these techniques efficiently were the ones most likely to emerge victorious.

As the afternoon wore on, Darel Cornelius was proving to be the most adept. As the number of Wordsmiths was whittled down from 64 to just 16, Darel was the obvious front runner as they went into the quarter finals. None of his matches had lasted more than a few minutes, and he had the crowd in the palm of his hand. Every blow he produced resulted in exultant cheering, every foe he vanquished was roundly booed as they stumbled from the arena in defeat.

If Max had disliked the tall, blonde Wordsmith before, he actively hated him now. Particularly as he could hear every squeal of delight emanating from Merelie whenever Darel word shaped his way convincingly into the next round.

It was obvious Darel would progress to the final, and sure enough, he defeated a husky Falion Wordsmith in barely five minutes during his semifinal, setting up a colossal confrontation with a Wellhome Wordsmith called Zachary Vorsted, who had to be seven feet tall if he was an inch.

Dusk had arrived by the time the stage was set for the epic climax to the Wordmeet.

As Vorsted came to the circle there were cheers from the Wellhome contingent, but as the thumping first chords of the Carvallen anthem once again erupted, the rest of the baying crowd did likewise. The ovation Darel got made the one Max had received hours earlier sound like a wet fart in a library by comparison.

The contest began, and it was clear that Vorsted would finally give Darel the challenge he had sorely lacked all day.

Max reluctantly found himself rooting for a Wordsmith from a different house as Vorsted time and again struck Cornelius with a series of deft Wordcraft strikes. Max was out of his seat as Darel teetered close to the edge of the ring for a moment, before shaking off the blows Vorsted was inflicting with an open palmed gesture that sent the incoming energy skating away to one side.

Max groaned as he sensed a turn in the tide of the fight. Vorsted had obviously put everything he had into that attack and it meant his defence was now severely weakened.

Darel stalked across the circle, the grass now blasted brown and black by all the expended energy from the day's contests. It was like a lion hunting its prey as he grew nearer to the wild-eyed Vorsted.

The Wellhome Wordsmith erected a barrier of Wordcraft in an attempt to block whatever attack Darel was planning. The Carvallen challenger was too wily for that though. Instead of directing a blast of energy at his opponent, Darel drew in as much energy as he could, before leaping into the air like a fish, his body arching gracefully as it reached the zenith of the arc and descended again down onto the hapless Vorsted.

The move was the most spectacular thing Max had ever seen.

What a bastard.

As he speared downwards, Darel launched a barrage of word power that blew Vorsted clear out of the circle, bringing the tournament to a triumphant close. Cornelius landed back in the centre of the ring on one knee as the crowd once again completely lost control of their faculties.

Darel stood, looking every inch the champion Wordsmith in his dark green Carvallen long coat. His blonde hair even ruffled in the wind a bit. Someone who had obviously studied dramatic timing to within an inch of its life fired up the Carvallen anthem one more time, adding to the exultant cacophony.

Max had to fight very hard to keep from throwing up.

Jacob stood and approached the plinth, waiting patiently for the rapturous applause and music to die away.

It did eventually, and he addressed the new Wordmeet champion. 'Darel Cornelius, I congratulate you on your victory here today. I have been present at many Wordmeets in my life, including the three I was fortunate enough to win myself.' This raised Max's eyebrows. He didn't know Jacob was that strong a Wordsmith. 'But no other contestant,' Jacob continued, 'and I definitely count myself amongst them, has ever put on a display as dominant as the one you have given us here today.'

The crowd cheered again and Darel smiled broadly. Max was surprised the setting sun didn't glint off his bloody teeth.

'We are proud to call you a member of House Carvellen,' Jacob told the Wordsmith, 'and even more proud to crown you the Champion of this year's Wordmeet!'

This time Jacob had to wait a full three minutes for the crowd to shut up. It didn't help that Darel did a lap of honour before returning to the centre of the ring.

'Is there anything you would like to say at this point, Darel?' Jacob asked.

Max was a bit taken aback when Darel stared directly at him. 'I ask only one thing, Lord Carvallen.'

Jacob noticed where Darel's gaze was fixed and his brow creased. 'And what is that, Wordsmith?'

'I ask only that the tournament goes one more match.'

Max stood. He knew what was coming next.

Darel took a deep breath and pushed out his chest. 'As reward for becoming champion I ask to compete in one-on-one combat with the man who saved our lands from Lucas Morodai and the Dwellers. I challenge Max Bloom to a fight!'

There was every chance the crowd would now need some form of incontinence pants. The deafening roar that filled the stadium actually made Max's ears ring.

'You can't do this Max,' Merelie told him, clutching one arm. 'Darel has done magnificently today, he doesn't realise what he's saying.'

'He seems pretty sure of himself,' Max replied, having to raise his voice to be heard over the crowd below.

'Yes, but he doesn't know what you are. He thinks you're like him. He doesn't know how much power you can tap into.'

Jacob calmed the crowd with outstretched hands. He addressed Darel again. 'Max Bloom is a guest of honour, Darel. He is not a contestant.'

Booing started at the rear of the stadium.

'I know my Lord, but surely he would still answer my challenge? He is not a coward, is he?'

The sharp intake of breath from several thousand people sounded like a jet fighter taking off.

'Oh Writer...' Merelie said in a quiet voice.

Jacob, who knew Max Bloom as well as his daughter, stood back from the plinth and put his head in his hands.

A chant started up in the audience. 'Fight! Fight! Fight!'

Merelie touched Max on the arm again. 'Are you okay?' she said in a small voice.

Max turned and gave her a dreamy smile. 'Oh my yes. I'm just fine Merelie. Why wouldn't I be?' His left eye twitched a bit as he spoke. Max turned and looked down at Darel. 'I'd be delighted to take you on mate. You just give me a few moments to get myself together and I'll be with you.' He gave Darel a cheery thumbs up and walked back up to the stairs that would lead him down to ground level.

For the first time in hours the crowd went completely silent. Merelie sat slowly back in her chair, nibbling one fingernail nervously.

Darel Cornelius stood proudly in the centre of the combat circle, awaiting his opponent.

There was a pause pregnant enough to give birth to an elephant.

Then, from everywhere at once - louder, harder and bigger than any of the anthems that had played thus far - music thundered into life, causing a few of the less prepared spectators to fall off their chairs.

A gigantic, chugging guitar chord shook the brains from people's ears.

The screeching voice of a man obviously in several degrees of agony came in over the colossal riff: '*Back in black, I hit the sack, I've been too long, I'm glad to be back.*'

The double doors below the VIP balcony burst open.

Max Bloom strode into the stadium, his entire body suffused in a silver corona of pure Wordcraft. Each footstep left a pool of silver in its wake, and a trail of energy hung in the air behind as he approached Darel Cornelius, who was now looking decidedly less sure of himself.

Max reached the circle and, just to really set things off, he levitated ten feet in the air and floated over to where Darel stood, lowering himself back to the floor just in front of the Wordmeet champion.

The strains of AC/DC faded, as did the glow around Max. He offered Darel a lop-sided grin. ''Evening chief,' he said conversationally.

Darel gulped. 'Good evening, Lord Bloom.'

Max sucked air in over his teeth. 'I'm no bloody Lord anything pal. You call me Max.'

'Okay… Max.'

'That's better. Now, what's all this about you offering me out for a fight?'

'A contest, Max. To see who is the stronger.'

Max nodded and began to walk around Darel, sizing him up. 'Well yeah. I mean why not? You've done really well today I guess. None of them poor sods could come close to you.' He arrived back where his little walk had begun and smiled at Darel again. 'If you really want a shot at me, I see no reason why you shouldn't get it.'

'I'm honoured.'

The smile dropped off Max's face. 'Don't be. I'm no Lord, but I'm no bloody coward, either.'

Darel blanched and stepped back.

'Now, I'm going to back up a bit and let you catch your breath, mate. After all, you're probably quite knackered, what with all that leaping around like a flipping porpoise. I'll just stand back here and let you compose yourself a bit.' Max favoured Darel with his best mean and moody expression. 'Then you come at me however you like.'

Max backed off, never taking his eyes off the Wordsmith. For his part Darel clenched his fists, closed his eyes and breathed deeply.

That's it. Pull it all in mate. I want your best effort.

Darel's eyes flew open, focused on Max and with an echoing scream he launched forward, word shaping a battering ram of energy headed straight for Max's head.

Which was all very well, and would probably have been very effective against any other Wordsmith, but this is Max Bloom we're talking about here, and there was a very good reason he was banned by Jacob from competing in the tournament in the first place.

Max blew the energy bolt apart with a somewhat contemptuous flick of the wrist. With his other hand he motioned towards Darel, and the blonde Wordsmith suddenly found himself frozen in mid-air. This elicited an awestruck gasp from the crowd.

Max grinned and started to revolve Darel in the air like a pig on a spit. He then rotated him around so he was upside down. Loud laughter started to erupt from the crowd.

'Please put me down Max,' Darel said in a small voice that barely carried to Max's ears over the noise the audience made. 'This is extremely embarrassing.'

Max feigned surprise. 'Oh? Is it? I hadn't noticed. I'm rather enjoying myself.' And he was. The chance to humiliate the good looking young man that Merelie had been practically salivating over all afternoon was proving too good to resist. He looked up at where his girlfriend sat to see her looking at him with a face like thunder.

Deciding he'd better put a stop to this little farce before it put him firmly in the dog house, Max brought Darel back to an upright position and started to lower him to the ground. 'There you go, buddy,' he said in a soothing tone.

'Thank you very much,' Darel said with relief. 'It's very apparent that I should never have - '

A loud crack reverberated around the stadium. Max felt something buzz past his left ear. Darel's face went slack and a blossom of crimson red burst across his chest. Somebody in the audience screamed. Max looked past Darel to see a man stood in the front row of the crowd. He looked in his mid-forties - the same age as Max's father. Spiked and thinning grey hair sat atop a sharp face that wore an expression of sardonic hate. He wore a long dark grey coat and a heavy black leather waistcoat. His arm was extended towards Max, holding something that looked completely incongruous in this parallel version of Earth.

He's got a gun.

There was another whip-crack explosion as the man fired the heavy black revolver again. Darel's body jerked in mid air and this time Max felt a sharp sting along his ribs as the bullet grazed his right side.

He let out a cry of surprise and pain. Darel's lifeless body dropped to the floor. Max word shaped and flung a barrage of energy at the sneering grey haired man, but he leapt out of the way with a speed Max couldn't believe.

More screams were coming from the crowd now. They weren't familiar with guns like the one this man held, but they knew a threat when they saw one.

From behind Max there was an explosion. Then another to his left, one to his right and one straight ahead. The enormous bookcases that ringed the stadium blew outwards in four places, sending books and wood flying in all directions. This brought a whole new level of panic to the crowd. It was pandemonium, with people climbing over each other to get out through the gates, which had been forced open by those at the outer edges of the throng.

Max stood straight, one hand to his side, looking for the gun toting madman who had murdered Darel Cornelius right in front of him. His gaze went to the VIP balcony, where there were equal levels of panic. Max could see Merelie being protected by Borne from panicked guests as they pushed past.

Jacob was now stood at the plinth again. 'Everybody calm down!' the Chapter Lord cried, but to no avail. 'Calm yourselves!'

Then Max saw the man with the gun again. He was standing below the balcony, revolver raised and pointed straight at Jacob.

Max acted on instinct. A spear of Wordcraft lanced out and struck the maniac's gun hand just as he pulled the trigger. The bullet struck the wooden canopy directly above Jacob's head. The gun itself went sailing twenty feet into the mass of bodies still trying to evacuate the stadium.

The gun wielding man snarled and Max felt him drawing in word power, before thrusting both hands out in Max's direction.

Darel's attempted volley of Wordcraft hadn't troubled Max in the slightest, but this maniac was far more powerful. The blow rocked Max on his feet, making him gasp out loud. If he hadn't instinctively word shaped a force field around himself it would have blown him across the stadium.

Max's assailant now ran right at him. From a concealed scabbard in the back of his long grey coat he pulled a vicious looking sword.

Bleary eyed and in pain from the bullet wound, Max had no time to counter with Wordcraft and instead dropped to the grassy floor as the blade whistled over his head. This gave him a few precious moments and he lashed out with fury at his attacker, sending the man spinning away across the circle of combat.

The interloper came to an eventual rest directly across from Max, with the sad shape of Darel Cornelius slumped between them.

'Seems like your reputation is deserved,' the grey haired man said with a thin smile.

'And it seems like you're a right dickhead who's about to get the living crap kicked out of him,' Max replied, the silver corona returning around his body. It whipped and curled in the air, powered by the abject rage suffusing Max Bloom. He rolled his sleeves up.

The man smiled. 'Oh, I think that'll have to wait for another day.' He looked up at the VIP balcony and a wide-eyed Merelie. 'Give my regards to Merelie for me, won't you?' he said and licked his lips.

Before Max could squash him like a bug, the man produced a blue League Book from his coat, flipped it open, and disappeared in a halo of blue light. The League Book fell to earth and was immediately consumed in fire, reducing it to ashes in a matter of moments.

Max ground his teeth and remembered a similar escape plan employed by a lunatic Morodai Chapter Lord. 'I bloody hate it when that happens,' he growled.

40

The panicked crowd had almost cleared the stadium by now. Max could see Chapter Guards running in from all directions. Merelie, Emerelda and Borne were also on the ground floor and hurrying over to where Max stood. Jacob and Halia were nowhere to be seen. They'd probably been hurried away by the Chapter Guards in the face of such a direct threat.

'Where in the Writer's name did he go?' snapped Emerelda as she joined him.

'No idea. One second he was there, the next he was gone. Used a League Book to get away.'

Emerelda looked shocked. 'Bloody hell.'

'My thoughts exactly.'

Merelie was by Max's side. 'Are you alright?' she asked, looking at where Max was holding his ribs.

'Yeah, I'm fine.' He went very pale. 'I have just been shot though.' Max removed his hand to reveal a long tear in his coat and pale cream shirt, which by now was looking decidedly bloody. 'I think I might just sit down for a second.'

Max's legs gave out from under him. Merelie cried out and went to ground with him. 'Somebody find the physicians!' she screamed.

Max waved a limp hand. 'I'm alright, Merelie. It's Darel... Darel's the one that needs help.' He looked over at the still form of his Wordmeet opponent. Borne was slowly draping a cloak over the boy's face.

'Oh shit,' Max said in a watery voice, and the world went black.

Part Two

Getting shot was not an experience Max Bloom had been through before, and judging from the way it felt as he swam back into consciousness, it was one he wasn't in a hurry to try again anytime soon. His whole right side ached with a dull throb and somehow getting shot meant you had to put up with a pounding headache as well.

'Merelie,' he mumbled. He felt a warm hand encircle his.

'I'm here Max. How are you feeling?'

'Well, I've watched a lot of action films, Merelie. I've seen Die Hard at least twenty times. John McClane never fainted dead away after being grazed by a bullet, and woke up feeling like hammered crud, so I guess I'm not doing all that well.'

'You can't be that bad if you're referencing pop culture, Mr Bloom,' Emerelda remarked from the other side of the bed.

'Fair point.' Max sat up slowly, wincing as his head throbbed even harder with the movement. 'Where are those physicians with the waggly healing fingers? My head's killing me.'

'Busy with the injured people from the awful events of this evening Max,' a third voice intoned. Garrowain stepped from behind Merelie. 'I'll provide you with some relief from the pain.' As he had done months before after the defeat of Lucas Morodai, Garrowain placed a hand on Max's head and whispered a few words. The relief was instantaneous. The headache disappeared, and the injury to his side felt far more manageable.

'You still haven't shown me how to do that yet,' Max said to the little man.

'You've been too busy with other pursuits, young man,' the custodian replied, making a point of not looking at Merelie.

Max wisely chose not to respond to that. He remembered what had happened at the Wordmeet. 'Darel?' he said.

Merelie's eyes clouded.

'Dead,' Emerelda told him matter-of-factly. 'Hit by two bullets. He stood no chance.'

'A gun Imelda!' Max pointed out, forgetting her real name in his horror. 'He had a flipping gun! A big, black thing like one out of a Western.'

'A revolver actually,' she corrected. 'One of the Chapter Guards retrieved it from the stadium. It's a Webley service revolver. Probably from World War 2.'

Max looked stunned. 'How do you know that?'

'It gets boring running a library you know,' she said by way of explanation. 'I went through a stage of reading books about the war.'

'It's a horrible thing,' Merelie remarked.

'Yeah, they generally are. Guns and wars,' Max said, which led him on to his next question. 'Who the hell was he? And how did he get a gun from Earth?'

'Questions which we would all like the answer to, my boy,' Garrowain said, stepping away now he had administered enough first aid.

Max's eyes narrowed and he looked at Emerelda in pointed fashion. 'Not the only ones either.'

'What do you mean by that?' she asked.

'The Gamelows. They told me about some deaths up where they're from? Said there had been other incidents? Sounds like the same kind of thing that just happened here to me...'

Emerelda folded her arms. 'Possibly.'

'So you knew about it?'

'Yes, Max. I did. My brother's been tearing his hair out trying to think of a way to stop it.'

'And none of you thought it was a good idea to tell me?' There was distinct anger in his voice now.

'To be blunt, no. Not everything in The Chapter Lands is your immediate concern Max. Besides, we have no idea who this person is, where he is from, or why he's committing these atrocities. Sending you blundering in with nothing to go on would probably only make the situation worse.'

'What, like Darel being shot and the Wordmeet exploding?'

Emerelda had trouble meeting his cold gaze. 'We didn't think it would escalate like that. It's been a few isolated incidents, where only a few people have been affected. Nothing like what happened today.'

'I could have done something, Imelda. I could have stopped this!'

'Enough!' cried Garrowain. 'This is getting us nowhere. You're aware of what's been happening now Max. Recriminations don't help anyone.'

'Garrowain's right,' Merelie agreed. 'The important thing right now is finding out who that maniac is.'

Max flung back the bed cover. 'Right then. I'm going to talk to The Cornerstone.'

Merelie tried to stop him getting up, but he pushed her arm away. 'Why?' she asked.

'Because the tosser didn't get that gun in The Chapter Lands, he got it on Earth. Which means he must have used Corny at some point.'

Emerelda exhaled quickly. 'Damn it, you're right.'

'You see how helpful I can be when I'm kept in the bloody loop?' Max said with a thin smile.

By the time they'd reached The Cornerstone's chamber in the Great Library, Max's side had started aching again. He tried to ignore the pain as he reached out to pick up the extraordinary book.

'What are you proposing to do?' Emerelda asked.

'Open him up and ask him if he knows who the bloke is,' Max replied.

'You really think that'll work? The Cornerstone is still a book after all, not a living being.'

He frowned at her. 'You've been around Corny for this long and you still don't think he's alive?'

She folded her arms. 'Just get on with it.'

Max opened The Cornerstone's cover. 'Evening Corny.' Silver light played along the book's edges for a moment. 'We've got a problem. Somebody – a bloke with grey hair, wearing a grey coat, with a thing for deadly weaponry – has used you at some point to go to Earth and get a Wensleydale surplus revolver - '

'Webley service revolver,' Emerelda corrected.

'Whatever… a big, nasty gun, anyway. We need you to show us when this happened and who he is mate.'

'Please don't call the most important book in the universe 'mate' Max,' Garrowain complained.

Max ignored the old man and concentrated on The Cornerstone's page, which was currently blank. 'Come on Corny. Don't let me down here,' he said, shaking the book in frustration.

Silver light started to flicker round the edges of The Cornerstone.

'It's building up to something,' Emerelda said, unconsciously backing away a couple of feet. Max noticed this and took a nervous gulp of air. The Cornerstone and he had an understanding, but he still wasn't entirely sure it wouldn't burn him to a crisp if it felt like it.

On the white page, writing started to appear very slowly. Normally, The Cornerstone would etch its words quickly and with no fuss. Now though, it was as if something was trying to stop it completing every single loop and line of the word it was creating.

'Something's being written,' Max said, holding the book at arm's length as the glow started to get too bright to have right under his nose. 'Looks like a V.'

'It's certainly taking it's time,' Merelie said.

'It's fighting against something,' Garrowain agreed. 'Almost as if there were an exterior power attempting to stop it from helping.'

'Bugger that. I want answers.' Max gritted his teeth and started to mumble under his breath, sending waves of word power into The Cornerstone. 'Here you go buddy. This should help you fight whatever it is off.'

The Cornerstone started to shake violently in Max's hand, but the writing did start to come quicker and the final letters of the word formed itself on the page. A huge final shudder rippled down The Cornerstone's spine before it settled back in Max's hands again.

He peered at the single word written on the page. 'What the hell is a Venhaligan?' he said.

Garrowain and Emerelda exchanged a meaningful glance.

'What was that?' Max asked, pointing a finger at the pair of them.

'Nothing,' Emerelda said.

'Rubbish! You exchanged a meaningful glance.' Max wagged the finger. 'Don't pretend you didn't, I saw it!'

'It's nothing to concern yourself with,' Garrowain said, trying to appease him.

Max slammed The Cornerstone shut and held it up. 'Nothing to concern myself with? Corny writes a mysterious word after I ask him who crashed the Wordmeet, and you tell me it's *nothing to concern myself with?*'

'Max has a good point,' Merelie said. 'And you two have suddenly started acting very suspiciously.'

Emerelda heaved a sigh and folded her arms. 'Sometimes I hate that book. It has a habit of making everyone's life more difficult.'

'Who or what is a Venhaligan?' Max asked, brow furrowed.

'It's a name. A surname to be exact,' she told him.

'The name of the man who killed Cornelius?'

'That's impossible I'm afraid,' Garrowain said.

'Why?'

'Because there is no way someone with that name could have used The Cornerstone to travel to Earth to retrieve that weapon,' he finished cryptically.

'That's right,' Emerelda agreed and fell to silence.

Max rolled his eyes. 'You're going to make me drag this out of the pair of you, aren't you?'

'Venhaligan is the name of a family who once wielded great power in the Carvallen Chapter Lands Max,' Garrowain told him. 'But they have been gone a very long time.'

'It seems like one of them has hung around though, doesn't it?'

'There's no way that person could have been from the Venhaligan family,' Emerelda said. 'No way at all.'

It was Max's turn to sigh. 'At the risk of sounding like a broken record... *why?*'

Garrowain held out his hands. 'I think at this point it would be better if we didn't say any more.'

'That's right,' Emerelda agreed.

'Oh, well that's bloody helpful isn't it?' Max snapped. 'Here I am trying to make sense of why some lunatic's going round killing people, and you two clam up like your solicitor has just arrived.'

'I think we should go and speak to my father,' Merelie said in a flat tone of voice. 'He should be able to provide us with the answers you two seem unwilling to give.'

'That will probably be your best course of action,' Emerelda agreed. 'Jacob has the authority to speak more on this subject. The custodian and I have said too much.'

'Oh yeah, ' Max said, rolling his eyes. 'You've really opened up and given us the juicy details haven't you?' He turned to Merelie. 'You know, just once... just *once*, I'd like it if people spoke plainly around here. It's a wonder any of you made it out of the dark ages.'

Merelie put a hand on his shoulder. 'Let's go to my father, he can sort this out.'

'Yes, alright. Let's go see how well Jacob can squirm his way out of telling me anything as well.'

And with that Max turned around and stalked off in the direction of the Library exit, holding his injured side and muttering under his breath about how unreliable people can be.

-2-

'That is not a matter up for discussion,' said Jacob Carvallen from behind his large polished green desk.

Max threw his hands up. 'See? See? I bloody knew it!' he moaned.

'The Cornerstone gave us the name father. It obviously thinks we should know what's going on,' Merelie said, eyes flinty.

The Chapter Lord took a long, deep breath. 'The name Venhaligan is not one I wish to hear spoken out loud in these chambers.' The anger in his voice was unmistakeable.

'That's as maybe Jacob,' Emerelda said, 'but Merelie is correct. The Cornerstone did provide Max with the Venhaligan name. Perhaps it would be wise to go along with its wishes.'

Jacob gave his sister a flat stare - which was returned in kind. Max looked from one to the other as a silent battle of wills took place. He saw Jacob's brow crease as he broke his sister's gaze.

'Our father made us promise that we would never bring up what happened again,' he said to her.

'He did. But that was before the most powerful book in the world virtually ordered us to. A boy is dead Jacob. We can stay silent no longer.'

Jacob looked to the ceiling and tapped his knuckle on the desk a couple of times in deep thought. 'Oh very well.'

'About time too,' Max muttered under his breath, drawing a look of irritation from Merelie's father.

The Chapter Lord looked to Garrowain, who stood at the rear of the room, watching proceedings with his usual calm demeanour. 'Custodian? Will you tell this dreadful story please? It was a bitter time in our family's past and I would rather not speak of it myself.'

Garrowain nodded. 'Of course my Lord. Your reluctance is perfectly understandable in the circumstances.' He then looked at Max. 'And so it falls to me to elaborate more on the name The Cornerstone gave you.'

'Good stuff,' Max replied, before a sour expression overtook his face. 'It's not going to take ages is it? You know what I'm like when it comes to long explanations.'

Garrowain rolled up his sleeves. 'Fear not Max. I will try to make it as entertaining for you as possible...'

And with that, he started to weave his hands in the air.

From the firmament emerged two hovering images that hung in front of the custodian, revolving gently in place. They were both circular crests, much like the proud green Carvallen one that reminded Max of a pair of antlers. These were the same colour, though in different shades from the deep sea green of the Carvallen house. One was a heavy, dark olive tone, while the other was a clear, vibrant shade that reminded Max of Spring. The olive crest depicted what looked like an open hand surrounded by fire, while the other brighter crest created the shape of a flower. Max couldn't decide what kind of flower though, it was somewhere between a tulip and a rose, as far as his limited knowledge of flora would allow him to guess.

'I've seen these crests before,' Merelie said. 'In some of the old Chapter House chronicles down in the Library.'

Garrowain smiled. 'Indeed my dear. While they are not spoken of in polite conversation, the houses of Venhaligan and Florren are still important parts of this Chapter House's past.'

'Florren?' Max said.

'That is correct,' Garrowain told him. 'Two fine and proud houses that were allied with ours from the day Symon Carvallen fashioned The Cornerstone.'

'Gotcha.'

'Sadly, in their attempts to gain favour with the ruling Carvallen lords, they became bitter enemies.' Garrowain smiled in misty eyed fashion. 'In some ways they were similar to the Montagues and Capulets. When I would read of those noble Italian families in the great bard's work, I would marvel at the way he almost seemed to be speaking of our own Houses and their strife with one another.' The old man smiled at Max. 'You know of the Montagues and Capulets?'

50

Max's expression couldn't have been more blank if you'd dunked his head in a bucket of Tippex. 'Er, were they on Hollyoaks? Only that's Monica's favourite show. I never watched it myself.'

'It's Shakespeare Max,' Merelie told him. 'Romeo and Juliet.'

Max waved a hand. 'Oh right. That movie with Sproutface DiCaprio in it when he was a kid?'

'Sproutface?'

'Yeah. Coz he's got a face that looks like a sprout.'

Merelie looked confused. 'Exactly what aspect of this person's face makes it look like a sprout? Is it green?'

'No, no. It's just round and... and...' Max threw his hands up. 'Oh, just trust me, he looks like a sprout.'

'I rather think we've strayed from the point,' Emerelda remarked.

'Sorry,' Merelie said. 'Carry on Garrowain, please.'

'Thank you my dear,' Garrowain replied, and returned his attention to the spinning crests - though you could tell he was still picturing a sprout atop a set of shoulders like everybody else in the room. 'Each house was presided over by men of great prowess and standing.' The crests dissolved into thin air, to be replaced by portraits of two men. Both looked grim. One was younger than the other, a fair haired man with soft features. The other was older, darker and had a face like chiselled granite.

'That one looks a bit constipated,' Max said, pointing at him.

Garrowain rolled his eyes. 'That is Colter Venhaligan, Max. The head of the family up until about thirty years ago.'

'What happened thirty years ago?' Max moved his finger over to the other man. 'Did these two kill each other?'

'If only it had been that straightforward,' Jacob said, his voice full of regret.

'To cut what would be an extremely long story short,' Garrowain continued, 'Colter Venhaligan and Xander Florren were born within a mile of one another. Both proud and powerful men, their rivalry extended back to their earliest years. When both rose to become heads of their house, that rivalry only intensified.'

'And got nasty?' Max guessed.

Garrowain shook his head. 'At first no. They were great friends to begin with. Then they started to discover the secrets of The Cornerstone. This led to differences of opinion that escalated wildly.'

'What kind of opinions?'

'None of us were ever entirely sure,' Garrowain said. 'All we know is they went from the firmest of friends, to hating each other within a matter of a few years.'

'And it was a hatred that would destroy them both,' Emerelda added.

Max folded his arms. 'This is starting to sound like the kind of story that isn't going to end happily.'

'Correct Mr Bloom,' Garrowain told him. 'Over the next few years the rivalry between Colter and Xander turned to malice, spite and true enmity. Both vied for approval and standing in Carvallen society, and both would seek to undermine the other at every opportunity. I could provide you with a litany of examples, but I fear all would sound petty and small-minded in the cold light of day.'

'My father eventually had to step in and ensure both behaved themselves,' Jacob said. 'The friction between them was threatening to engulf the Chapter House entirely. My father was a patient man... but only to a point. He had to make sure things didn't spill over into bloodshed.'

'Indeed my Lord, and a fine job he did too.' The custodian offered his master a smile before his face grew grave again. 'Far worse was to come though. One day - we know not how - Xander Florren discovered that Colter Venhaligan was stealing from the Carvallen treasury to bribe the Morodai's.'

This drew a sharp intake of breath from Max. 'Why would he get involved with those bastards?'

'Because Colter wanted trade agreements with them that would make him one of the richest and most powerful men in The Chapter Lands,' Jacob said, his voice dripping with barely suppressed loathing. 'By bribing the Morodai, he figured he could secure his position as my father's one true right hand man.'

'But Florren discovered his theft,' Merelie said.

'And reported it to your grandfather, yes.' Jacob balled a fist and slammed it on the desk in front of him. 'The whole thing still makes my blood boil.'

'Venhaligan was summarily arrested once Florren provided the evidence of his crimes,' Garrowain told them. 'He was immediately imprisoned.'

'A week later Colter committed suicide,' Jacob said. 'The shame of it all was too much for him to bear. He slit his own throat with a dagger his wife Viana smuggled in to him on a visit.'

Merelie gasped and put a hand to her face. 'That's awful.'

'More awful was what Viana did next.' Jacob nodded at Garrowain. 'Pray continue custodian, I apologise for my interruptions.'

'Thank you my Lord.' Garrowain's head dropped. 'What Viana did is a source of huge shame to everyone in these lands. Mere days after her husband's suicide, Viana ordered an attack on the Florren household in the middle of the night. She slaughtered every member of the Florren family, and the staff who served them.'

'Christ,' Max said and exhaled heavily.

'She did not escape herself though,' Jacob added through clenched teeth.

'No indeed my Lord. Viana Venhaligan died in the house that night herself.'

Max was incredulous. 'She went in on the attack?'

Garrowain nodded. 'Yes. The assault was led by her eldest son, but Viana must have been consumed with such hate for the Florren family that she went along to see them die with her own eyes.'

'Who killed her?' Merelie asked in a small voice. Max could see that this story was having a profound effect on her. She just wasn't used to this kind of treachery and violence from families in her own land.

'We're not sure,' Garrowain said. 'The details from that night are hazy to say the least. The Florren household was more or less burned to the ground during the battle, so it was hard to know what went on under that roof. What we do know is that every member of the Florren household perished, as did Viana Venhaligan and her two sons Marran and Randal. This, in and of itself, was a tragedy. Marran was destined to be a leader of men, and Randal was a fifteen year old boy who showed huge potential in Wordcraft. Their mother sent them and the Florren family to their deaths for no good reason that night.'

Max folded his arms. 'And then the whole thing was covered up, right?'

'And what would you have had us do?' Jacob snapped. 'Both families were dead. There was no-one left to answer for the crimes committed that day. My father, in the best interests of the Carvallen Chapter House, saw fit to keep the ghastly details from public consumption. There was no reason for this to get out.'

'Except they weren't all dead, were they?' Max said.

'What do you mean?'

'A man has been killing people for apparently no reason in the past few weeks, and murdered Darel Cornelius today with a gun from my world. When The Cornerstone was asked who it was, he told us it was somebody called Venhaligan.' Max stared back at Colter Venhaligan's portrait where it still hung in the air in front of him. 'Somebody did survive that night... and now they're back.'

'That's impossible boy,' Jacob told him. 'No-one from either family survived. The search was extensive. Our best Wordsmiths were set to the task. My father himself led the investigation, such was the scale of the crime. No-one would have been able to hide themselves from him. No-one at all.'

'Oh? The same way Lucas Morodai hid what he was up to until it was too late?' Max said.

'Max! There's no need to drag that up again!' Merelie said, her face flushing red.

'Sorry.'

Garrowain rubbed his chin, lost in thought. 'The hand gun,' he eventually said.

'What of it?' Emerelda asked.

'I fear there may be credence to Max's theory. The Venhaligans and Florrens were the only two families, aside from the Carvallens, allowed access to The Cornerstone at the time of your father's rule. What limited travel between the two worlds there was usually involved someone from one of the three houses.'

Max snapped his fingers. 'That's how they got the gun!'

'It would seem to be a logical conclusion,' the custodian said. 'A further leap of logic would suggest that somebody did indeed walk away from that hideous night at the Florren house.'

'Somebody with a grudge,' Merelie finished for him.

Jacob sat down heavily in his polished chair. 'Even if this were true, why wait so many years to make your presence felt? The Florrens were murdered nearly thirty years ago.'

Garrowain shrugged. 'That I do not have an answer to my Lord.'

Max was counting on his fingers. 'How old did you say the two Venhaligan kids were?' he asked the old man.

'Marran was eighteen I believe. Randal was fifteen.'

'And the bloke who shot Darel looked what? Mid to late forties? Could have been either of them.'

'Or somebody else entirely,' Jacob said, though there was now doubt in his eyes.

'But as Father said, why wait all this time?' Merelie asked. 'And who would he be seeking revenge on anyway? Garrowain said all the Florrens were dead.'

Max didn't have an answer for that. 'No idea,' he said to her in frustration. 'Maybe I can get Corny to cough up more info if I ask.'

'I doubt it,' Emerelda said. 'That book likes you for some reason, if it could have told us more, it would have. I can't see it holding back information that would help us at a time like this.'

'So we're left with a name, a dead body, two extinct families and nothing else to go on,' Max replied.

'That's about the size of it.'

'Sod it.'

Jacob stood. 'All this talk of the past will not help us track this man and his cohorts down. It frankly doesn't matter who he is or where he comes from, we just need to find him and bring him to justice.'

Max couldn't argue with that. He and the Chapter Lord disagreed on many things, but both liked the simple, straight forward approach whenever possible.

—

'And that starts with the League Book he carried,' Garrowain said. 'My fellow custodians are already seeking answers as to where it came from, and where it might lead. I should join them in that purpose.'

'Can you do that?' Max asked. 'Even though it burned to a crisp?'

Garrowain clasped his hands together. 'I do not know. Travel by League Book leaves a trace that can be picked up on, but only if the conditions are just right. It takes enormous skill.'

'Then we shouldn't keep you any longer custodian,' Jacob told him.

Garrowain bowed, bade them all farewell and left Jacob Carvallen's chambers.

Max blew air out of his cheeks. 'Right. What do we do then?'

'I'm going to assist Borne with improving security,' Emerelda said. 'If that bastard comes back, we'll be ready for him.'

'Agreed,' Jacob said. 'And I will spend some time pouring over the recent terrorist incidents to see if I can glean anything further that may assist us.'

Max nodded. 'Sounds fair enough.' He scratched his nose and sighed.

Merelie recognised a Max Bloom cry for help when she saw one. She linked his arm in hers. 'Perhaps we could return to my chambers and read more about the two families Max? Something might come up if we do.'

He smiled, relieved to be given some sort of purpose. 'That's a great idea Merelie.'

'And stay there, both of you,' Emerelda said. 'The last thing I need is you two getting yourselves into trouble with all this going on.'

Max looked disgusted. 'How in hell could we get into any trouble?'

'Max Bloom, you could get yourself into dire straits locked in a room with the lights off,' she replied. 'Now go away the pair of you. There's a lot of work to be done and we've spent way too much time flapping our gums already.'

'Come on Max.' Merelie started to drag him to the door. Lacking any good reason to stay longer, Max let her spirit him away.

Jacob watched them go out of the door before turning to his sister. 'Let us hope this matter can be resolved swiftly before Mr Bloom can get into that trouble you spoke of.'

Emerelda surprised her brother by laughing. 'To use a phrase I picked up over on Earth Jacob... you've got no hope and Bob Hope. And Bob Hope is dead.'

'Who is Bob Hope?'

Emerelda opened her mouth to explain, then thought better of it. Some things had no chance of translating across dimensions, no matter how much you tried.

'It's horrible,' Merelie said as they walked along the gallery towards her chambers.

'What is?'

'Two families tearing each other apart like that.'

'I guess,' Max said.

'You don't think so?'

'Well, yeah. It's pretty nasty and all. But people can do nasty things to one another if they think they've got a good enough reason.'

'Maybe on Earth Max, but here in The Chapter Lands it just doesn't happen.'

'Not in *Carvallen* Chapter Lands Merelie. I'd bet my comic book collection that it happens all the time over where the Morodai are. Draveli's lot as well, for that matter. It just probably comes as a shock to you because this place is a good area to live in. Not everyone's so lucky.'

Merelie pushed the door to her chamber open and stood at the threshold, digesting Max's words. 'You're right. Sometimes I forget how lucky I am.'

Max shrugged. 'Don't beat yourself up about it. You can't help being the daughter of a Chapter Lord.'

They went into Merelie's chamber and she closed the door behind them. Max felt his heart rate rise. This was par for the course any time he was left alone with Merelie in private. It didn't seem to matter how many times the situation occurred, it still sent a small thrill of excitement through him. Being alone with Merelie usually meant there were shenanigans of the most pleasant kind to be had.

'Wordcraft me down those two big brown books at the top of the bookcase to your left Max,' she told him 'We have a lot of reading to do.'

Merelie's words quelled any sense of excitement Max felt. She was all business this evening. There would be no shenanigans happening any time soon.

With a sigh he looked up at the heavy volumes above his head and plucked them both simultaneously from their resting place, floating them down to the table in the middle of Merelie's room.

'Thanks,' she said with the kind of dazzling smile that shenanigans were invented for. 'These are the two volumes that comprise Adric Mold's Houses Of Carvallen. They are a list of all the most powerful families in our Chapter Lands, dating all the way back to the foundation of the House when Symon created The Cornerstone.' She slid one book over to Max. 'You find the Florrens in that one while I look up the Venhaligans in this.'

Max stared disconsolately down at the enormous thick book presented to him.

Max Bloom, as has been well established, is not much of a reader. Before his first contact with The Chapter Lands he'd read three books, and to be brutally honest, not much has improved since, despite becoming a sorcerer who relies on the power of the written word to fuel his considerable abilities.

Many have *tried* to get him to read more. Merelie has loaded him down with books on several occasions - all of which he has completely ignored. His grandfather Charlie has also plied him with editions of various literary masterpieces that now form a haphazard pile next to his bed back home. His mother even bought him a Kindle for Christmas, in the vain hope that the clever technology of ebooks might stir some passion for reading novels inside him. It hadn't worked. Touchscreens and USB ports were for things you played video games and Blu Rays on, as far as Max was concerned. If he was going to actually read a book, it would be the good old fashioned paper kind.

And anyway, the Kindle gave off a strange aura when he held it in his hand. His mother had loaded it with about twenty books, and while Max could feel the word power emanating from the sleek grey device, it felt oddly constrained and *thin* compared to the robust sensation he always got when handling a hardback. It was rather like the difference between a burger made of beef and one made of tofu.

Merelie caught sight of the distraught look on Max's face. She rolled her eyes. 'You really are going to have to embrace reading at some point you know. It's in your blood.'

'So is iron, but you don't see me knocking out any horse shoes on an anvil do you?'

'Just sit down and read Max. We have to find out more about what happened today.'

'Yeah, yeah. Alright. No need to nag me.'

He sat down and wrenched the cover of the large brown book open. The dust that flew up from its pages elicited a loud sneeze and a brief coughing fit.

Books didn't like Max, so Max didn't like books. It was a simple as that.

Nevertheless, if he did want any shenanigans of any kind tonight, he'd better do as he was told. With tongue stuck out in concentration, Max started to leaf through the huge volume.

It was in alphabetical order, which was helpful. He skimmed past all the letters leading up to F and opened the book to a page featuring a family called Fabbamore. Then came Fardel, Felstren, Finbar and eventually Florren.

'The Florrens get a lot more pages devoted to them than the others,' he pointed out.

'Powerful family. Lots to write about.'

Max sighed again. There were at least twelve pages of closely written text between him and the end of this job. This was going to take forever.

Forever actually turned out to be about an hour and a half, by which time another small but obtrusive headache had formed above his right eye.

'This is no bloody good,' he said, slamming the book shut. 'There's almost nothing here to help us. Mold doesn't cover any of the animosity that existed between Xander Florren and Colter Venhaligan. The chapter about the family stops just after the birth of Petren Florren anyway.'

'Petren?'

'Their youngest boy. He was only fourteen when he died in the fire.' Max pushed the book away. 'About the only thing this book does help explain is why the poor old Gamelows were targeted before the Wordmeet.'

'Why?'

'Turns out they were closely allied with the Florrens back in the day. If our killer is somebody from the Venhaligan family, it stands to reason he'd start by taking his anger out on those who chose to side with his main enemy.'

'Certainly makes sense.'

'That's about all there is of any use though. The rest of the book is just dull and unhelpful.'

Merelie nodded and closed her own book. 'Same with the Venhaligans. If Mold knew anything about the conflict he wasn't letting on in here. The whole chapter is just about lineage and land ownership for the most part.'

'Yeah. If I tried to form any Wordcraft from this thing it'd come out beige and flat.'

Merelie yawned and stretched. 'I've had enough of this. We're not going to learn anything from these. We just have to hope Garrowain is more successful.'

Max perked up a bit. If this was the end of the book reading, maybe it meant they could move on to more enjoyable pursuits.

Merelie rubbed her eyes. 'I'm going to bed Max. I need sleep.'

Sod it.

'Okay.'

Merelie misinterpreted the heaviness in Max's voice. 'Don't worry,' she told him, taking his hand. 'I'm sure Garrowain and my father will come up with something to help us soon.'

'What?'

'That's why you look so sad, isn't it?'

'Er... yeah. Of course it is.'

Merelie stood, leaned over the table and gave Max the kind of kiss that would, in other happier circumstances, have been the first step on the path to shenanigans. 'Are you going to stay in the chambers my father provided for you in the north tower?' she asked him.

What? The ones your dad made sure were as far away from you as possible?

'Yes, I'll stay there tonight. With all this going on I don't want to leave you when there's some maniac about. Corny will blast a quick message to Grandad I'm sure.'

Merelie made a face. 'You really shouldn't use it as a messaging service Max.'

'He doesn't mind.'

'Maybe not, but it's just not right and proper.'

There were many things about today that just weren't right and proper. Chief among them now was the fact he was about to leave Merelie's chamber shenanigan free.

'We'll have breakfast together tomorrow morning,' she said to him as she guided him over to the door. 'Maybe a good night's sleep will give us a bit of perspective on what happened today.'

'Yeah. Perspective. That's what we need.'

At the door, Merelie put a hand on his arm. 'Poor Max. This whole thing really has hit you hard, hasn't it? You look so downcast.'

'Absolutely. I can honestly say, that I really wish this day had gone *very* differently.'

'I know.' She kissed him again. 'Tomorrow will be better with any luck.'

Max thought about the trudge up several flights of stairs that awaited him, and the rather chilly chambers at their end. 'I really hope so.'

He walked out through the door and bade Merelie goodnight, before ambling off back down the gallery towards the north tower.

Coming up the main stairs from the large hall below was Borne, looking tired and heavy footed. 'Good evening Max. Have you been with Merelie?'

'Yep. Sadly, she's decided to go to sleep now.'

Borne's shaggy eyebrow shot up. If Merelie had misinterpreted the reasons for Max's misery, Borne most certainly did not. 'You seem decidedly unhappy about that.'

'Yeah. You could say that.' Max noticed the Arma's rapidly darkening demeanour and snapped out of his glum mood almost instantly. 'Still, it's good you're here now. Means I can happily leave, knowing she'll be protected all night!'

'Indeed. I will be in the chamber next to hers, listening for sounds of *any* intrusion.' Borne's eyebrow arched even more. Max got the hint.

'Well, night then Borne.'

'Good night Max.'

The Arma passed Max by and walked towards the chamber he slept in next to Merelie.

'Crap,' Max said under his breath, before continuing to his own room - which you couldn't place further away from his girlfriend and still be under the same roof if you tried.

Merelie lay in her bed, her mind whirling with all the information that had been dropped on her today in her father's study.

Until now, she had always thought of the Houses who sat under her own as being an honourable bunch, but now it seemed that even they were capable of treachery and deceit. She was uncomfortably reminded of the Morodai, a comparison that made her skin crawl.

The deliberate cover up almost made her feel worse. It was one thing to think that people unrelated and unknown to her could behave in such a manner, but the idea that members of her own family could have conspired to keep the unlovely history between families Florren and Venhaligan a secret made the rest of her flesh crawl along with her skin.

With a deep sigh, Merelie resolved to find out more tomorrow with Max's help. Together they should be able to piece together a more accurate version of events, she was sure of it. Maybe then they would have a better idea of who the murdering maniac was that had interrupted the Wordmeet.

This thought led her on to the fate of Darel Cornelius. Tears welled in her eyes as she remembered watching those horrible bullets punch their way through Darel's body. She couldn't stop replaying the look of pained surprise that crossed his face as the life left his body.

Merelie had seen people die at the hands of somebody wielding Wordcraft, but to see someone's life ended by that weapon from Earth made her sick to her stomach. Such an ugly, black, graceless thing it was. She feared for any world that could produce such a tool of destruction, and use it repeatedly throughout their history. Earth held many fascinations for Merelie, but the gun was definitely not one of them.

It had nearly taken Max's life as well. Darel's death was awful, but if Max had been struck a mere couple of inches to the left...

It didn't bear thinking about.

With these unhappy thoughts running through her head, Merelie dropped into a rather fitful sleep, ending this terrible day with the hope that tomorrow would be better.

Bright blue light awoke her from a dark dream. In it, she had been sat in the middle of the Wordmeet stadium, cradling Max Bloom as he died in her arms. In one hand he held a gun, in the other The Cornerstone, which was bleeding from between its pages. Max was looking up at her with an expression of terror that wrenched her heart.

It was almost a relief to be brought out of the nightmare by the bright, flashing blue light that now consumed her entire room.

Merelie sat up and shielded her eyes from the glare. She looked over to the source of the light - one of her bookshelves on the opposite side of her chamber. There, she could see that a book had fallen from its place on the top shelf, and was now open on the floor in front of it.

Oh Writer, that's a League Book!

Merelie was up out of the bed and running towards the door in a split second. She was fast, but not fast enough.

From the League Book sprang a figure. It was the man who had killed Darel that afternoon!

The intruder now stood between Merelie and the door, an evil leer on his face. 'Good evening Merelie,' he said. 'I would like a word with you, if you don't mind.'

'Borne!!' Merelie shouted.

The man waved a dismissive hand and Merelie's bed immediately shot forward, crashing through her table and slamming itself into the chamber door, blocking it completely. She could sense Wordcraft emanate from the pile of broken furniture, indicating that the man in front of her was holding the barrier in place. 'Don't bother calling for your Arma, young lady,' he said. 'I fancy he won't be able to break that door down until my business with you is done.'

'What do you want with me?' Merelie asked, backing away and starting to draw in word power from the books around her.

'For starters, you can stop attempting to word shape,' the man said and flicked one finger out at her. Merelie screamed as her head rocked backwards as if slapped by an invisible hand. Still she tried to draw in enough force to counter the intruder. One of his eyebrows shot up. 'Not one to give up easily, are you my girl?' he said.

The chamber door shook on its hinges as something battered into it from the other side. 'Merelie!!' Borne shouted from the hallway.

Merelie's attacker laughed. 'And your Arma appears to be equally stubborn!

Merelie levelled her gaze at him. 'When he does get in here he's going to rip your arms out of their sockets,' she told him.

The man shook a finger. 'I rather think not, young lady. He, and the rest of your father's men, can throw themselves at that door all they like. They're not getting in here with us.'

Merelie's eyes narrowed. 'And how about Max? You think your little display of power is going to hold him back too?' She was rewarded with a flicker of uncertainty in the man's eyes. It was a pleasure to see the slightly smug expression drop off his face for even a second.

'Max Bloom can't help you either,' he said and walked forward. 'You're coming with me.'

'Never!' Merelie spat and word shaped. A ball of pure energy spun itself out of thin air and flew towards the intruder, intent on pushing him back and crushing him against the wall.

In a slashing motion he brought one arm down, cutting the energy barrier neatly in two. It flew past him on both sides. Her intruder shook his head. 'Tut tut, my dear. You'll have to do a lot better than that.'

Merelie backed away towards the window as the man stepped closer to her. He held out one hand and balled it into a fist.

Merelie felt a heavy blow land on the back of her neck... and the world went black.

-4-

Max didn't like the look of the toilet.

Sure, it ostensibly did the same thing as one you'd find in any average house on his version of the planet, but the Chapter Land equivalent tended towards a more complicated design that he didn't think looked all that efficient - or hygienic. There were more pipes for starters. Max had no idea what most were actually used for, or where they led to, but more pipes meant more chances for things to leak, which didn't sit well with him at all.

Then there was the flush mechanism. The ones in his Grandad's house were reassuringly solid. Big shiny chrome handles that you pushed with confidence, with the sure and secure knowledge that the cleansing sound of water flushing away your deposit would follow immediately after.

Here though, there was some kind of pulley system going on that Max couldn't make head nor tail of. Also, when you did yank the chain that dangled disconcertingly to your left side, there was a squeaky noise, the sound of cogs whirring and a slight rumbling that vibrated its way up through your legs.

Max eyed the toilet with suspicion as he attended to a middle of the night visit. As he went about his business he hummed AC/DC and tapped one foot.

Where Merelie had found it hard to sleep because of the day's events, Max had dropped off earlier almost immediately. While she fretted that deceit and treachery could exist in her world, Max was well aware it existed in his, and therefore wasn't really troubled by it in the slightest.

Max finished up and pulled the flush chain carefully. Once the rumbling had ceased he walked away again, safe in the knowledge that the damn thing wasn't about to explode in his face.

Without warning, he felt a colossal burst of Wordcraft coming from the other side of the Chapter House as he walked back to the bed. Someone had expelled a huge amount of energy and Max's sensitivity to the incredible power source had picked up on it easily.

In an instant he was wide awake. A few seconds later he was dressed in his usual black hoodie and jeans and was striding towards the door as quickly as possible. His head darted from side to side as he tried to identify where the burst had come from. The door to his chamber flew open with a flick of his wrist and he was off down the corridor.

As he jogged through the galleries, he felt another two or three bursts of Wordcraft, helping him to pinpoint exactly where in the Chapter House they were coming from.

Sudden fear overwhelmed him. It was Merelie.

Merelie was in danger. He didn't know how he knew this, he just knew he was right.

He had to reach her chambers as quickly as possible.

Now Max was no longer jogging, he was sprinting. Round corners and up stairs he ran, desperate to get to Merelie as soon as he could.

With a sudden cry of frustration he realised he'd gone down the wrong corridor and a long stone wall lay between him and the large Chapter House hall that Merelie's chambers led off from.

'Sorry Jacob,' Max whispered under his breath, before smashing a hole through the foot thick stone wall with a Wordcraft laden punch.

He was through the hole and flying across the empty space between him and the gallery where Merelie lived in a split second. He could see Borne smashing into her doors with his shoulder.

'Borne! Move!' Max ordered. The Arma looked around wide-eyed, saw Max coming with his fists held out in front, and swiftly jumped out of the way.

Like a human battering ram, Max crashed straight through the doors, obliterating the heavy bed beyond.

With eyes glowing silver with pure fury, his head whipped around the room. 'Merelie!? Where are you? Are you alright?'

No answer came.

Borne climbed over the wreckage behind him. 'Is she here?'

'No!' Max turned to look at the Arma. 'What the hell is going on Borne?!'

'I heard her scream my name, but I couldn't get through the door. There was a man's voice, some bright blue light... and then silence. I was still trying the door when I saw you coming and got out of the way.'

'A bright blue light?' Max asked.

'Yes.'

'That means a League Book was used here...'

Max searched the room with his eyes, eventually alighting on the League Book lying at the foot of Merelie's bookcase. The instant he saw it, the book spontaneously burst into flame.

'NO!' Max cried and leapt over to it. As the flames started to lick up its spine, he grabbed it up, trying with all his might to extinguish the flames with word power. It took more effort that he would have liked, but he managed to wrest the fire under control, and put it out before it managed to do more than scorch the cover of the book.

With a grubby thumb, Max wiped the ash away from the title on the front of the cover and read it.

VENHALLAS.

That was where Merelie had been taken, wherever it was. Max flicked the cover open, preparing himself to be transported through the League Book to the other side.

Nothing happened.

'The fire must have damaged it too much,' Borne said.

'Son of a bitch!' Max spat and kicked a three foot wide hole in Merelie's wall.

Through the wreckage of the door came several Chapter Guards and their master Jacob Carvallen. 'What in the Writer's name is going on here!?' he demanded.

'Merelie has been kidnapped sire!' Borne moaned. 'I have failed you!'

'Give it a rest Borne,' Max said, still breathing heavily as he tried to control his rage. 'He was a powerful Wordsmith, you couldn't have stopped him even if you had got in here before he took her.'

'Took her?' Jacob asked, fear writ large across his face. 'Someone has taken my daughter?'

Max nodded. 'Yes. I'm sorry Jacob. He used a League Book.'

'Who did?'

'I'm guessing it was our friend from today. He used a League Book to escape me at the Wordmeet as well, before destroying it with fire. The one we found in here tried to do the same thing, but I managed to stop it in time.' He shook it at Jacob. 'It's knackered now though. Doesn't work anymore.'

Jacob scowled. 'How did somebody get a League Book in here without Merelie knowing?'

Borne grunted. 'Diversion.'

'What?' Jacob demanded.

'He used a diversion today to get the book smuggled in here.'

'Oh hell...' Max said in a low voice, realising what Borne was saying. 'That's right. The Wordmeet was just a distraction. He crashed it so nobody would be paying attention to the Chapter House, giving someone else time and space to smuggle a League Book up here.'

Jacob looked horrified. 'Are you saying Darel Cornelius died just to give someone the chance to kidnap my daughter?'

'That's about the size of it,' Max said in a grim voice. Then he remembered the title of the League Book. 'Where is Venhallas?'

'Venhallas?'

'Yes. That's where this thing is supposed to go when it's not damaged.'

'Venhallas was the seat of the Venhaligan family. It's their ancestral home.'

Max ground his teeth. 'And where will I find it exactly?'

'About an hour's airship ride north west of here,' Borne told him. 'It's close to the entrance of Seven Mouths.'

'Seven Mouths?' Max asked.

'The largest river in the nearby Chapter Lands.'

Max's geography wasn't up to much, but even he knew what that river was called back home. 'The River Severn, you mean? Venhallas is at the mouth of the River Severn? Pretty much where Gloucester is?'

Max had been to Gloucester with his parents when he was a small boy. There was a lot of cheese there, as he recalled.

'If that is what it is called on your world Max, then yes,' Jacob told him.

'Right.'

Max threw the League Book to Jacob. 'Get that to Garrowain. See if he can get it working again.'

'And what are you going to do?' Jacob asked.

Max looked back to Borne. 'An hour's airship ride, you say?'

'Yes. More or less.'

Max looked to Merelie's window. With a slight twist of his head, he neatly pulled the entire window frame out from the stone archway, floated it down to floor level and rested it against the wall. 'How long do you think it'll take to get to it powered just by Wordcraft, Borne?'

'I have no idea.'

Max's eyes began to glow silver. 'Let's find out, shall we?'

Summoning all his enormous power to one single purpose, Max Bloom floated into mid air.

'Be careful Max,' Jacob warned. 'Find my daughter and bring her back to me.'

'It's a promise,' Max told him, before setting his sights on the horizon, where the morning light was just starting to show.

As he considered what he was about to do, Max whistled a few notes of a catchy tune quietly.

'What is that?' Borne asked.

'Oh nothing,' Max said. 'Just psyching myself up a bit.'

Max whistled a few more bars of the Superman theme, before taking a deep breath and launching himself out into the cool early morning air.

As the world swam back into focus, Merelie knew she was in trouble.

You never wake up with a throbbing headache in a cage suspended thirty feet above a flag stoned floor and think you're going to have a fun day.

She looked up and saw that the cage swung from a thick chain that disappeared into the gloom above her head. Then she looked down and saw that a large grey box was fixed to the underside of the cage. Strapped to this was a strange looking glass device, filled with what looked like a silvery vapour.

Beyond her confines was a large, and what looked like abandoned, hall. It was similar in design to the ones back home at the Chapter House, though on a smaller scale. She could see a long, dark and dusty oak dining table below her, surrounded by broken chairs. Filthy cloth banners hung from the stone walls at intervals between enormous opaque windows. The long white banners were all embossed with the same dark olive green coat of arms Merelie had seen Garrowain conjure out of thin air in her father's study, featuring the open hand surrounded by fire.

This must be the home of the Venhaligan family.

'Admiring the decorations, are we?' a strong voice drifted up to her from the floor below.

Merelie looked down to see her kidnapper enter through a large set of rotting double doors at the end of the hall. He was followed in by four other men, all clad in black armour and sporting the same coat of arms.

'Where am I?' she called down.

'Why... you are in what was once one of the most glorious houses in your father's Chapter Land!' he replied, opening his arms expansively to take in the room around him. The man kicked a tarnished chalice out of the way as he walked towards her. 'It has admittedly seen better days I'll concede, but the space is still impressive I think.' He stopped right under Merelie. 'Impressive enough to contain you and your cage anyway, little songbird.'

'Bite me,' Merelie told him, doing her best Max Bloom impression.

The man laughed and ran a hand over his balding and spiky hairline. 'Such language! Surely your father would not approve?'

'My father doesn't approve of a lot of things I do,' Merelie replied. 'Using my Wordcraft for violent ends being very much one of them.'

Merelie began to draw in word power, intent on smashing this cage to smithereens. Unfortunately, there was hardly any of the ephemeral energy source present for her to use.

66

The man below her laughed. 'I wouldn't bother. I had every book removed to an extremely safe distance. There isn't one for miles around us. It takes someone with the power of your irritating friend Max Bloom to use Wordcraft in this place.'

'Dammit,' Merelie whispered under her breath and stopped her attempts to muster some kind of attack. 'Who are you?' she asked the man beneath.

This elicited another laugh, this one tinged with some bitterness. 'A question you need never have asked, had certain events of the past not transpired.'

'You mean Colter Venhaligan betraying the Chapter House?'

Instantly, humour gave way to rage. 'My father did nothing of the sort!' the man screamed and put a fist right through the thick oak dining table beside him. Splinters of wood flew through the air, forcing two of the man's companions to duck out of the way.

Merelie was shocked. 'Your father?'

Her captor breathed out slowly, calming his anger, and looked back up at her. 'Yes, Merelie. Colter Venhaligan was my father.'

'So, you're Marran?'

This time, grief clouded his expression. 'Have the years aged me so badly? For you to think that I am my own older brother?' Again, a hand ran through what remained of his hair. 'No. I am not Marran.'

'Randal then? You are Randal Venhaligan?'

'You seem to know far more about my family than I thought, my girl.'

Her eyes narrowed. 'Yes, far more than I'd like.'

He chose to ignore that. 'I am indeed Randal Venhaligan. Son of Colter and Viana. Brother to Marran. The only survivor, I thought, of the tragic fire that consumed my family all those years ago.'

'A fire which you and your mother started... right after she'd murdered an entire family of innocent people.'

The rage flared again. 'You think they were *innocent*? Were it not for those people my father would still be alive!'

'Your father? The man who tried to betray my Chapter House, you mean?' Merelie was very satisfied with the look of uncertainty this brought from her captor. 'Didn't think I knew that, did you? That Colter tried to sell his own people out to gain power?'

Venhaligan clenched a fist and immediate wracking pain seared through Merelie's head. She screamed and crashed to the floor of the steel cage.

'Enough,' Randal said. 'I did not bring you here so you could insult my family.'

Fighting back a wave of nausea that threatened the reappearance of last night's dinner, Merelie sat back up. 'Then... then why did you bring me here?'

An expression of insufferable smugness appeared on Randal Venhaligan's face. 'Why in the world would I kidnap the daughter of the Chapter Lord, and lady friend of the most powerful Wordsmith in history? Come now Merelie. You're an intelligent girl. Why do you think I'd do it?'

Merelie thought for a few moments, then rolled her eyes and sighed. 'Bait.'

'Exactly!'

'Well, that's an incredibly stupid plan,' she sneered. 'You don't bait the two most powerful men in The Chapter Lands. Especially ones who can lay waste to this building and you in it.'

Venhaligan folded his arms. 'Oh, don't worry yourself about the details, my dear. I have ways and means in place to ensure my safety when your loved ones come calling. In the meantime, I have other matters to attend to.' He indicated to the four silent armoured men who had come in with him. 'My associates here will keep a careful watch on you now you've awoken. Please don't do anything that would cause them to harm you. A dead Merelie Carvallen is as good a worm on a hook as a live one.'

Venhaligan let those words hang in the air for a few moments, before turning to leave the hall.

'Go to hell,' Merelie whispered quietly.

'Already been there, my girl!' Venhaligan called back over his shoulder as he walked through the broken double doors.

It took Borne, Jacob and Garrowain a good ten minutes to calm Emerelda Carvallen down. By the time they had, she'd destroyed two of the long comfortable couches in the Chapter House hall close to Merelie's ruined bed chambers.

'How the hell could you let this happen!?' she screamed at Borne. 'Where the hell were you?!'

Borne hung his head in shame. He knew better than to argue.

'In point of fact, my dear,' Garrowain said, 'Borne could have done nothing to prevent this happening. He had no knowledge of the presence of a League Book in Merelie's room.' He held the singed book up to illustrate his point. 'If anything, the fault lies with myself and the rest of the custodians. In all matters related to Wordcraft we are where the buck stops, so to speak.'

'This was nobody's fault,' Jacob snapped. 'Someone has been planning this for some time.'

'That much is certainly true,' Emerelda agreed. 'To murder an innocent boy just as a distraction...'

'It is a crime that will not go unpunished,' Jacob promised her. 'Our first task is to get Merelie back safe and sound though.'

'Max is way ahead of us on that front,' said Borne in a low voice. Regardless of blame or not, he still keenly felt the guilt of allowing his mistress to be kidnapped.

'Can he reach her that way Garrowain? By flying that large a distance?'

The Custodian shrugged. 'Mr Bloom's powers exceed anything I can properly comprehend my Lord. It may well be true that he has that capability.'

'It certainly looked that way as he went out of the window,' Jacob said.

Emerelda folded her arms. 'Flying is one thing. Navigating is another. I'm sure Max can fly around like a loon all day if he wants. Actually doing anything constructive with it is another thing entirely.'

Jacob nodded ruefully. 'I fear you may be right.' He looked at Borne, who was now lost in thought. 'Borne?' No answer. 'Borne!'

The Arma shook himself back to alertness. 'Yes my Lord?'

'Go and prepare an airship with a dozen Chapter Guards. I want it ready to launch within the hour. Max may be ahead of us, but that doesn't mean we can't follow and mop up after him if needs be.'

Borne, relieved to have some purpose, snapped off a salute and strode out of the room.

'Well done Jacob. He'd have just moped around here like a little boy until someone slapped some sense into him,' Emerelda said.

'Whether sending an airship will do any good is another thing entirely.'

'Better than us just sitting around here waiting for Max to do something explosive,' she pointed out.

'Agreed.' The Chapter Lord turned back to his head custodian. 'Can anything be done with that book? If we could use it, we could even beat Max to Venhallas.'

Emerelda groaned. 'And walk right into a trap you mean?'

'The point is moot I'm afraid,' Garrowain responded. 'The book appears to be completely inert.' He saw the look of disappointment in his master's eyes. 'However, I will take it down to the Library and see if I can do anything with it.'

Jacob smiled gratefully. 'Thank you Garrowain.'

The Custodian left, leaving brother and sister alone in the hall.

'We'll get her back Jacob,' Emerelda said, seeing the look of distress on her sibling's face.

'We'd better. The last time the name Venhaligan was involved, an entire family of good people died.'

'The Florrens didn't have what we have though.'

'And what's that?'

'An angry Max Bloom.'

Part Three

Maps.

Maps are extremely *useful* things.

Maps show you the way to a desired location, providing a clear and concise route to your chosen destination. They can, when used properly, take a great deal of the stress and worry out of a long journey.

Max Bloom hovered uncertainly thirty or so feet above a wide gravel highway that lay next to a seemingly endless green field, and deeply wished he had a map.

If he were being honest with himself, he'd have to admit that the rage at discovering Merelie kidnapped had sent him off rather half-cocked, and ill prepared for the task at hand. It's all very well being clever enough to work out that Venhallas is where Gloucester would be back on Earth, but this isn't really all that useful when you have no idea how to get to Gloucester anyway.

Max looked up the long gravel highway and scratched his head, wishing with all his might that somebody in this crazy alternate dimension had invented some kind of Wordcraft powered sat nav.

He was brought out of his muddled thinking by the sound of movement behind him. Coming up the highway was a large cart, being powered by a complicated looking metal contraption bolted to the front just above the wheels. Max had little engineering experience, but he fancied he recognised a small steam engine when he saw one.

Sat atop the cart on a wide bench was a woman of questionable vintage, wearing a black shawl and cloak. She could have been anything from sixty to one hundred and sixty by the look of her. In the cart behind her was a selection of house wares that included metal pots and pans, cutlery sets, wash boards, earthenware plates and large pottery milk jugs. There was also a small brown pug, who was sat on his haunches among the myriad kitchen utensils, looking up and regarding Max with an expression of deep distrust.

The old woman was singing loudly. Well, it approximated singing anyway.

The subject of her song was a lady, a gentleman, and the interesting things they got up to in the woodshed on a bright summer's morn. As the cart got nearer to where Max hovered, the song descended into what could only be described as audible pornography, and Max thought he'd better put a stop to it before he suffered some kind of severe emotional trauma.

'Er, excuse me?'

The song immediately stopped and the old woman's head whipped around. 'Who's that? Where are ye?' she said.

Ah...

This could be difficult. Max had temporarily forgotten that he was in fact floating high above the ground. He feared that the surprise of seeing an eighteen year old wearing a faded black hoodie and equally battered Nike trainers hovering above the old lady's head might cause a fatal heart attack. Still, Merelie was in danger, so he really didn't have time for niceties.

'Er, I'm up here.'

The woman looked up in the air, just in front of where Max floated. 'Is that you Writer?' she said in a tremulous voice. 'Have ye come to claim me on this road before I reach home, ye cruel godling?'

'Um... look back a bit,' he advised.

She did so and saw him. Max gave her a little wave. 'Morning,' he said.

The old woman look relieved. 'Oh, it's just you Max Bloom. Ye gave an old woman a start, and no mistake.'

Well this was unexpected.

'How do you know who I am?' he asked in amazement.

'What? A young man dressed as you are, hanging in mid air above my head in all defiance of the laws handed down to us by the Writer himself? Well there's only one person in all The Chapter Lands who that could be, as far as Mother Witcham is concerned.'

'Who's Mother Witcham?'

'I am, you cloth headed fool. Come down here so we can talk properly, will ya? My neck's getting an awful crick in it.'

Max did as he was bid, floating down to sit next to old Mother Witcham on her cart. 'So you've heard of me then?' Max said, sounding almost disappointed.

'Of course! Why, there's not a town between here and the north that hasn't heard of Max Bloom, the Wordsmith from another world!'

This disturbed Max greatly. Given that this dimension didn't have Sky News or the internet, he rather hoped his celebrity hadn't gone that far. He was more or less content with the fact people knew who he was in and around the Carvallen Chapter House and the surrounding city, but the idea that this entire country could pick him out of a line up was just a tad disturbing. 'It's the hoodie, isn't it?' he said to Mother Witcham, pulling at it. 'It's a dead giveaway around here.'

'And the strange shoes, my boy. The surly expression and bad haircut don't help either. You're an easy one to describe to others.'

Max was about to complain over the bad haircut remark, when he remembered what he was here for in the first place. 'Do you know the way to Venhallas?' he asked.

Mother Witcham's eyes narrowed. 'Why be ye wantin' to go to that place? It is full of ghosts.'

'Right now it might be full of kidnapped girlfriend, so I need to find it.'

'Miss Merelie has been kidnapped?' the old woman said in horror. 'Why that must be awful for you! After all, 'twas her who brought you to this world with The Cornerstone, was it not?'

Max gave her a suspicious look. 'You know, for an old lady who sells kitchen utensils, you seem to know an awful lot about things that aren't your business.'

Mother Witcham contrived to look shocked. 'Why, whatever can ye mean, young Mr Bloom?'

'I'm not buying all the yeeing and yaaing either,' he replied. 'If you're just a weird old lady with a cart full of crap and a slightly distressed looking dog, then I'm Batman.'

Mother Witcham let out a disgusted grunt, sat up straight in her seat and dropped the semi-baffled expression. 'Alright, no need to shout it about. It's a good disguise. Gets me in and out of places with no questions asked, if you know what I mean.'

'Who the hell are you really?'

'None of your damn business Max Bloom. Not everything in The Chapter Lands is your concern. Suffice to say that selling frying pans is only a part-time job.'

'And what do you do for the rest of the time?'

Mother Witcham stared Max down. 'I make cheese.'

'Cheese?'

'Yes. Lots of cheese,' she said matter of factly.

'Don't believe you.'

'No, I'm sure you don't. But right now, don't you have more pressing concerns than what an old woman does with her spare time?' Mother Witcham's arm shot out ramrod straight and pointed off towards a couple of low lying hills about four miles away. 'Venhallas lies behind those hills. Big bugger of a place. Mostly black and shiny, and what isn't has long since fallen down. You can't miss it.'

Max looked in the direction she indicated. Clenching his jaw, he stood up and floated back into the air.

'Thanks very much,' he said to the strange old woman.

'Not a problem,' she replied.

Max gave her a look. 'I have a feeling we might meet again at some point.'

Mother Witcham returned the look with interest and a fair amount of top spin. 'Quite possibly Mr Bloom. Quite possibly.'

Without another word she pressed her foot down on a paddle beneath her feet and the strange cart lurched into motion again. Max wanted to question her further, but thoughts of Merelie's predicament prevented him from doing so. He set his eyes on the horizon and flew off in the direction of the two hills the old woman had pointed out.

-2-

Garrowain placed the burned League Book on a pedestal and stood back. He couldn't for the life of him think how the book remained intact, but did not function as it was supposed to.

It was as if somebody had simply removed all of its magical power without destroying its physical shape. This should be impossible. The very nature of Wordcraft is woven into the fabric of every book. While the book exists, so should the power. Even League Books - which weren't really books when you got right down to it, but methods of transport - should always retain some essence of the word source in them. But this one seemed to have been leeched of all its power completely. Even here, in the centre of the great Carvallen Library, the League Book did not give off even the merest trace of the energy source that otherwise spun and twisted its way among the stacks, invisibly linking every book it touched.

The scorched League Book was like a void in space. An area of negativity that made Garrowain's teeth itch.

This was all highly disturbing. It indicated that whoever had created or modified the book had a mastery over Wordcraft that was unprecedented - as far as Garrowain was aware. Coupled with the will to kill innocent people to achieve an end, he could not think of a more dangerous adversary for Max Bloom and the Chapter House.

His eyes flicked over to The Cornerstone where it sat on its own plinth at the centre of the chamber. The strange and marvellous book had been rather quiet of late. It had gone about its job of ferrying Max to and from Earth, but had done very little else until today. This was very unlike The Cornerstone. It was only Max's interrogation into who had killed Darel Cornelius that had awakened it after a good few weeks of apparent slumber. Garrowain didn't quite know why, but the lack of activity actually worried him. It was almost as if the book was girding its loins for something dreadful that it saw looming on the horizon, even when nobody else could see it.

Giving both Cornerstone and League Book a final contemplative look, the head custodian turned and walked out of the chamber deep in thought.

As soon as his back was turned, the plinth The Cornerstone sat on started to rotate slowly so that it faced the damaged League Book. A flicker of silver light played across the magical book's cover as the plinth settled into place.

The Cornerstone didn't have eyes, but you can bet vital parts of your anatomy it was watching anyway.

Venhallas looked exactly like old Mother Witcham had predicted. It was indeed black and shiny, what there was left standing of it.

Time, weather and the forest that surrounded the once imposing great house had done a thorough job of wrecking a large majority of its vast bulk. As he flew towards it Max could see entire buildings collapsed and overgrown with greenery. Only the centre of Venhallas had apparently escaped the worst of nature's onslaught. There, surrounded by a maturing collection of beech trees stood a wide, square building, ornamented with many bold crenulations and ramparts. The stone it was made from was polished, jet black granite. It reflected the bright light of the sun back into Max's eyes.

If Merelie was anywhere, she would be in that building.

Max slowed his approach, looking for signs of movement. He saw none, but nevertheless knew that there were people down there, probably watching him.

The whole thing screamed 'trap!' in a very loud voice, but Merelie was down there somewhere being put through God knows what, so if it was a trap, Max would just have to spring it and hope it wasn't a fatal one.

He landed a good hundred metres away from the only building left standing and gave it a long hard look.

There were two ways this could be handled.

He could surreptitiously make his way towards the set of shattered main doors, using the trees and other foliage for cover, or he could take the more direct approach and announce his arrival loudly. Given that Max suffered from hay fever now and again, and some of the flowers growing in clumps around the trees looked decidedly laden with pollen, the direct approach seemed the sensible way to proceed.

Let's face it, Max would have gone that way whatever, but it's always nice to have a justification for your actions.

Max created a protective blanket of Wordcraft around his body, and started to make his way forward. He was forced to concede that the blanket wasn't particularly thick. He couldn't sense any books close to him and was uncomfortably reminded of that day in the Morodai library when Lucas Morodai had cut him off from the word source, until The Cornerstone had opened its pages and filled him with the power he needed to defeat the villainous Chapter Lord.

This wasn't quite the same. Max had honed his Wordcrafting skills to the point where he could draw on the word source wherever he was, no matter how many books were immediately present. It still didn't make him comfortable to think he'd have to strain himself here in Venhallas though, should anyone offer him resistance.

Shrugging off such thoughts Max walked towards the building, ready for any kind of attack that was coming his way.

As he reached the shattered oak doors none had come. Everything remained suspiciously silent.

Max took a deep breath, rolled up his sleeves and entered the building. As he did so he felt a strange but subtle feeling of pressure, as if something was preventing him from entering. He pushed his way forward and the sensation disappeared. Whatever barrier had been erected to prevent his entry, it hadn't taken any real effort to break through it.

The first thing Max saw as he made his way into the gigantic hall was the cage high above his head. The next thing he saw were the four heavily armoured and helmeted guards walking towards him.

'Max!' he heard Merelie's voice call down to him from the cage.

'Merelie! Are you alright?' he called back up to her.

'Other than being kidnapped and having to swing around all day in this cage? Fine thanks!'

If she was being sarcastic it couldn't be all that bad.

'Just hang on while I take care of these goons and I'll get you down from there!'

'It's not them you have to worry about!'

'What do you mean?'

'I think she's referring to me,' a voice said from behind Max in the doorway he'd just stepped through.

Max spun around to find himself face to face with the man who had shot and killed Darel Cornelius.

'Oh, you are about to get your head kicked in, pal,' Max said as silver lightning flashed in his eyes.

The man held out a hand. 'I'd stop right there if I were you! Performing any acts of Wordcraft in this hall would go very badly for Merelie!'

'What are you on about?' Max asked.

'Felt something odd when you came in did you?' the man asked him, obviously referring to the weak barrier that Max had pushed through easily.

'Yeah. Some sort of protection against me getting in. It didn't work.'

The man barked a short laugh. 'It wasn't meant to keep you out Max! It was meant to trigger the detonator on the bomb strapped under Merelie's cage.'

Max's blood ran cold. He looked back up at the cage, and could see the large grey box affixed to its underside.

'Don't worry yourself!' The man reassured him. 'Providing no external Wordcraft is performed in this hall, the explosives will not detonate. The trigger will only react if you do anything with all that power of yours.'

'Merelie! Is he telling the truth?' Max shouted up.

Merelie looked back down at the grey box beneath her. The silver vapour that had filled the small glass device next to it had turned a sickly shade of purple. 'I... I think so. There's a weird glass bulb here with stuff in it. It was silver before, now it's gone purple.'

Great, thought Max. *More bloody purple.*

'That would be the device arming itself Max,' the man continued, walking past him towards the centre of the room. 'It's a rather clever little apparatus, even if I do say so myself. Distilling word source into a vapour and capturing it in a bottle was difficult. Programming it to respond to the use of Wordcraft was even harder.' He found a chair amongst the detritus on the ground and tipped it upright. 'Should it detect even the slightest use of aggressive magic in this hall, the glass will shatter, sending a charge directly into the four pounds of TNT contained in the box next to it.'

Max was aghast. 'TNT?'

'Oh yes! My father didn't just bring service revolvers back with him on his visits to Earth. There were all sorts of interesting things he found over there that he thought he could put to good use in The Chapter Lands if he ever needed to.'

'Your father?'

'He's Randal Venhaligan Max!' Merelie called down to him as she tried to sit as far away from the grey box as possible. 'He's Colter Venhaligan's youngest son!'

Randal Venhaligan performed a florid bow. 'Pleased to make your acquaintance.'

'I'd be more pleased to make your face into a pizza,' Max replied.

Randal rolled his eyes. 'You try to be polite and this is what you get.' From his belt he produced another revolver and pointed it at Max. 'Have a seat young man.'

'You like your guns, don't you?' Max said in derisory fashion as he walked over to the chair and slouched into it. 'Guns are a coward's weapon... in case you weren't aware.'

Randal shrugged. 'They provide a handy shortcut when necessary.' His eyes flicked up to the bomb above their heads. 'Especially in situations where Wordcraft isn't advisable.'

Max nodded. The point was a valid one. 'So you're Randal Venhaligan. The only person to survive the fire that killed the rest of your family and the Florrens. How did you get out?'

'Luck, Max. Pure, unadulterated luck. I was overcome by the fumes and blacked out. When I awoke I was lying in the garden at the rear of the house. I have no idea how I came to be there.'

Max sneered. 'So you got to watch your mother's handiwork up close then? Got to see all those people die right in front of you?'

'What else could I have done? I was a scared boy.'

Max grunted. 'Yeah, and here you are... all grown up and the last survivor of a war your two-faced father started.'

Randal was in Max's face in an instant, the gun held against his temple. 'You're wrong on two counts, my cocky little Wordsmith. My father was a *great* man... and I was not the only survivor that night.'

'What do you mean?'

Randal Venhaligan stood upright again and regarded Max with a curious expression. 'You have his eyes. That's how I knew.'

'What?'

'The first time I saw you, at the Carvallen Chapter House after you'd defeated the Dwellers and Morodai. I was there in the crowd as they cheered you.' The gun fell to Venhaligan's side as he became lost in thought. 'I wasn't cheering though. I was looking right at you. Lost in the horror of it. Because you look *so much* like him. Especially the eyes.'

'Do you intend to start making sense any time soon?' Max asked him. 'Or shall I just sit here and wait for the men in white coats to come and cart you off?' His eyes strayed down to the gun.

'Your father Max. The day I saw you, I knew your father must still be alive, and had escaped me.'

Max's eyes snapped back up to Venhaligan's face. 'What the hell has my dad got to do with all of this?'

Randal's eyes went wide in shock. 'You don't know, do you?' He laughed. 'Oh my, this is just too rich for words!'

'Max...' Merelie called down to him from above.

Randal looked up. 'Ah, it seems Merelie wishes to join the conversation. Why don't we bring her a little closer?' He nodded at one of the armoured guards, who went over to a crank in the corner and began to lower Merelie's cage so it hung just above their heads.

Max stood up as the cage stopped its descent. 'I said... what does my dad have to do with any of this?'

Randal rolled his eyes again. 'For such a smart little sod, you can be incredibly dense Wordsmith.' The gun came back up, levelled at Max's face. 'And you might want to sit back down again. *Right now.*'

Max did so reluctantly.

'The second I saw you, I knew he must have survived,' Randal continued. 'Must have gotten out of the fire... maybe the same way I did. The more I learned of you and where you came from on the other side of The Cornerstone, the more I knew he must have fled to Earth all those years ago. There he must have started a new life. Grown older, found a woman and fathered a child that looked just like him.'

Max was still completely confused. 'Who are you talking about?'

'Max...' Merelie repeated slowly. She was a lot quicker on the uptake than he was. 'He's talking about Petren Florren.'

'The youngest kid? What about him?'

'Petren Florren escaped the fire and fled to Earth,' Merelie said, her voice low and shaky. 'Oh Writer.'

'What?' Max said.

'That's the real reason why The Cornerstone chose you last year. Your bloodline is from The Chapter Lands after all...' she trailed off, her hands going to her face.

Max thumped the arm of the chair. 'Will someone please start making some sense around here?!'

'I'll handle this, my dear,' Randal said to Merelie. 'I rather think this revelation is somewhat difficult for you to explain properly, given your current state of mind.' He stared back down at Max. 'Have you ever wondered where you get your surname Max? Where the name Bloom comes from?'

'Not really.'

'The study of family names has always fascinated me. Take the name Florren for instance. It's a very, very old word from our Chapter Land's past. It means the bloom of a flower. Pretty word, really. I can see why your father didn't want to let go of it entirely.'

At last, things fell horribly into place in Max's head.

Peter Bloom had told his family that he was the only child of two people killed in a car crash when he was fourteen. He'd even shown them pictures of the man and woman he claimed were his parents.

'You're lying,' Max said flatly.

'I'm afraid not.' For the first time Randal Venhaligan sounded almost sympathetic. 'Your father lied to you. He fled The Chapter Lands after he committed his crime and obviously created a new life for himself in your world. I was blissfully unaware of any of it until I saw your face and knew you were Petren Florren's son.'

'What crime?' Merelie asked. 'What crime did Max's father commit?'

Randal's head lowered. The hand not holding the gun clenched. 'The murder of my mother. On the night of the fire I saw Max's father deliberately push my mother from a balcony, straight into the flames below.' The gun came up again, this time shaking slightly at the barrel. 'I have cursed Petren Florren's name for nearly thirty years, thinking he had escaped me in death. But then his offspring came to The Chapter Lands, and I knew I still had my chance for revenge.'

Max dry swallowed. He could detonate every cartridge in that gun with a flick of the wrist, but doing so would set off the TNT that would kill them all. He cared little for his own life in that instant, but the thought of Merelie being consumed in the explosion was enough to make him sick. If Randal Venhaligan wished to pull the trigger and end Max's life here and now, there wasn't a damn thing he could do about it.

'Go on then,' he said, voice shaking. 'Kill me. That's what you want, isn't it? That's why you brought me here.'

From beyond the barrel of the pistol, Max could see a triumphant smile spread across Randal Venhaligan's face. He could see the man's finger tightening on the trigger and closed his eyes.

'Max!' Merelie wailed and reached a hand down to him through the thick bars of the cage.

The gun hammer fell with a click. Max opened one eye and was astonished to see he wasn't dead.

Randal laughed and threw the gun to one side. 'You see, that's the problem with Earth weapons... once you run out of bullets, they're as useless as a paperweight. If only my father had brought more back with him!'

Max, now feeling on slightly firmer ground given that the imminent threat of death had been removed, responded in time honoured tradition. 'Yeah... and if only your father hadn't been such a slimy, two-faced sack of gerbil droppings, then none of us would have been in this situation in the first place.'

The punch was hard, fast and straight to the point. Max's head rocked backwards.

'Ha!' he said, putting a hand up to his bloody lip. 'All you tossers are the same. You all spout the same old crap, trying to sound clever and above the rest of us, but the second somebody winds you up, you start chucking the punches around just like everybody else.'

Venhaligan was in Max's face again in an instant. 'I suggest you try to kerb that mouth of yours. Let's not forget that with a single gesture I can send all three of us straight into oblivion.'

This time, Max pushed forward in the seat, making Venhaligan lean back again. 'You don't strike me as the martyr type, mate. But why don't you try and prove me wrong?'

For a split second, for the merest of moments, all their futures were held in the palm of Venhaligan's hand. But true to Max's word, this man was no martyr, and he stood away from Max, straightening his long grey coat and smoothing his thinning hair as he did so.

'Enough of this. I never brought either of you here to kill you.'

'Then why did you?' Merelie said, half in fear, half in exasperation.

Randal looked up at her. 'I needed you to get Max here my dear, and I needed Max away from the Carvallen Chapter House so no-one would stop my next move.'

'Which is?' Max asked.

'Oh, you'll find out soon enough.' Randal nodded his head in the direction of his four armed guards, who immediately walked forward to surround Max. They all carried the evil looking cross bow guns favoured by all the Chapter Guards Max had ever met. 'Now, you will stay sat here for as long as I deem it necessary. I highly doubt you have the physical prowess to overcome four highly trained warriors without the use of Wordcraft.'

Max nodded. 'No, no. You're probably right.' He favoured the guard standing in front of him with a look of decided malevolence. 'Let's just hope for their sakes that bomb doesn't get disarmed while they're still in the same room as me.'

The guard, who was more intelligent than his role suggested, knew a horrific threat when he heard one and flinched back slightly before recovering his composure.

'Yes. Quite,' Randal said. 'Nevertheless, I recommend you just sit there and ponder on the gravity of your combined situation.'

'My father will be coming here to rescue me, you monster,' Merelie said. 'And he doesn't have to use Wordcraft to kill you and your underlings. He has many Chapter Guards of his own.'

'I don't doubt it my dear! In fact, I'm relying on his desire to save you as equally as I was relying on the same desire from Max here.' Randal's smug smile made Merelie want to slap him across the face. 'With both Jacob Carvallen and Max Bloom gone from the Chapter House, it will be very quiet, don't you think?'

'What are you going there to do?' Merelie asked.

'The Cornerstone,' Max told her. 'He wants The Cornerstone.'

'Why?'

'Yes, why Max?' Randal said. 'Why would I need The Cornerstone?'

'You're going after Petren Florren. You're going after my father.'

From beneath his coat Randal produced a blue League Book. 'My, my. You really *are* a smart little boy, aren't you?'

'Don't call me boy.'

Randal bowed apologetically. 'This has been a fascinating conversation, but I really do have to go now. Important matters to attend to, you understand.'

'Bite me,' Max said.

The smug laugh returned in spades. 'Merelie already offered me the chance to do that, but I'm afraid I must turn you down as I did her!'

And with that Randal Venhaligan strode towards the doorway. 'Remember! No Wordcraft in the boundary of this hall if you want Merelie to stay in one piece!'

He was just stepping through the doorway when Max whistled long, loud and sharp. Randal turned back. 'Something more to say?'

Max sat forward. The guards moved back. 'Just one thing, and you'd better listen good and hard. We *will* get out of this little trap of yours. I *will* find you. And if I do... *when* I do... ' Max's voice lowered and his hands clenched on the arms of the chair, '...I *will* pull your head out through your arse.'

This elicited a confused look from Venhaligan, who seemed about to respond, but then closed his mouth, shook his head, and left the building.

'You're really going to have to come up with a better threat than that you know,' Merelie told him as she slumped back, sending the cage rocking to and fro.

'Quite probably,' Max agreed and sat back as well. He gave the Chapter Guards surrounding him a good, hard look. 'So, how much does it take to betray your countrymen and follow a madman?' he asked them. 'A bar of gold? Two? Maybe five?'

None answered, but the bow guns were raised slightly. 'Fair enough,' Max said, raising his hands.

'He's going to use that League Book to get into the Chapter House. The same way he did when he kidnapped me,' Merelie guessed.

'Yep. I suppose that was his plan all along. Get me out and get in himself.'

'And once he gets there, he'll fight his way through the building to The Cornerstone and use it to get to Earth. I'm so sorry Max.'

'He won't have much of a fight I don't think.'

'Why?'

Max looked up at her. 'Who's the first person your dad would have given that League Book to?'

'Garrowain, of course.'

'And where would Garrowain have taken it?'

'Well, the Library... *oh no*.'

'My thoughts exactly.'

'And there's not a damn thing we can do about it all the time this bomb is under me.'

'That's about the size of it.' Max folded his arms and tipped his head back. 'Not to worry though. I reckon our predicament is about to get a whole lot better.'

'What makes you say that?'

Max looked up again and smiled broadly at the four men holding them prisoner. 'Because I can hear an airship, that's why.'

Borne stood in the front section of the airship cabin, staring ahead at the bright blue morning sky and chewing one knuckle in a combination of suppressed rage and shameful guilt.

While it was easy for Max Bloom and the others to tell him that there was nothing he could have done to prevent Merelie's kidnap, it didn't make him feel better in the slightest.

Borne was Merelie's Arma, and as such any harm that came to her was a failure on his part, no matter how it came about.

'You'll go through to the bone if you're not careful,' said Emerelda as she joined him.

Borne lowered his hand and stuck it in his belt. 'A fair point,' he replied.

The Wordsmith and one time librarian looked up at the bulk of the airship above their heads and gave an involuntary shiver. 'I don't like these things. Never have,' she told him.

'Why?'

'I spent a good portion of my life in a world where something called The Hindenberg Disaster happened. Trust me, if you knew what I was talking about, you wouldn't want to be trapped in this giant balloon either.'

'We've never had any problems with them,' Borne said to her.

'No. What with all that Wordcraft helping to power them, they are considerably safer than the ones back on Earth, which were full of the most explosive gas they could possibly find... the idiots.' Emerelda pointed a finger up at the bulk of the air balloon above them. 'But you mark my words Arma, punting around several hundred feet off the ground in a giant balloon is never, ever a good idea. No matter how it's powered.'

'You think too much Emerelda.'

This was greeted with an arched eyebrow. 'Oh? And what have you been doing for the past hour since we left the dock?'

Borne sighed. 'Another fair point.'

Emerelda looked back out of the window. 'I think you're about to get the chance to put thought into action though Borne,' she said, staring down to their right at the land below.

There, coming into view between two large hills was the dilapidated remains of Venhallas. Instead of chewing on one knuckle, Borne started to crack them, a grim look on his face.

Jacob came forward from the control station behind them and joined them both at the viewing platform. 'There it is. Venhallas. This is the first time I've ever been here.'

'And the last with any luck,' Emerelda said.

'How do you wish to proceed my Lord?' Borne asked.

Jacob stared down at the vast complex of tumble down buildings for a second. 'We will land on the outskirts and make our way in slowly from there. I don't wish to risk Merelie's life by charging in like a bull.'

'What about Max?' Borne said.

'Max Bloom will be here somewhere,' Emerelda replied. 'I just hope he's not done anything stupid in the time it's taken us to get here.'

It was Jacob Carvallen's turn to arch an eyebrow. He then turned to the Chapter Guard stood behind the raised control station. 'Begin making your descent Captain. Land us in that large open area just beyond what remains of the west gate.'

'Yes my Lord,' the thick set captain responded and started to turn the heavy wheel in front of him.

As the airship turned and began to descend Jacob looked back down at the buildings below and started to chew a knuckle.

'Oh, don't you start doing that as well,' Emerelda told him. 'There might be people down there who need punching.'

From the ground Randal Venhaligan looked up into the morning sky and saw the airship coming towards them.

'Ah... right on time,' he said in a very self satisfied manner.

A tall, dark haired and muscular man dressed in Chapter Guard armour came towards him, walking across the weed infested courtyard outside the hall where Max and Merelie were trapped. Randal nodded as the much larger man approached.

'Hello Mitigir. I trust your men are in position and ready?'

'They are.' The large man lifted his grizzled face to look at the rapidly nearing airship. 'Not a moment too soon. We seem to have company.'

'Indeed we do. The kind I hired you and your men to protect me from.'

Mitigir shifted the hard chest piece of body armour and cracked his neck. 'You will get your money's worth, don't worry.'

Randal smiled. 'I'm sure I will. Just keep them busy for the next few hours while I work, that's all I ask.'

'Not a problem.'

Randal Venhaligan wasn't as confident in Mitigir and his men, it had to be said. They may be dressed as Chapter Guards, but most were brigands, thieves and wastrels that Randal had picked up in the watering holes of the local towns. Most would be ill prepared to deal with Jacob Carvallen and a troop of his highly trained warriors. Still, you worked with what you had. They only needed to put up enough resistance to provide a decent distraction.

'I hope you are right,' he told Mitigir. 'But just to lend you a helping hand before I leave...'

Randal turned to the airship, took a deep breath and held both hands out in front of his face, palms facing one another. There, a ball of fire started to form, constructed from pure Wordcraft. A weaker Wordsmith would not have had the power to create such a tightly packed sphere of destruction with no books in the close vicinity, but Randal Venhaligan had been born with great skill, and the intervening years of never-ending hate and thoughts of revenge had honed those skills to a *very* sharp edge.

He flung his hands out, sending the ball of fire crackling straight towards the airship. Immediately, he created another and sent that flying at the vast bulk above his head as well.

Not even looking up to see where they went, he turned back to Mitigir. 'There, that should help you out.' The League Book was once again retrieved from a deep pocket in the lining of his grey coat. 'Now, I have business to attend to elsewhere. Once I am gone, make sure this book is kept safe. ' He had to pause for a second as the two fireballs struck the airship with colossal force. '...as I was saying, make sure this book is kept safe.'

'Yes Randal,' Mitigir replied staring up at the drama that was unfolding above their heads.

'Good lad,' Randal said and flipped open the League Book.

Once he had disappeared into its pages, Mitigir gathered it up, stuck it behind his chest plate and ran as fast as his legs would carry him away from the airship that was about to crash onto his head.

'Borne, have the men line up at the exit,' Jacob said. 'I want them ready to fan out onto the ground the second the airship touches the ground.'

'Yes my Lord,' the Arma replied.

Jacob looked back at his sister. 'You and I will follow, Emerelda. There may be need for our Wordcraft.'

'I don't doubt it for a second,' she replied, and resisted the urge to chew on her knuckle. This was the first time Emerelda would have to use her skills in battle since that Dweller business, and she wasn't looking forward to it one little bit.

Still, at least they would be on the ground soon. No matter what Borne said, she really didn't like being on this airship at all.

Jacob picked up on her nerves. He placed a hand on her shoulder. 'It will be alright. We will find Merelie and punish the man responsible for taking her.'

She covered his hand with her own and looked back out at Venhallas below them. 'I know. I'll just be glad when we're off this - ' She saw the fireball screaming up towards them from the ground. *'Bloody hell!'*

Randal Venhaligan's fireball punctured the airship's underside right in front of their eyes. The cabin shook wildly as the shockwave rippled its way along the inflated structure above them.

87

'We're under attack!' the airship captain shouted.

'That much is fairly obvious!' Emerelda spat back at him as she tried to steady herself against the metal wall of the cabin.

'Don't worry,' Jacob said. 'The airship structure is very strong. We can take a direct hit like that and still be okay.'

'What about two direct hits?' Borne said as he peered out of a side window.

'Why do you say that?' the Chapter Lord asked.

Borne gave his master a grave look. 'We all may want to hang on to something,' he said.

The second fireball slammed into one of the enormous rotor blades that powered the airship through the sky. The whole vessel lurched sideways as it took the impact. Jacob and Emerelda were thrown to their feet, as were a majority of the Chapter Guards.

The airship started to spin as it headed towards the ground at a fatal speed. The captain gained his feet again and began to yank several levers at the control station, which was now sparking and sending billowing clouds of smoke into the cabin.

'Use the landing rotors!' Jacob commanded, fighting his way past the tangle of Chapter Guard arms and legs to the control station. 'We have to slow the ship's descent!'

He joined his captain and started to pull on a large lever next to the steering wheel. It didn't want to move, no matter how hard he yanked at it. Swearing under his breath Jacob concentrated and augmented his efforts with some finely tuned Wordcraft. The lever did move now, and with a reluctant squeal it locked into place.

To Emerelda, the sound that followed this was like two thousand vacuum cleaners being turned on at once. The airship began to right itself and everyone was thrown to the floor of the cabin again as its descent dramatically slowed.

'I see someone!' Borne shouted, looking out of the window. He could see Mitigir running across the courtyard below him, now a mere fifty yards below his feet.

With a roar, Borne slammed down the latch that held the cabin door in place and smashed the door open with his foot.

'Borne!' Jacob yelled at him. 'What are you doing?'

'Making amends my Lord!' the Arma shouted back.

As the airship hit the stone courtyard with a jarring thump, Borne leapt from the doorway in pursuit of the armoured brigand.

'Sounds like something's coming boys,' Max said, arms behind his head and legs splayed out in front. It was apparent that, from the way the previously steadfast guards were now shuffling about nervously, they were not the trained killers Max had considered them to be. The armour was impressive, but it didn't seem like the human beings inside it were at all.

From somewhere outside and above them, there was a tremendous explosion.

'Oh dear, sounds like whatever it is, it's really *big* and *mean*,' Max continued, and looked up at Merelie. 'Would you say that's your father paying a visit?' he asked her.

'Why yes Max, I do believe you're right. That does sound like my father Jacob Carvallen, the most powerful man in The Chapter Lands, with access to both Chapter Guards and powerful Wordsmiths.'

There was more shuffling of feet from their captors now. At least two of them were also looking around at the exit.

Max nodded sagely. 'Yes, that's right, isn't it? Those Chapter Guards are a merciless bunch, aren't they? I can see them cheerfully blowing to pieces anyone who'd harm a hair on your head.' Max snapped his fingers. 'And I bet Borne is with them too!'

'Borne? You mean my Arma, Max?' Merelie replied. 'The man who once ripped his way through an entire crowd of Dwellers to save me?'

'Yeah, that's the one!'

Another explosion rocked the building to its foundations. A decade's worth of dust was shaken from the ceiling and deposited on their heads.

Max coughed loudly and bow guns that had been lowered and forgotten temporarily were raised again. 'Oh, I don't think those are going to do you much good when our friends come barging in through that door lads.'

'Shut ya mouf,' said one of the guards.

'We ain't supposed ta talk to 'em!' Another hissed at him.

'Yeah? Well, I ain't gettin' paid enough to listen to 'im flap his gums all the time.'

'Will you idiots be quiet?' a third guard piped up.

'Don' tell me to be quiet Meggins!' the first said.

'No bleedin' names! No bleedin' names, you twonk!' Meggins spat back.

'Oh sod off Meggins. We only brung you along coz Pimlicker was sick again,' the second guard said in a disgusted voice.

'That ain't true!' Meggins protested. 'Mitigir wanted me along. I'm an assit to the team, he said.'

This drew a sharp intake of breath from all three of his compatriots. The first guard pointed at him. 'You said the boss's name! You're such a tool Meggins!'

'Yeah! Thas right Gorman, you tell 'im!'

Gorman swore. 'No bloody names Vilbert!'

'Well you just said mine too!' Vilbert wailed.

Max exchanged grins with Merelie. This was huge fun. He only wished he had his iPhone with him so he could film it all and put it on YouTube. 'Lads, lads, lads!' he said, gesturing for them all to calm down. 'Don't argue amongst yourselves.' He gave them a winning smile. 'You're going to need all your strength to fight off our friends when they get in here in a minute.'

'Absolutely,' agreed Merelie. 'I figure Borne will snap Meggins's neck first, before stabbing Vilbert in the heart and kicking Gorman's head off. Sound about right to you Max?'

'I should think so! Then the one who was clever enough to keep his name a secret will probably piss himself and run away.'

'His name's Arfur,' Vilbert told him. Arfur groaned loudly, but elected to keep quiet and await further developments.

Further developments were certainly happening, in the most dramatic way possible.

Borne hit the ground running, only stumbling slightly to compensate for the hard landing the airship had taken. He saw Mitigir sprint around the side of the huge central hall of Venhallas and roared after him as the airship's balloon began to deflate above his head.

As he rounded the corner himself he could see his quarry labouring under the weight of the armour he wore and redoubled his efforts to catch him. Borne was helped when the other man stumbled on a tree root that jutted out from one of the cracked flagstones that surrounded the hall.

Barely breaking his stride, Borne reached Mitigir, grabbed him by both shoulders and propelled him into a tree. The mercenary only saved himself a broken neck by moving his head at the last minute, as his shoulder struck the beech with a mighty thump.

'Where is MERELIE!?' Borne screamed with rage and picked Mitigir up again, throwing him this time into the hard black stone wall of Venhallas. It was the man's back that took the brunt of the collision this time, the impact of metal on stone echoing around the overgrown courtyard.

Mitigir held up one hand. 'Enough! I'll tell you where she is!'

Borne bent down to his fallen enemy. 'Where?!' he demanded.

Mitigir smiled, blood erupting from his lips as he did so. 'Up my arse, picking daisies,' he said and laughed.

The mercenary expected Borne to fly into a rage and throw him into something else but what the Arma did next was a hundred times worse. He stood up, put his hands on his hips for a second, sighed and then delved into his belt.

'If there's one thing I've learned from Max Bloom in the past year,' he said as he rummaged around in the belt lining for a few moments, 'it's that sometimes it's better not to just resort to brute force, but to be more creative with your efforts.' He produced a pencil.

'What's that?' Mitigir asked, his voice unsteady.

'This?' Borne shook the pencil. 'This is a pencil.'

'And what are you going to do with it?'

Borne leant back down and held the pencil up between them both. 'Well now, unless you tell me where Merelie Carvallen is, this pencil is going to gain immediate entry into some very uncomfortable places, my friend.'

Mitigir looked into Borne's eyes and gulped. He knew where he stood with extreme and brutal violence. Pencils were another thing entirely.

-4-

Jacob and Emerelda emerged from under the collapsed airship balloon held up by several of the Chapter Guards, and looked around.

Suddenly, from behind the stout trunks of several trees dotted around the expansive courtyard came about thirty men, all armed to the teeth and running straight towards them brandishing weapons high above their heads.

'This would be the welcoming committee then,' Emerelda said and turned to face them.

'Indeed,' Jacob agreed. The last of his dozen Chapter Guards had come out from under the collapsed airship and were lining themselves up in standard formation.

'Captain?' Jacob said to the heavy set man in charge of the assembled troops. 'Would you kindly have your men take care of that lot? We'll lend some Wordcraft support if needed.'

The Captain of the Guard withdrew his bow gun. 'It'd be a pleasure my Lord.' He turned to the dozen men lined up in front of him. 'Standard free-form combat gentlemen. Let's show these fools how stupid it truly is to attack Carvallen Chapter Guards.'

All thirteen men strode forward to meet the oncoming hoard.

The ensuing fight was short, nasty and entirely predictable. Four of the brigands managed to get lucky and make their way past the Chapter Guards, but all were dispatched with a little light Wordcraft from the Carvallen siblings. Even the lack of books in the vicinity wasn't quite enough to weaken their word shaping sufficiently to give the mercenaries a chance of victory. All were rendered satisfactorily unconscious in no time at all.

'Well that was easy,' Jacob pointed out as he watched his Captain administer a final thumping knock-out blow to the last mercenary left with his faculties still intact.

'Hmmm. Possibly too easy?' Emerelda said. 'This whole thing has the distinct whiff of a diversionary tactic again,' she pondered.

'Agreed. Our enemy seems to be relying on the same gambit over and over.'

'With some considerable success so far,' Emerelda remarked.

'True. But it never pays to be predictable.'

Jacob looked across the courtyard to see Borne reappear, jogging towards them and carrying what looked like a League Book.

'Merelie is in the building,' he said as he reached them. 'I've just thoroughly questioned the man who was the apparent leader of that lot.'

'You sure he's telling the truth?' Emerelda asked.

Borne adjusted his belt. 'Very sure Emerelda.' He held out the League Book. 'He had this with him. Said it was the way his employer had left the battle earlier.'

Jacob took the book and opened it. 'It appears to be lifeless. Our enemy has certainly mastered the ability to control the capabilities of our League Books.'

'Maybe Max can do something with it,' Borne said.

'Maybe so,' Emerelda agreed. 'First things first though... let's go see that Merelie is safe.'

Max listened to the short lived battle going on outside with a half smile on his face. Every few seconds he would throw a quick glance over at Meggins, who seemed the most nervous of the guards.

None of them looked exactly comfortable with proceedings though. The foot shuffling continued, and you could sense a great deal of thinking going on in those helmeted heads. Max wondered how much each man had been paid for their role in this escapade, and whether it would be enough to make them stand their ground when Jacob Carvallen and his Chapter Guards appeared at the doorway.

'Sounds like they're wrapping things up out there,' Merelie said. She was now lounging back against the cage wall, a degree of boredom having replaced the abject terror of the unexploded bomb beneath her.

'Yep,' Max replied, wincing as he heard a strangled scream filtering through from the bright morning outside. 'I'd say things are about to get very interesting for our four friends.'

'We tol' you to shut up!' Vilbert squealed.

'Now, now Vilbert. Don't strain yourself, you're going to need all your energy for when our friends show... *ah!* Speaking of which!' Max said delightedly and pointed over to where Borne had stalked into the hall.

'Borne!' Merelie cried.

The Arma took one look at his caged mistress, a further look at the four men surrounding her and exploded there and then on the spot.

Max pantomimed a look of unmitigated horror and crept around to hide behind his chair. 'Look out lads! Here comes the pain!'

The Arma screamed with rage and ran straight at the guards.

'Try not to kill all of them!' Merelie suggested.

This was too much for both Vilbert and Meggins. The two men screeched, dropped their bow guns and went clanking off towards the back of the hall. Max was amazed to see Gorman and Arfur stand their ground. This was something of an error on both their parts. Gorman was pole-axed by a punch that would have knocked out three elephants before he even had time to get a shot off. Arfur did indeed manage to fire his bow gun at Borne, but the Arma dodged the missile and was on his enemy in a split second, tumbling the other man to the ground and smacking his helmet into the flagstones repeatedly.

'I think - ' Merelie started.

Smash

'I think he might - '

Crash

'I think he's probably - '

Bash

'I'd say he's definitely unconscious by now Borne,' Merelie eventually said. 'You can tell by the way one leg is twitching like that.'

Max saw Emerelda and Jacob appear with the Chapter Guards in tow. He thrust out one hand. 'No Wordcraft! If you use any in here it will trigger a bomb!'

'Not a problem,' Emerelda told him. 'There's so little word source around we weren't even going to try.'

'Merelie!' Jacob cried and hurried over to the cage. He looked up at his imprisoned daughter. 'What have they done to you, my girl?'

'I'm fine father, just feeling a little claustrophobic. Also, there is a rather large bomb underneath me, which I wouldn't mind getting away from as soon as possible.'

'And how are you Max?' Emerelda asked.

Max flopped back into the chair. 'Pretty damn hungry as it goes actually. I don't suppose anyone thought to bring any breakfast with them?'

Jacob arched a familiar eyebrow. 'You're well then, I trust. In my experience any man who is thinking of his stomach is not one suffering with injury or malady.'

Max's eyes widened slightly. Jacob had never referred to him as a man before. He felt quite proud.

This feeling was immediately and inevitably punctured by the ex-head librarian of Farefield. 'So, you didn't stop Darel's killer then?' she said to him.

Max gave her a disgusted look. 'Well I couldn't, could I? Not with that bloody thing set to go off if I so much as wiggled my fingers.' He pointed up at the bomb.

Emerelda studied the device. 'It looks nasty, I'll grant you that.'

'So we should do something about getting rid of it,' Borne responded, having come back from the other end of the room where he had deposited what was left of Vilbert and Meggins in a tidy pile for the other Chapter Guards to come and clean up.

'Agreed,' Jacob said. 'We'll get Merelie out of that contraption and as far away from that explosive device as possible. Then we can discuss what has happened here.'

Max grimaced. 'You're really not going to like it. Randal Venhaligan is insane, clever and wants my father dead.'

Emerelda blanched. 'Your *father*?' she said in amazement.

'Yep. Turns out I'm not such a complete stranger to The Chapter Lands after all.'

As the Chapter Guards went about repairing the airship to make it ready to travel again, Max and Merelie filled the others in on Randal Venhaligan's revelations about the Bloom family.

When they were done, Jacob stroked his chin and looked across the courtyard to where his men worked. 'You know, I've always been troubled by why The Cornerstone would pick a complete stranger from another world to save us from the Dwellers. Now I understand its reasoning far more.'

'It also explains why Max is so bloody powerful. The records state that Wordcrafting was always strong in the Florren line,' Emerelda added.

'Pity really,' Max said.

'Why?' Merelie asked.

'I always felt, you know, a bit *special* before. Saviour from another planet and all that.'

Merelie rested a hand on his shoulder. 'You'll always be special to me, Max,' she said, eliciting a retching sound from Emerelda.

'Thanks,' Max told her as he glowered at her aunt.

'So now we know the who and the why,' Jacob said, 'we just need to know what comes next.'

'Emerelda was right,' Max piped up. 'This was yet another diversionary tactic. Randal just wanted us all out of the Chapter House so he could do what he wanted there without any opposition.'

'And you did exactly what he thought you would,' Merelie said, '...rush to save me and leave The Cornerstone undefended.'

'We could have done nothing else,' her father said. 'Whether it played into his hands or not.'

'He's a smart git, I'll give him that,' Max remarked. 'The airship's knackered, the League Book Borne retrieved is useless to us, and my sense of direction is apparently appalling, so even I can't get back to the Chapter House fast enough to stop him. Randal's got a free run at Corny and there's not a damn thing we can do about it.'

'Not quite a free run,' Borne rumbled. 'He still has Garrowain to contend with.'

'Indeed,' Jacob said. 'So we must not lose hope. The head custodian may prove obstacle enough to Randal Venhaligan, and may well delay his plans long enough for us to return home and deal with him.'

'Let's hope so,' said Max in a dark tone. 'If Garrowain can't stop him and he travels to Earth...' He left the sentence hanging. They all knew the potential consequences if Randal Venhaligan reached Max's father.

The thick set Captain of the Chapter Guards came lumbering over. 'The airship is sufficiently repaired my Lord. It just requires air.' He looked pointedly at Max, who rolled his eyes.

'Alright, alright, I'll fill it up,' he said and walked off, gathering his Wordcraft in as he did.

'He's hiding it well, but I can tell he's worried,' Merelie said, watching him go.

Emerelda put an arm around her shoulder. 'Don't worry girl. We'll be in the air soon and with any luck Garrowain will have delayed Randal long enough for Max to have a proper go at him.'

Merelie smiled. 'That'd be nice. I know Max felt powerless earlier. All he could do was throw threats around. It'd be good for him to bash Venhaligan into the nearest wall for a while.'

They stood in silence for a moment watching Max re-inflate the airship with the Wordcrafting skills he had been born with.

'Threats, eh?' Emerelda eventually said.

'Yeah.'

'Not the one about pulling his head out through his bottom?'

'Yes... unfortunately.'

'That would never work, you know. It's not anatomically possible.'

'Tell Max that.'

Within a few minutes the airship was up and ready to go, and they were airborne again shortly after, making headway south to the Carvallen Chapter House and whatever awaited them there.

As they sped away as fast as the ship could carry them, Max looked back at the ruined hulk of Venhallas from the open aft window. His hands were white where they gripped a hand rail below.

Now that he had some time to think about Randal Venhaligan's words, Max's mind was aflame with a mixture of curiosity, anger and fear.

How could his father have kept his true lineage a secret for all these years?

Had Peter Bloom actually murdered Viana Venhaligan, as Randal had suggested?

Was his father aware of Max's abilities? He'd certainly shown no signs of it in the year that had passed since Max first journeyed to The Chapter Lands.

And how much did The Cornerstone know of all of this? Did it bring him here in the first place because it knew Max was the son of a Chapter Lander?

All these questions whirled around Max's head as Venhallas shrunk from view. As did a building sense of urgency. If he knew which direction the Chapter House was, he'd fly straight out of this window right now and power his way back there.

Suddenly, one crystal clear notion entered his head, temporarily quelling all other thought.

I don't know if I can stop you Venhaligan, Max spoke to his enemy in the vaults of his mind. *But I can sure as hell make sure you have no home to come back to.*

With a whisper, a gesture and a mirthless smile, Max sent a spear of Wordcraft arcing back at the hall of Venhallas. It flew straight through one of the large windows and immediately set off the bomb that Randal Venhaligan had placed under Merelie's cage.

The entire building erupted in a ball of flame, shooting chunks of stone, earth and wood in all directions. The explosion was so strong the shock wave rocked the airship as it sped southwards.

Max turned to see everyone staring at him.

'Whoops,' he said in a flat tone.

Part Four

To Garrowain, there was no better way to clear one's mind than a bit of book cataloguing.

Now, this may sound like the kind of pursuit that would make watching paint dry seem exhilarating by comparison, but in the mind of a librarian, nothing quite matched the thrill of making sure that all the gardening books were on the same shelf and in alphabetical order.

Go into any municipal library and study a librarian as they do this, and you will see them step back at the end of their task with a self satisfied nod and a sigh of contentment. They will then look around guiltily to make sure no-one was watching, so it's best to hide yourself behind the big print books so as not to be seen.

This morning, Garrowain was delighted to leave the malfunctioning League Book and all the problems that came with it, and spend a constructive half an hour engaged in the rather mindless task of ensuring the new stock of books from House Wellhome were properly placed in the right aisles of the enormous Carvallen Library.

He hoped that by engaging his mind in such a straight forward task, it might throw up an answer as to how to get the League Book working again. This was often the way of things with the head custodian. When he needed a little inspiration, it often came when his brain was occupied with another, less taxing job.

Thus far today though, no answers had leapt into his head to fix the problem, which was disconcerting to say the least. Usually the mundane task of cataloguing successfully took his mind off whatever issue he was trying to resolve, so that his subconscious could have a go at it. The process was not working this time however. No matter how much Garrowain tried to forget about the name Venhaligan and the broken League Book, his brain simply wouldn't let him. Even putting several aisles of distance between him and the scorched book helped very little.

Part of him was also worrying about Merelie Carvallen's safety. The girl was such a joy to be around, the thought of anything happening to her at the hands of the villain who had killed poor Darel Cornelius was horrifying. Garrowain just had to console himself that Max Bloom was on the case.

To tell the truth, he wasn't entirely sure whether this made him feel better about the whole thing or not.

He put down the copy of Whittling The Wellhome Way on the trolley in front of him and heaved a long and heavy sigh. Maybe he was getting too old for all of this.

His reverie was broken by a junior custodian running up the aisle towards him. 'Garrowain! Garrowain!' the young, skinny boy wailed at him.

'What is it Bevens? Has the Guardian eaten your lunch again? Only I keep telling you not to leave it in the dark magic section.'

'No! No!' Bevens cried in horror. 'That League Book you brought down here is about to explode!'

'What?!'

Garrowain was off and running back towards The Cornerstone's chamber as fast as his ancient legs would carry him. Young Bevens may have been several decades his junior, but there was no way he could keep up with the head custodian as he powered his way back to where the League Book was apparently about to blow up.

Garrowain reached the archway leading to the chamber and threw his hands up in front of his face to protect his eyes from the bright, searing blue light that now emanated from the book where it still sat on the pedestal he had placed it on earlier. Its cover was thrown wide open, indicating someone - or something - was trying to transport themselves through the rift in space time created by the book.

Two other subordinate custodians were attempting to get closer to the League Book in order to shut it.

'Get back you fools!' Garrowain warned. 'You can do nothing to stop this!'

Bevens came alongside him. 'We must flee then master!'

'You take Primley and Gasforth with you boy. I will stay here and await whoever attempts to enter the Library.' Garrowain moved forward to stand directly in the blue light coming from the book. 'I am curious to see who holds such power over this League Book that he can prevent even me from unlocking its secrets.'

'But you might be killed!' Bevens said, ushering his compatriots away.

'Many have tried my boy. Many have tried. Now be off with you. We have a guest about to arrive.'

Bevens gave his master one last frightened look, before ducking out of sight and running off to hide somewhere far away with stout walls.

Garrowain watched him go, and returned his attention to the League Book, which was now vibrating and jumping around on the pedestal like a mad thing. The custodian looked quickly over to The Cornerstone to see if it was reacting to all of this. It was completely still, but Garrowain was sure it was watching carefully and awaiting developments.

'I hope you have a better idea of what's going on here than I do,' he said to the book. 'If I fail, it may come down to you to stop this monster.'

If The Cornerstone agreed with the old man, it didn't show any signs of it.

Suddenly the League Book flew into the air and from it, in a burst of blue light, appeared Randal Venhaligan.

Garrowain decided that a pre-emptive strike was probably the best way to start negotiations, so he sent a volley of Wordcraft directly at Venhaligan, who was still somewhat discombobulated by the instantaneous journey from his ancestral home.

Randal flew back into the stone wall behind him, but was still aware enough of his surroundings to cushion the impact with Wordcraft of his own, and dropped to his feet with little sign of damage.

'Ah,' he said. 'You must be Garrowain. Pleased to meet you.' His greeting was backed up by his own surge of word power that barrelled its way across the intervening space between them in an instant. Garrowain was equally prepared for this however and barely slid backwards on his soft slippers as it struck him.

'I wish I could say the same of you,' the old man replied. 'But I fear your murder of Darel Cornelius has left me unwilling to show you much courtesy.'

Randal laughed. 'Fair enough custodian, I like a man who talks straight. Let us skip the pleasantries and get right to business.' He pointed over at The Cornerstone. 'I want that.'

'Indeed? I very much doubt it wants you.'

Randal looked confused. 'How could it want anything you old fool? It's just a book.'

Garrowain looked positively delighted. 'And that, my nasty little friend, is why you will lose this fight sooner or later... whatever happens here today.'

Randal sneered. 'Enough talk. Give me the book.' He walked forward, fists clenched.

Garrowain looked around the stone room. 'This is a very ancient chamber, my friend. I would rather see it undamaged. Let's take this encounter elsewhere shall we?'

Garrowain's arm flew out and The Cornerstone rocketed across the chamber into his hand. At the same time he picked up the pedestal it was sat on with Wordcraft and flung it at Randal Venhaligan's head. The tall, grey haired man ducked the ballistic pedestal with ease, but it was enough of a distraction to allow Garrowain to run out of the chamber and down the Library aisle.

It occurred to Garrowain that this was not the first time he was forced into an unseemly run through this Library with an enemy close on his heels. If this was to become a regular occurrence he'd have to start wearing more appropriate footwear. Perhaps he'd ask Max Bloom to secure him a pair of those outlandish canvas 'trainers' he always wore around the Chapter House.

Happily, unlike the last time this had happened, the Library Codex was in fully functioning order and Garrowain had every space-warping section in which to lose his opponent. He ran into the Main Hub where the Codex lived, flipped the book open and hastily wrote 'dark magic' on its pages.

As the library magically reordered itself to allow Garrowain entry to the section he had requested, Randal Venhaligan came flying through the other open door, looking like he wanted to hit something very hard. 'Give me the book old man, and maybe I won't boil your blood in your veins.'

Garrowain backed towards another doorway that was now suffused with silver light. 'Hmmm. To do that requires great talent and power my friend. One wonders if you truly possess such.'

'Don't doubt what I am capable of Garrowain. I have had years since the death of my family to perfect my skills in every Chapter Land I visited. I am more than a match for you.'

'The death of your family?' Garrowain regarded the other man closely for a second. 'A Venhaligan you are then. And young when Lady Viana attacked the Florren house no doubt.'

'Old enough to see everyone I loved die.'

'Then Randal Venhaligan is your name.'

'At your service.' Randal's eyes glowed with contained power. 'Now give me The Cornerstone or die where you stand old man.'

The doors behind Garrowain flew open. He backed into them. 'Come and get it Mr Venhaligan. If you can.' And with that the custodian turned and fled into the shadowy and mysterious aisles of the dark magic section, where he hoped the Guardian Of The Stacks was on patrol... and itching for a fight.

'Come back here!' Randal screamed and gave chase once more.

Garrowain didn't bother trying to confuse his pursuer with a lot of twisting and turning through the stacks. He had a feeling Venhaligan could follow him wherever he went. It was becoming very apparent that this man had levels of Wordcrafting power that rivalled Max Bloom, and was therefore not a man to be toyed with.

A direct confrontation would lead to inevitable defeat, and Garrowain could not afford for The Cornerstone to fall into his hands. He did not know why Venhaligan sought access to Earth, but it couldn't be for any good reason. A murderous Wordsmith unleashed on the unsuspecting people of Farefield would be disastrous, and needed to be avoided at all costs.

With this all in mind, Garrowain sprinted towards where the Guardian had last been sighted two days ago. The ephemeral creature was hard to coerce at the best of times, but Garrowain hoped an intruder in its midst would annoy it enough to come to his aid.

Randal had suspected that the wisened old custodian would prove a problem.

Getting Max Bloom and the rest of the Carvallen gang out of the Chapter House was simplicity itself, once he'd taken Merelie from them. It never ceased to amaze Randal how love could be such a weakness if pressure was applied in the right place. Seemingly sensible, formidable people could be reduced to mindless puppets when a loved one's life was put in jeopardy. The rag tag bunch of miscreants he'd hired to keep them busy would probably last about as long as a naked flame in a hurricane, but it would be time enough to gain access to The Cornerstone and make his way to Earth.

That is, if he ever managed to catch up to Garrowain, who could produce a turn of speed that far exceeded his ancient stature. Randal had predicted that removing the head custodian from the Chapter House would have been nigh on impossible, and that the old man would be bound to take the League Book to the library once he had it in his wrinkled little hands. What he hadn't bargained for was that the old bugger was a slippery customer and knew these library aisles far better than he did. He'd been prepared for a fight... not for an extended chase.

Randal didn't like the look of the strange mist hanging above his head either. It reminded him of the billowing smoke rising from the Florren residence the night his mother had been killed by Petren. Also, he could swear there were noises coming from the strange ceiling of fog. Noises that to a more imaginative person would sound like rough tentacles rubbing alongside one another.

Up ahead, Randal could hear Garrowain's soft slippers padding their way along the corridor, and he quickened his pace to catch up.

Surprisingly, he found the old man standing at the end of a particularly long aisle, The Cornerstone held in both hands and an expectant look on his face.

'Given up your attempts at escape have you old man?' he said, approaching him.

'Oh my yes. I'm am a very old man and completely exhausted,' Garrowain replied, sounding neither. 'Why don't you come and get the book and put this old man out of his misery?'

Randal slowed down. Something was very wrong here. The old duffer was giving up way too easily. Why go through all that effort to run away, if you're just going to throw the towel in before the first blow is struck?

'What are you playing at custodian?' Randal asked.

'Me? Nothing my boy,' Garrowain answered innocently.

'You're up to something.'

'No, no! Not at all. I'm doing absolutely nothing.'

'Why don't I believe you?' Randal had stopped completely now, a good twenty feet in front of Garrowain. The hackles on the back of his neck were standing on end.

'I couldn't possibly imagine,' the custodian said, still with an air of good natured innocence.

Randal's hand shot out. 'Throw me the book. Now.'

'Or?'

'Or I will lose patience with you very fast old man, and do something you will regre - '

Randal's threat was cut off by the sound behind him of something heavy falling to the smooth grey stone floor of the library with a very loud bang.

'What was that?' he said, head spinning round. In the distance, he could see and hear more heavy shapes hitting the floor with sharp, echoing thumps.

'That?' Garrowain replied, straining to hear. 'Oh that's nothing. Don't worry yourself one little bit about that.'

'What is it?!' There was a high pitched tremulous tone to Randal Venhaligan's voice that hadn't existed before. Garrowain found it very gratifying.

'Seriously my boy, it's nothing. Just a centuries old demonic entity that really doesn't like to be disturbed. We call him the Guardian Of The Stacks, and it sounds like he wants to make your acquaintance.'

More books hit the floor, this time much louder and much closer. If Max Bloom were here he'd probably be laughing by now. Though on second thoughts, he probably wouldn't, given that his own experiences with the bizarre creature have been universally terrifying.

'Where is it?!' Randal demanded, backing up towards Garrowain.

The custodian clicked his fingers. 'Oh yes! That's right, I forgot. It's also invisible.'

To Garrowain's left, a small section of library shelf swung open. 'Good luck!' he hollered to Randal Venhaligan before disappearing into the gap. The library shelf swung back into place with a very secure click.

As Randal looked back down the passageway to see the falling books get nearer and nearer, faster and faster, he was forced to reflect for the first time that this revenge business might be more trouble than it was worth.

Nevertheless, if one sought to defeat strong opponents, one must be prepared to withstand their best assault. He stood his ground, gritted his teeth and awaited the arrival of the Guardian.

This turned out to be about as wise as standing on the tracks awaiting the arrival of the three fifteen from Paddington.

With an almighty and deafening roar, the Guardian Of The Stacks charged into Randal, picking him up and propelling him down the library aisle at astonishing speed. Books flew in all directions, several managing to clout the renegade Wordsmith about the head and shoulders before he was able to summon up a protective barrier of Wordcraft.

It was just as well he did as the Guardian then proceeded to start shaking him around like a rag doll, smashing him into the hard, ancient library shelves at bone breaking velocity. Then he was tossed into the air, right up into the nebulous mist that hung above the whole library. Up there Randal could briefly make out the kinds of dark, shifting shapes that give people nightmares, no matter how powerful and dangerous they are. One shape started to resolve itself into what looked like a hand with ten fingers on it. Randal had the presence of mind to lash out a bolt of Wordcraft to scare it away before it could grab him by the head and squash it like a grapefruit.

With that problem disposed of, he still had the issue of falling thirty feet down onto the stone floor of the Library, where the Guardian was no doubt ready for round two if he managed to survive the fall.

This was *not* the way his plan was supposed to be unfolding.

It was time to take steps to rectify the matter.

Any other man would have panicked, screamed and flailed around in mid air before inevitably breaking every bone in his body on contact with the floor. Randal Venhaligan was no ordinary man though.

He drew in a deep breath, sucked in all the word source he could from the books around him, and slowed his descent to such a degree that he came to earth with his feet lightly touching the floor.

'Now,' he said to the still enraged Guardian, 'I think it's about time you were taught some manners.'

Garrowain stood listening by the bookshelf that separated him from the fight going on over on the opposite side. He'd kept up with the Guardian's attack on the intruder in the hopes that he could step in once the invisible monster had done enough damage to stop Venhaligan's charge, but not enough to outright kill the man. Garrowain had questions, and he wanted the chance to ask them - preferably to a man chained to the nearest stout stone wall and nursing several painful injuries.

Sadly, the fight wasn't going entirely the way the custodian had envisioned.

At first it had all gone swimmingly, but once Venhaligan had gathered his wits about him and fought back, things had gone downhill fast.

Garrowain didn't like to admit it, but here was a man who's abilities nearly measured up to Max Bloom's. A frightening concept when the man in question was clearly extremely angry and somewhat unhinged.

And he was definitely putting manners on the poor Guardian Of The Stacks it appeared.

The creature was bellowing now in a mixture of anger and pain. Its great bulk slammed into the enormous, thick book shelf, sending the volumes it held across the floor every which way. Garrowain had to dodge a particularly large black volume of necromancy before it dropped onto his head and put a real dent in his day.

The custodian could feel the hairs on the back of his neck rise as a vast amount of Wordcraft was discharged a mere few metres away from him. The Guardian screamed, this time just in pain. Garrowain couldn't believe it, but there was every chance he'd have to intervene in this battle just to save the poor thing.

No, he stopped himself. *You should get away with The Cornerstone while you still can. If this man gets his hands on it, there's no telling what damage he will do in Max Bloom's world.*

Garrowain started to back away from the battle on the other side of the bookshelf. He didn't think he had long to get away now. Venhaligan sounded like he had well and truly bested the giant demon. Still, he would have to find a gap before he could come after Garrowain again.

Then the bookshelf exploded.

Garrowain was violently thrown across the aisle he stood in, slamming into the shelf opposite with a scream. His head connected with the hard wood of one shelf, and several ribs broke as they struck the level below.

A storm of paper, wood and stone whipped in all directions. Inside the maelstrom was an empty space that could only be the body of the Guardian Of The Stacks, which had been thrown through the gigantic bookcase as if it were a rag doll through a wax paper screen. It hit the opposing bookshelf with a thunderous crash and came to rest on the grey stone floor, either dead or unconscious.

Randal Venhaligan walked through the hole he had just punched in a centuries old bookcase with the look of a man well satisfied with his work. He pointed one long finger at where he thought the Guardian probably was. 'Let that be a lesson to you. A good dog is a disciplined dog. Be thankful I didn't tear you to pieces.' His attention swung round to where Garrowain was trying to sit up. 'And as for you old man, enough fun and games with your pet. I will take what I came here for, with no further delays.' Randal stalked up the blasted aisle towards the custodian, his long grey coat flapping about him.

Garrowain attempted to stand, but the whole left side of his body was agony, and blood from the head wound blurred his vision. As Randal reached him and bent down to grab The Cornerstone from his clutches he attempted to drive the man away with a surge of Wordcraft.

'Oh stop it,' Randal said irritably. 'You're probably dying as it is, so you'll want to preserve your strength as much as possible.'

'I will... I will not let you take The Cornerstone,' the old man wheezed, still trying to back away.

'Yes you will, and you'll be damn glad I don't crush what's left of the life out of you for keeping it from me,' Randal said.

He took hold of the strange green book and pried it from Garrowain's fingers. Standing with his prize, he smiled, blew some wooden splinters off it, and returned his gaze to the injured custodian. 'While it would give me some pleasure to watch you die in front of me, I still have need of your services custodian.'

Garrowain grimaced. 'I will do nothing for you, maniac.'

'Now, now. Let's not descend into name calling,' Randal replied in a disapproving voice. 'When I use this book to travel to Max Bloom's Earth, I need you to do two things for me. The first is to keep The Cornerstone safe for my return, and the second is to prevent Max Bloom from following me.'

'I'll do the first, but the second would not be easy, even if I agreed to do it.'

Randal grinned. 'Oh, you'll do it Garrowain. You'll make sure Max doesn't follow me, because if he does, I will kill every last person he cares about in that world. If he stays here, only his father has to pay the price for what he did to my mother, but if I see The Cornerstone open and Max Bloom appear... ' He left the threat hanging in the air.

'His father? Your mother?' Garrowain asked, confused.

'I don't have time to explain it to you now, I'll let your friends do it when they return.' Randal looked up and closed his eyes for a second. 'Which, unless I'm very much mistaken, is happening just about now.' He opened The Cornerstone and pointed at Garrowain again. 'Remember, stop him from following me. I will have The Cornerstone on the other side with me the whole time, and there is no way Max Bloom can pass across the void without me killing him and anyone else I choose. I'll do it if I even get a *hint* that he's coming for me. I have a task in that world that I will not be prevented from completing, no matter what the cost.'

Garrowain's eyes narrowed. 'I warn you Venhaligan, that world is not like ours. Your path to vengeance may not be as smooth as you think, Max Bloom or no Max Bloom.'

'We'll just see, won't we?' the other man replied and tried to flip open The Cornerstone's cover. It resisted though, starting to shake in his hand and project waves of hectic silver light from its pages.

'You think your protective magic will stop me?' Randal sneered.

Garrowain managed a weak smile. 'You truly know nothing of that book do you? I wish you all the luck in the world... you're going to need it.'

Randal ignored this and concentrated his power on the book for a few moments, shaping hard lashes of Wordcraft across its cover. Eventually, The Cornerstone capitulated, and reluctantly allowed Randal to open it.

He read the last few moments of his life and disappeared in a blaze of silver light.

The Cornerstone, it's job reluctantly done, drifted back into Garrowain's lap, just as the old man lost his fight to stay conscious, and collapsed back onto the hard smooth floor, his eyes rolled back into his head.

-2-

The Carvallen airship sped towards the Chapter House, cutting a swathe through the mid morning clouds as it went. Max could see the tall tower looming in the distance, the city laid out around it and gleaming in the sun.

He jiggled around on the spot, impatient to get off the airship and back into action.

'Try to relax Max,' Merelie told him. 'I'm sure Garrowain and the custodians have the situation under control.'

'Really?' Max said. 'You've got more faith in them than me.' He returned to looking out of the window at the city ahead. 'I should have flown back on my own. I shouldn't have stayed with you lot.'

'You would've got lost again,' Borne argued, no doubt correctly. 'And even if you hadn't, you would have only arrived just ahead of us. And Merelie is right. Garrowain knows what he's doing.'

'I'm sure he does Borne, but so does Venhaligan.'

'He's just one man,' Borne replied.

'So was Hitler,' Max pointed out.

The airship entered the city's airspace and headed for its mooring point atop the great Chapter House. As it reached the giant building and slowed to docking speed, Max's remaining patience fizzled out. 'Screw this for a game of soldiers,' he said. 'I'll meet you all in the Library.'

Without another word, he gathered his Wordcraft around him, opened the exit door and flew out, headed downwards towards the main Chapter House gates twenty stories below.

'What the hell is he doing?' Emerelda snapped from the control console.

'Being Max Bloom?' Borne replied.

Emerelda threw her hands up. 'We should be careful about going in! We don't know what Venhaligan has set up for our arrival. There could be booby traps!'

'If there are, Max can handle them,' Merelie said.

'Yes, I'm sure he can. But can the rest of the bloody Chapter House, girl?' Emerelda told her in a cold voice.

Max sped through the building, headed straight for The Cornerstone's chamber as fast as he could fly down the long stone corridors between the main gates and the Library entrance.

Flinging the Library doors open with a gesture, he took a deep breath, preparing himself for whatever may lie beyond.

As he entered the well appointed atrium he heard and felt an enormous explosion coming from somewhere within the Library itself.

'What the hell's going on?' he barked at a custodian, who was running across the room with a look of blind panic on his face.

'Someone has broken into the Library!' Bevens the custodian cried. 'Garrowain is locked in a pitched battle with him!'

Max snarled and doubled his speed, flying through into the Main Hub where the Codex still lay open. Glancing at what was written on the book's pages he gulped, steeled himself, and flew into his least favourite part of the Carvallen Great Library, head darting everywhere for signs of books falling from shelves.

It took him only a few minutes to find evidence of the Guardian's presence. Piles of discarded hardbacks were strewn across the floor, indicating that the Guardian had been here and had moved along the aisle Max now sped down. He forced himself to slow as he caught his first sight of the debris and damage caused by Randal Venhaligan's chastisement of the terrifying invisible beast.

Max word shaped the obligatory shield around his body as a precaution and dropped to his feet.

As he neared the centre of the destruction Max could hear the low rumble of the injured Guardian's breath. His mouth dropped open as he came upon the enormous hole punched through the high bookshelf. Passing through it, he could see the shape of the Guardian where it was still slumped against the bookcase opposite, covered in bits of paper, splinters of wood and thick, black dust.

Max walked up to the creature and laid one hand on what could have been a leg. This was the first time he'd ever touched the thing and was surprised to feel a soft, leathery texture under his fingers. It was rather like touching an expensive sofa.

'What did he do to you?' Max whispered.

The Guardian stirred and gave voice to a plaintive growl.

'Max?' a cracked voice filtered down the aisle towards him.

'Garrowain?!' Max cried and ran towards the source.

The custodian was battered, bloody and looked close to death. 'Oh crap,' Max whispered, kneeling down next to the old man and taking his hand. He saw The Cornerstone in the old man's lap and clenched his jaw.

'Good to see you, my boy,' Garrowain said, coughing up blood as he did.

'Don't try to talk,' Max said in a calm voice, not taking his eyes off the scuffed green book that had changed his life.

Garrowain saw where Max was looking. 'He has gone across. I'm so sorry Max.'

'We'll worry about that after we've taken care of you.'

It was taking every ounce of Max's willpower not to grab Corny, throw the book open and take off after that murdering piece of scum, but Garrowain's life hung in the balance, and he couldn't be left until someone came and took care of him.

'I need to go and find help Garrowain,' Max said, looking at the custodian's ragged head wound.

'I think... I think I may not have time for you to do that,' Garrowain replied, trying to give Max a comforting smile.

Max let out a sharp breath. 'What the hell do I do?'

Garrowain tried to reply but a coughing fit overtook him, blood spilling from his mouth as his body was wracked with pain.

'The healing craft...' Max said. 'The thing you did when Morodai broke my hand and when Venhaligan shot me. How do you do it Garrowain?'

'It takes... it takes many years of training to perfect such a subtle craft Max.'

'Okay. Well, I figure we've got about a minute.'

Garrowain tried a smile. 'It will have to be the accelerated program then.'

'What do I do?'

'You must concentrate on transfering your own sense of well being into Wordcraft. It takes - ' The old man was wracked by another coughing fit. 'it takes years to first understand how your body works and feels before you can help others.'

'Great.' Max hung his head. They didn't have minutes, let alone years. He looked back down at The Cornerstone. 'When in doubt, ask the magic book,' he said hopefully, picking his little green friend up.

'Right Corny, big one for you,' Max said, flipping the book open. 'Gazza here is in a really bad way and I need your help to transfer some of my... er, nice healthy stuff into him so he doesn't pop his clogs. Can you help me with that?'

The book flashed silver along its length.

'Cracking.' Max put the book on the floor and laid one hand on it. He asked Garrowain to do the same.

The custodian placed a shaking, bloodied hand on the page, staining it. 'Oh... Oh no,' he said in a weak voice, 'I've damaged the page.'

'I doubt Corny cares much,' Max told him. 'Now close your eyes and keep your fingers crossed.'

At first, nothing happened, but slowly Max started to feel a strange tugging sensation that began in his chest and made its way down his arm into his hand. He felt the disconcerting sensation of something being *drained* and instantly felt exhausted. Conversely, some of the colour was returning to Garrowain's cheeks and his breathing had become less laboured.

The process continued and Max felt exhaustion sink into his bones. It was all he could do to keep his head up.

'It's working my boy!' Garrowain said, his voice stronger. 'Well done!'

's'okay,' Max mumbled, unable to articulate more.

'Oh Writer!' Garrowain cried when he saw the damage being done to Max. 'Stop now! You'll go too far!'

The custodian now had enough strength to push Max away from The Cornerstone. He did so, and Max slumped back into a sitting position. He fought against the overwhelming fatigue to look at the restored custodian. 'Good stuff,' he said wearily. 'Nice t'see you back, Gawwa... Ganna... Garrower... oh screw it.' His eyes went blank, and he collapsed unconscious onto the grey stone floor.

It was with some regret that Max drew himself out of a dream involving him, Merelie in a bikini, and the kind of shenanigans that couldn't be conducted in public without risking immediate arrest.

'Munnamummarr,' he said as the world swam back into view.

The vision of Merelie in her bikini still floated in his mind's eye and as consciousness took hold, a content smile spread across his face. Then he saw Borne looming over him and the pleasant vision was shattered. It's rather hard to think about your girlfriend semi-naked when her muscular bodyguard is standing over you with a dour expression on his face.

'He's awake,' Borne rumbled.

'Max!' Merelie said and came to sit by him on the long couch he was laid out on. She wasn't in a bikini, but he was very happy to see her anyway.

'Where am I?' he asked.

'The Library atrium. We found you next to Garrowain and brought you out here.'

'How is he?'

Merelie's face clouded. 'Still very sick. We managed to speak to him briefly, but now he's fallen into a sleep no-one can wake him from. But the physicians say he will survive thanks to what you did.'

'Good.'

Max rubbed his head for second, then remembered why he'd been in the Library in the first place. 'Venhaligan!' he exclaimed and tried to sit up. This resulted in the world spinning at a rapid rate of knots, so he laid back down again, thinking better of it.

'Gone through The Cornerstone and into your world. Emerelda tried to follow, but The Cornerstone wouldn't let her.'

'It'll let me through,' Max told her.

'Probably,' Emerelda said, joining them, 'but Garrowain was told that if you did, Venhaligan would kill you the instant you appeared... and would then kill your family too.'

'Emerelda!' Merelie said, shocked.

'He needs to know what the score is Merelie. There's no point in beating around the bush.'

Max sat up again, this time ignoring the spinning sensation. He didn't have time to be sick. 'The bastard's going to kill my family anyway.'

'No. I don't think so,' the ex librarian replied. 'He seems intent on revenge against your father. Nobody else interests him, unless they get in his way.'

'I don't care!' Max spat. 'I still have to save dad! Where's The Cornerstone?'

'You can't boy!' Emerelda thundered. 'He'll have it with him. The instant you appear, he'll blow you to smithereens. Think about it!'

Max considered Emerelda's words. She was right. Using The Cornerstone to cross dimensions always discombobulated you for a moment on the other side. Time enough for Randal Venhaligan to get a killing blow in.

'Damn it!' he snapped and punched the back of the couch.

'There must be something we can do?' Merelie said, tears in her eyes. 'We can't just let Max's father die.'

Emerelda shook her head. 'I don't know girl. Venhaligan holds all the cards here.'

Max could feel tears of frustration well up in his eyes. Venhaligan did indeed hold all the cards. There wasn't a damn thing he could do right now to stop the madman without getting himself killed.

Max would just have to wait, and pray for a miracle.

-3-

Nugget was not by and large a curious dog.

He'd reached the age when curiosity had taken a back seat to comfort, so it was rare for the big black Labrador to stick his nose into places it wasn't wanted.

Today however, Nugget was feeling quite frisky. The combination of a sunny warm day, a hearty breakfast of burned bacon, and a mid-morning nap had combined to turn the usually lumbering old dog into a puppy again. And puppies do love to stick their noses in places where they're not wanted.

Specifically a fox's den, in this particular case.

Charlie had walked Nugget through the copse at the edge of town hundreds of times before, but this was the first time the dog had discovered the fox's hideaway. As such, it was of incredible interest. Frankly, Nugget was slightly disgusted with himself that he'd never smelled it before, and wanted to make up for his glaring oversight with some concerted digging. The fox wasn't particularly happy with this, as it had been sleeping off a particularly large pigeon when Nugget came calling.

The Labrador growled when he saw the fox at the back of the den. He'd dug out a hole big enough to stick his head through, but nothing else could squeeze into the gap.

The fox returned the growl with a high pitched whine, bearing its teeth as it did.

It was only a little fox, but it wasn't scared of the big lumbering black dog. He'd seen it many times before as it crashed clumsily through the copse, and had dismissed it as just another overfed creature that belonged to one of the horrible two legged things.

'Nuggie!' Charlie Pearce called from behind.

Nugget ignored his master, intent on the little red fox in front of him.

'Nugget! You come out of there and leave that poor fox alone!' Charlie ordered.

In Nugget's doggy brain a battle was waged. On one side was his ancestral wolfish nature, which wanted to keep digging into the fox's hole so he could eat the little sod. The other side of Nugget was the good dog, who knew he should listen to his master and do what he was told.

With a snort, Nugget withdrew his head and loped back to Charlie. A thousand ghostly wolves from centuries past howled in shame and misery.

This was all very well, but Nugget couldn't really care less about his wolf ancestors. Charlie Pearce gave him biscuits, and when it came right down to it, all the wolves in all the world couldn't compete with someone who gave you a garibaldi when you wanted one and patted you on the head.

'Good boy,' Charlie said, handing over the biscuit and administering the requisite pat. 'Let's get home boy, shall we? I do believe Grand Designs is about to start, and I do enjoy watching how pretentious Kevin McCloud can sound walking around a converted barn.' This suited Nugget fine. The puppy-like curiosity was wearing off now, and there was a place on the comfortable couch back home with his name on it.

———

It only took the pair ten minutes to get back to the house, and Nugget trotted happily up the driveway, safe in the knowledge that a lunchtime nap was on the cards.

He stopped dead in his tracks. Something was *very* wrong.

Nugget's hackles went up and a low growl emitted from his mouth.

Fat, old and dopey he might be, but there was still wolf in him yet, and the wolf knew when danger was close.

'What is it Nuggie?' Charlie asked, coming to stand next to him.

Charlie looked towards the house and saw why Nugget had stopped. The front door was open.

Charlie Pearce would be the first one to admit that he was getting old, and that with the onset of advancing age came a certain amount of forgetfulness. He knew that remembering birthdays and other important anniversaries was becoming harder, and that on at least two occasions he had spent a good thirty minutes looking for his car keys. But what Charlie also knew was that this descent into good natured senility had not gone as far as forgetting to lock the front door when he took the dog out for a walk.

He was one thousand percent sure that he had closed and locked it half an hour ago, so it was understandable when his heart rate rocketed as both man and dog approached the porch very cautiously.

'Now don't do anything stupid Nuggie,' he whispered to his best friend. 'You're too old and fat to be taking on burglars.'

Nugget gave him one of his legendary reproachful looks... though it was a bit half-hearted to be honest. Nugget would be the first one to concede his guard dog days were probably a good few years behind him, and he could still remember that business last year with the strange men in funny costumes. He had no intention of finding himself in the pantry covered in mouldy potatoes again.

Nugget crept across the threshold, the low growl still vibrating its way up from his gullet.

Nothing appeared to have been disturbed, but there was the smell of electrical discharge in the air.

Charlie followed his dog through the house and into the living room. 'I don't hear anyone,' he said. 'And there doesn't appear to be any sign of damage or theft from what I can tell.' He lifted his head. 'Is anyone here?!' he shouted, immediately tensing as the last syllable fell out of his mouth. 'If you are in here, I suggest you leave before I set my large and undoubtedly vicious guard dog on you!'

Nugget rolled his eyes. There was nothing like a bit of false advertising to ruin your day.

There was still no sign of movement from anywhere in the house. Charlie relaxed his shoulders a little. 'How peculiar,' he said to the empty room.

To Nugget, there was still something wrong though. The living room felt different, and he wouldn't be able to relax until he nailed down what it was. He padded into the centre of the room and began to sniff. That strange smell of electricity still hung in the air, and seemed to be stronger when he turned his head towards the bookshelf.

Nugget walked over to it and looked up.

There was the source of his disquiet. Where Max's magic green book should be there was an empty space.

'Wuff,' Nugget said by way of explanation, and looked from Charlie to the gap in the row of books.

Max's grandfather understood the message and immediately saw what his dog was getting at. 'Oh dear Lord!' he exclaimed and came closer. 'But where has it gone boy? Do you think Max took it?'

'Wuff,' Nugget commented. If Charlie could speak Labrador he would have known that the dog thought Max had nothing to do with this.

'But why would he leave without saying anything? And why leave the front door open like that?'

Nugget whined. It was as big a mystery to him.

Charlie sat down in his armchair and rubbed his chin. 'I have a feeling that there is something going on boy... and I don't think we're going to like it one bit when we find out what it is.'

Nugget laid his head on his master's lap. 'Wuff,' he said, in total agreement.

-4-

If there was one thing Peter Bloom loved to do on a Saturday morning, it was buy garden gnomes. This might not sound like the kind of hobby you'd want your friends to know about, but Peter was not the kind of man to really care what other people thought of him.

After all, you don't watch your family killed in front of you by a mad woman, escape certain death by crossing dimensions, and start a new life for yourself in a strange and alien world, without developing a very thick skin. All that was thirty years ago, and the scars had well and truly healed over as far as the boy who was once Petren Florren was concerned.

He had a good job, a nice house, and a healthy family. He'd certainly like to have more time to play golf, and would like to see more of his wayward son, but other than that, things were pretty peachy all round. There were still the nightmares. The ones where he was always choking on the thick, acrid smoke - but their frequency had lessened as the years had gone by, to the point where he could cope with them without too much stress. Where once they would keep him awake for days on end, now they were largely forgotten about by lunchtime.

And there was no Wordcraft in Peter Bloom's life anymore. For that he was whole-heartedly grateful. He had hated the never-ending lessons in the magical arts of his people when he was a child. The only Wordsmith tutor Peter had ever liked was Farran Witherbed, but he had left when Peter was still small, to act as The Cornerstone's custodian on Earth.

He'd seen the Wordsmith again of course, when the old man had looked after him in the first few years of his exile on Earth. Peter had always been eternally grateful for Witherbed's help - including the fact that the librarian had kept Peter's presence on Earth a secret from everyone until his death.

After the events that had destroyed Peter's family and his youth, he had been glad to leave The Chapter Lands and Wordcraft behind completely, vowing never to return to either.

There were few books in the Bloom household, and that was just fine as far as he was concerned.

What there were though, were plenty of garden gnomes. In the garden, anyway.

The collection had now reached somewhat ridiculous proportions, with over forty of the weird little things scattered around the edges of the lawn, buried into the flowerbeds at semi-regular intervals. Amanda hated the very sight of them, but to Peter they were quite wonderful, especially the ones based on famous fictional characters.

There had been heated arguments between husband and wife over what he was allowed to keep in the garden. What with Peter's equal obsession with old toilet bowls full of flowers, it had begun to resemble the kind of place you'd keep children away from at all costs.

Eventually Amanda had issued an ultimatum. It was either the gnomes or the toilets... not both. Peter had agonised for three whole days before reluctantly giving up the toilets. There was just no way he could sacrifice his gnome collection.

The latest addition to that collection was sat on the back seat of the car as Peter pulled into the driveway. He'd just picked it up from the garden centre outside of town and was delighted with his new acquisition.

It was a Batman gnome.

Bat-gnome, if you will.

A squat little representation of The Dark Knight, it hunched over a small pottery gargoyle with an expression that struck fear into the hearts of all criminals. The gnome-shaped ones anyway. In his head, Peter already had a place picked out for the little bugger - right on top of the compost heap, where it could look down on the rest of the gnomes and keep them in line.

He parked the car and retrieved his new prize from the back seat. Bypassing the house completely, he went round to the garden, placed Bat-gnome on top of the compost heap and stood back to admire his handiwork.

The gnome looked resplendent.

With a cheery smile plastered across his face, Peter unlocked the back door and went into the house. He went through the kitchen and into the living room.

There, tied to two dining chairs on either side of the table with gags across their mouths, were his wife and daughter. Behind them stood a ghost, and on the table was a very familiar green book.

-5-

Twenty minutes earlier Amanda Bloom answered the phone to her father, who was sounding quite... *odd*.

She was used to Charlie Pearce being eccentric, and lacing every sentence with an abundance of extraneous verbiage, but today he just seemed a bit distracted and not himself.

'Good morning Amanda,' he opened the conversation with when she answered the phone. This was the first oddity. Charlie never called Amanda by her name. She was always 'daughter of mine', 'most exalted offspring', or 'fruit of my loins'. Frankly, she could usually do without the last one, it sounded a bit creepy.

'Morning dad,' she replied. 'Are you okay?'

'Oh yes. Yes, yes, yes. Why do you ask?'

'Because we only spoke yesterday. Has something happened?'

'Something happened? Um... no. Nothing's really happened. Just wanted a quick chat, that's all.' He cleared his throat. 'Is Max there?'

Clue number two that something was up. It was never Max, it was always Maxwell.

'Is he not with you?' Amanda asked, her voice slightly raised.

'No. No, he's not.' Charlie paused for a couple of seconds. 'So you've not seen him today then? Possibly carrying a book of some kind?'

'What? No dad. Not seen him today.' She started to fiddle with her necklace. 'Is something wrong with Max, dad? Is he in some kind of trouble?' One eye twitched. 'Again?'

'Trouble? No, he's in no trouble Amanda. I was just wondering if you'd seen him today. With a book. A green book. It might have been glowing a bit.'

'Glowing?'

'Oh, it doesn't matter, my dear. I just missed him this morning before he went out and was wondering where he was.' Another pause. 'He promised to play a game of chess with me.'

'Max? Play *chess*?' Amanda gripped the phone tighter. 'What's he gone and done this time dad? Be honest with me.' Her blood ran cold. 'Has he gone and got a girl pregnant?'

'Good God no! Don't be so ridiculous!'

'Then what *is* going on?'

'Nothing! I keep telling you that. I was just ringing to see if you'd seen him that's all.' Amanda then heard the sound of muffled barking. She supposed it was Nugget, but from the sounds of things it could just as easily have been her father holding the phone away from his head and making fairly unconvincing woofing noises. 'What's the matter Nugget?' he said back into the phone. 'Oh dear! Nuggie says my waffles are burning, I'd better go Amanda!'

'Waffles?'

'Yes. Love the things. Very moorish. Speak to you later, sweetheart.'

'Okay dad. If you do see Max, tell him to come by and visit his mother. I haven't seen him all week.'

'Will do! Bye!'

Charlie banged the phone down, leaving Amanda partially worried for her father's sanity, and partially worried for Max's good standing in society.

She returned to her vacuuming in the lounge, resolving to pay her father a visit later that afternoon to get to the bottom of whatever it was that was making him sound so weird.

'Mum!' Monica called down from upstairs.

'What?' she replied with the sure and certain knowledge that she was about to be ordered to fetch something.

'Can you get me one of the milkshakes from the fridge? A chocolate one?'

'Come down here and get it yourself, you lazy little toad!' she snapped back up the stairs. 'I'm cleaning!'

Monica had reached her teenage years, and had thus turned into a malevolent demon of ill device, bent on driving her mother stark staring mad. 'But I'm doing homework!' the demon called down by way of explanation for her apparent laziness.

'And I still have to get the lounge tidied before your father comes home and messes it up again!'

'You're so unfair!' Monica shouted, immediately followed by the sound of stomping teenage feet coming towards the stairs.

'I'll give you bloody unfair madam,' Amanda whispered with gritted teeth. She felt a paper round was in Monica Bloom's near future, whether her daughter liked it or not.

Amanda's waspish mood was exacerbated by the sound of the doorbell.

'Oh for crying out loud, what now!?' she said, dropping the vacuum with a clatter and stalking across the living room and into the hall. There she narrowly avoided a collision with a stomping teenager, who huffed at her on her way past to the fridge.

Amanda approached the door. Through the frosted glass she could see a tall man in a long grey coat. If her head had been clearer and she hadn't felt so harassed, she might have paused before opening the door, given the way the figure loomed disconcertingly in the doorway. As it was, her mind was preoccupied with her father's strange behaviour and her daughter's truculence, so she threw the door open without thinking, and came face to face with the man who sought to murder her husband.

'Does Petren Florren live here?' the man said, not bothering with any pleasantries.

'Excuse me?'

'Petren Florren?' Then he clicked his fingers. 'Of course he wouldn't be called that here would he? Bloom! His name would be Bloom!'

'Do you mean my husband Peter?' Amanda said.

'Yes! Peter! Of course. Peter Bloom. He lives here then?'

'Yes, this is the Bloom residence.'

The man clapped his hands together. 'Excellent! I was worried that the residual trail of Wordcraft Max leaves in his wake wherever he goes had dissipated too much to follow. This place had the highest concentration other than the dwelling I found The Cornerstone in, so I thought it must be important to him.'

'Max?' She *knew* it! Max was in trouble and this man was here to speak to her about it. *He was probably the poor girl's father!*

'What's my son done now?' she asked the stranger, preparing herself for the worst.

'Many things, I'm sure my dear. But none of them are of interest to me. It's his father I have business with today.'

'Peter? Are you from the company then? Only it's the first day off he's had in months.' Amanda folded her arms. She thought she was on firmer ground here. 'I really wanted him to have a clean break for a few days, as he was promised. What with that Korean deal going south, he's had a terrible time of it recently.'

Randal Venhaligan stepped across the threshold and grabbed Amanda Bloom round the throat. 'Trust me woman, it's about to get a lot worse.'

Peter Bloom's legs gave out from under him. He fell back against the living room wall, his eyes locked on The Cornerstone where it sat on the dining table. Then he looked up at his wife and daughter, both tied to the chairs on opposite sides of the small dining table the Bloom family only ever used at Christmas. A moan of dismay, laced with both recognition and disbelief, escaped his lips.

Randal Venhaligan smiled. 'Now that was just the reaction I was looking for!' he crowed.

Peter tried to steady himself, both against the horrible scene in front of him and the tide of memories that seeing The Cornerstone had unleashed in his head.

'Who... who are you?' he managed to say, his attention flicking from Amanda to Monica, both of whom had eyes full of fear and confusion.

Randal actually contrived to look hurt. 'Now that's not very nice, is it? You pay an old friend from the past a visit and he doesn't even recognise your face. I admit my hair is greyer and thinner, and the lines on my face are deeper, but I still have those proud Venhaligan features, do I not?'

Now Peter's legs gave out completely and he slumped to the floor. 'Randal? Randal Venhaligan?'

'A ha! The light dawns!' Randal hung one arm around Monica, who shuddered under his touch. 'It's a real pleasure to see you again Petren. A *real* pleasure.' He squeezed Monica's shoulder. 'Now, only one question remains... which one of the people you love most do I kill first?'

Peter stretched out a hand. 'Please Randal. Please don't hurt them,' he implored. 'They've done nothing.'

'No. They haven't, have they? It's sad how the innocent have to be punished for the sins of the guilty.'

'They don't know anything about what happened Randal,' Peter said, voice quivering. 'It's me you're angry with. It's me who escaped.'

'Yes! You escaped didn't you? Fled the scene of your crime to this charmless little world and built a new life for yourself, while I lived hand to mouth back home in The Chapter Lands, starving hungry and cold.' As he spoke Randal's hand gripped Monica's shoulder tighter, making her cry in muffled pain through the gag tied across her mouth.

'I didn't... didn't know...' Peter replied.

'No! You didn't, did you? You just murdered my mother and scurried away like a rat!'

'Your mother killed my entire family!' Peter spat, anger in his voice for the first time.

Randal's hand tightened even further on Monica's shoulder. 'Steady Petren. Let's not forget who's in charge here.'

120

Peter's anger was immediately quashed. 'You're right Randal. I'm sorry. Just please don't hurt my family.'

'You love them then?'

'Of course, they mean everything to me.' Tears coursed down Peter's cheeks.

Randal leant forward. 'Not enough to tell them the truth though, eh? Tell them who you *really* are?'

'Please...'

'Not very fair, is it Petren? That your wife and daughter will die not knowing your true name? Your proud lineage? Let's rectify that, shall we?'

Randal crossed over to Amanda and ripped off her gag.

'Peter! she cried.

'Amanda! Sweetheart. I'm so, so sorry.'

'What does this man want?' Amanda asked. 'He says he *knows* you? Says... says he knows *Max*?'

Peter started with shock. 'Max? What has Max got to do with this?'

This elicited a bout of laughter from Randal Venhaligan that took a good minute to wrest under control. 'You're not serious surely?' he said, wiping away the tears of mirth. 'You're not telling me you know nothing about what your son is?'

'What do you mean?' Peter said in confusion.

'Like father like son! Both lying to their family about who they really are!' Randal slammed a hand on the dining table, which jolted The Cornerstone across its shiny wooden surface closer to Monica. 'Your son,' Randal continued, 'is the most powerful Wordsmith in Carvallen history, Petren. You should be proud!'

'Max is a Wordsmith?' Peter said in a disbelieving voice.

'Indeed he is! And without him I would never have found you.'

'Peter,' Amanda said, her voice shaking, 'what's a *Wordsmith*?'

This sent Randal Venhaligan off into another gale of laughter. 'Incredible!' he shouted with delight and smacked his hand on the dining table again. The Cornerstone jumped, and bumped against Monica Bloom's tied down hand. 'Why don't you explain to your woman what a Wordsmith is, Petren?' Randal asked. 'Why don't you try to explain who you are and where you really come from?'

Peter looked at Amanda's tear stained and terrified face. He opened his mouth, and then closed it again unable to speak.

'No? Cat got your tongue? Let me have a go at it then!'

Randal grabbed Amanda across the face and brought her head round to his. 'Your husband has lied to you for years, my dear. His real name is Petren Florren, and he is from The Chapter Lands, a place only accessible using that green book on the table there. Petren comes from a world full of magic, the kind you read about in books. He fled it thirty years ago after killing my mother in cold blood.' He now stroked Amanda's cheek gently. 'I do feel sorry for you, you know. To be lied to for so long. By both your husband and your Wordsmith son, it appears.'

'Please Randal. Leave her alone,' Peter pleaded again, struggling to his feet as he did so.

Randal's head whipped round. 'You're right of course Petren. She isn't the reason I'm here.' His eyes burned. '*You* are.'

Slapping Amanda contemptuously across the face, Randal reached out an open hand towards Peter. He word shaped, and Max's father flew back against the living room wall, his head punching a hole through the plaster.

'Peter!' Amanda screamed.

Randal crossed over to the dazed man and picked him up by the throat. 'Now *Peter*,' he said, rage burning in every syllable, 'I'm going to strangle you slowly in front of your wife and child. Let's see what gives out first. Your windpipe or their sanity.'

Amanda screamed again as Randal Venhaligan started to choke the life out of Peter Bloom.

Throughout this entire confrontation so far The Cornerstone had remained silent. It had watched developments with detached interest, taking in events as they unfolded around it.

Max's papery friend was, if nothing else, a patient creature. After all, it was made from tree pulp, and trees are extremely long lived things - until someone comes along and turns them into a book, that is. Long life breeds an enduring outlook on the world. Trees move slowly and deliberately, with the kind of persistence that can send roots into the heaviest, largest rocks - cracking them in half with seemingly no effort.

Randal Venhaligan looked like a particularly difficult rock to crack, so The Cornerstone had decided to remain quiet and wait for the right moment to act. That moment had now come.

It was the girl. She was the key here.

From the moment Randal Venhaligan had stepped into this house, The Cornerstone had sensed Max Bloom's little sister, and found the same power buried deep within her as it had in Max when he'd entered Farefield library.

She didn't quite have Max's massive reserves of natural Wordcrafting ability, but there was more than enough for it to work with, once Venhaligan was distracted enough not to notice what it was doing.

That moment came when the enraged Wordsmith had begun to educate Petren's terrified wife about The Chapter Lands.

In its dry, alien voice, The Cornerstone spoke in Monica's mind.

'Monica Bloom. I would speak with you.'

'Aahh! Who is this?!' she replied in her head, her eyes wide.

'I am The Cornerstone.'

'The what?'

'The book by your hand.'

Monica looked down at the shabby book on the dining table. 'You're a *book*? I'm talking to a *book*?'

'Yes. Please try to control your disbelief. We do not have time for it.'

Monica jumped as her father was slammed into the living room wall. 'Daddy!' she screamed silently.

'Monica! Calm yourself and listen! Your father will die if you do not do exactly what I say.'

'What?! What do I do?!'

The Cornerstone glowed silver along its edge, and its cover flipped open.

'Read Monica Bloom. Read what is written on my pages. It's time your brother was unleashed'.

Monica looked down at the strange book and read the words on its page:

Monica looked down at the shabby book on the dining table. 'You're a book? I'm talking to a book?'

'Yes. Please try to control your disbelief. We do not have time for it.'

Monica jumped as her father was slammed into the living room wall 'Daddy!' she screamed silently.

'Monica! Calm yourself and listen! Your father will die if you do not do exactly what I say.'

'What?! What do I do?!'

The Cornerstone glowed silver along its edge, and its cover flipped open.

'Read Monica Bloom. Read what is written on my pages. It's time your brother was unleashed.'

Monica looked down at the strange book and read the words on its page:

To Monica Bloom's surprise, shock and dismay, the world exploded.

Part Five

Max paced.

Then he paced some more.

To mix things up a bit, he stomped for a while. Then went back to pacing, because it suited his mood better.

'You'll wear a rut in the stone if you keep doing that,' Emerelda observed from where she stood next to The Cornerstone. They had returned it to its pedestal in the chamber at the centre of the Library, figuring that when and if Randal Venhaligan returned, it was best to keep him confined in an area they could control.

'It's been over an hour now. Venhaligan could be doing anything on the other side.'

'If he's even found your family Max,' Emerelda said. 'Earth will be a very confusing place to somebody from The Chapter Lands, even a maniac like Randal Venhaligan.'

'Men driven by vengeance rarely worry about the scenery,' Jacob pointed out unhelpfully.

Merelie got up from where she was sat in an alcove and went over to Max, taking his hand. She looked back at the others. 'There must be something we can do?'

'Only Garrowain knows enough of The Cornerstone's capabilities to even suggest a way to cross over without endangering Max or his family further,' Jacob said. 'We can do nothing until he awakens.'

'*If* he awakens,' Max replied darkly.

'He will,' Emerelda told him. 'It will take more than a monster like Venhaligan to put him out of action for long.'

'And in the meantime I get to stand here and think about all the horrible things that son of a bitch could be doing to my family,' Max said.

Emerelda's usually icy demeanour gave way to genuine sympathy. 'I know Max. I'm so sorry. I wish there was something else we could do.'

Max glowered at The Cornerstone. 'Come on, you stupid book. Help me out here.'

'That's hardly fair Max,' Emerelda chided. 'The Cornerstone can't be blamed for what's gone on here.'

'It could have put up a bit more of a fight,' he grumbled, not knowing that at this very moment it was starting a conversation with his little sister.

'It does seem a bit odd that it let Venhaligan through to Earth without fighting him more. It certainly put up more of a struggle against the Dwellers,' Merelie added.

'Agreed,' Borne rumbled. He had been his usual quiet self during this conversation about magic things he had little interest in, but when it came to matters of physical violence, he always had an opinion.

Jacob stood in front of The Cornerstone with one eyebrow raised. 'Perhaps it knows something we don't.'

'I know that if we don't do something soon I'm likely to use it anyway... and to hell with the consequences,' Max told them and went back to his pacing.

'No you won't Max Bloom,' Emerelda replied. 'You're smart enough to know that kind of decision will get your family killed, otherwise you would have done it already.'

Max didn't know what to say to that. Emerelda had him pretty well pegged. It was all very well making threats and promises in order to make yourself feel a bit better, but he ultimately knew that his hands were tied, which was frustrating to the point of immobility.

'Look!' Jacob exclaimed and backed away from The Cornerstone, which had begun to glow silver.

Max heard the chorus of a million voices all raised in song. This was the sound of The Cornerstone making its presence felt.

'Get back guys, Corny's up to something!' Max cried.

The Cornerstone's green cover flew open and lightning began to flick out from its pages, earthing itself on any surface it could find, including - painfully - the end of Max's nose.

'What is it doing?' Emerelda said as her hair burst from its usual tight bun and started dancing around in the static air.

'Something big,' Merelie responded. 'It only starts singing like that when its feeling melodramatic.'

Sure enough, the lightning started to crackle brighter and faster, sending out tendrils in all directions. They all had to back out into the aisles surrounding the chamber to avoid them.

Then, with a final exultant cry of the entire chorus, The Cornerstone spat a dazed and terrified Bloom sibling into The Chapter Lands for the second time in the space of a year.

Randal Venhaligan's hand tightened around Peter's throat. He felt a surge of triumph as it did.

After all these years of waiting, he was about to end the life of the man who had effectively ended his. Viana Venhaligan had been Randal's whole world. A cruel woman to everybody else, she doted on her youngest son, and there was nothing she would not have done for him. They had been inseparable from his birth, a duo that even excluded other members of the Venhaligan family most of the time. Colter was often heard to say (in private, beyond the ears of his wife and child) that Viana only loved two things in this world: Randal and everything Randal did - up to and including what he had deposited in the toilet. This always produced a roar of approval from Marran, the eldest son, who took far more after his father and despised his sibling's relationship with her as much as Colter did.

In truth, Randal had barely batted an eyelid when his father had killed himself, despite what he'd told Max. The same went for his brother's untimely demise under a flaming roof beam as he mounted the main staircase of the burning Florren household. But when Petren Florren had pushed his mother off the second storey balcony into the maelstrom below, he had lost his mind.

'Please...' Peter pleaded in a whisper, trying to push Randal away with one weak hand.

'Now, now, Petren. Do try to take this like a man, won't you? You don't want the last thing your wife sees to be you mewling like a newborn kitten. It just wouldn't sui - '

Behind him, Monica Bloom screamed. As she did silver light filled the room, blinding them all.

'No!' Randal raged and dropped Peter, lunging for Monica and The Cornerstone. It was too late though, the girl was already being sucked into the vortex before Randal could reach her. As he slammed into the table the girl disappeared completely, and The Cornerstone's cover slammed shut, detonating a blast of targeted Wordcraft that cannoned Randal Venhaligan across the living room, smashing into the fifty inch LCD TV that took pride of place above the mantelpiece.

The chair Amanda was sat in toppled to one side, depositing her on the ground, close to where her husband was holding his neck and gasping for breath.

'Amanda,' he wheezed painfully and crawled over to her.

She was unconscious, knocked senseless by The Cornerstone's explosive transportation of her daughter to another dimension. Peter held out a trembling hand and placed it on her neck. Her pulse was still strong and regular.

He grabbed the edge of the dining table and hauled himself to his feet. His back was agony from where Randal had catapulted him into the wall, and he could feel slick warm blood trickling from the gash at the back of his head. The worst was his throat though. It felt like trying to swallow a cheese grater.

On his feet properly for the first time since he had seen his wife and daughter tied up, Peter Bloom looked first across the shattered living room to where his enemy now stirred on the floor, then down to The Cornerstone which still sat on the table, smoking slightly.

'You bastard,' he said, with venom in his voice. It was hard to decide which one of them he was talking to.

The Cornerstone insolently flashed silver light twice in quick succession from between its pages.

In that instant, the horrors of a dark and cold night three decades ago came flooding back.

Waking from a deep sleep to feel the smoke choking his lungs...

The headlong rush along the corridor screaming for his mother and father...

The sight of Viana Venhaligan, her eyes ablaze, walking through the fire towards him...

Seeing what was left of his parents, burning like effigies on a pyre...

Saving the life of someone he should have left to burn with them...

The escape to the Carvallen Chapter House...

Sneaking into the Great Library, and the journey through The Cornerstone, with the heat of the fire still on his skin...

Petren Florren could feel the hate bubbling back up inside him now, as he stood in Peter Bloom's house, reliving the horrors of the past that he had done so much to bury deep within himself. Peter's head spun, unable to cope with the sudden influx of memory. Tears fell from his eyes, both for the family he had left behind in the ashes, and the family he had now, torn from him by both book and man.

In an act of primal rage, Peter grabbed The Cornerstone and threw it with all his might across the room at Randal Venhaligan. 'Go away!' he screamed. 'Leave us alone! I am not Petren Florren anymore!'

Randal, who had been sitting up, was struck across the forehead with the book, making him grunt in pain. A bloody gash to match Peter's appeared where the edge of The Cornerstone impacted against his temple.

'Oh no, cully. You don't get away from me that easily,' Randal admonished, shaking a finger at Peter as he rose to his feet again. He wiped blood away from the cut above his left eye and picked up The Cornerstone.

Randal strode back towards Peter, who shuffled around to put the dining table between himself and the madman who had destroyed his home. Randal threw the green book down between them and leant on the table, wiping more blood away as he did so.

'I think we should wrap proceedings up now Peter. It appears that I have outstayed my welcome.' His eyes flicked down to The Cornerstone. 'Something tells me this book disapproves of what I'm doing here.'

'That book is evil,' Peter replied.

Randal chuckled. 'For once, you and I completely agree on something.'

'It's evil because it's *Wordcraft*.' Peter spat the word out, as if disgusted to have it on his lips. 'And Wordcraft is the most hateful thing in the universe.'

'What makes you say that?'

Peter stumbled slightly where he stood. 'Because it makes men like you, and women like your mother. Because it makes families like ours.'

'And it can kill Petren. Don't forget that.'

Peter smiled. It was a smile completely devoid of humour. 'How could I Randal? How could I ever forget?'

Randal thrust out a hand and caught Peter round the throat again, this time in an invisible ligature of pure Wordcraft. 'Enough talk. Enough words. Now you die.'

Peter looked down at Amanda, who was beginning to stir, and wished he could have had one more minute in her arms before the darkness took him.

'Monica!' Max cried as his little sister popped into existence.

He ran back into the chamber and over to where she was still sat tied to the dining room chair, her head lolled back between her shoulders. He pulled the gag from her mouth, put his hands on her shoulders, and with tears coursing down his cheeks he shook her, trying to bring her back to consciousness.

'Max! Stop that! Emerelda ordered, and pushed him away. 'You'll only make matters worse. She's had a bad trip through The Cornerstone, the last thing she needs is you shaking her to pieces.'

'Is she.. is she...' he said, unable to finish.

Emerelda rolled one of Monica's eyelids up. 'No, just knocked out. Somebody get me some water, we'll try to bring her out of it.'

'Max? Who is this?' Jacob asked.

'My sister. My sister Monica.'

'But why has The Cornerstone brought her here?'

Monica's head came up and her eyes flew open. 'MAX!' she screamed. 'The book says you have to go through!' Her eyes focused for the first time on her older brother. 'It says go through Max! Mum and dad need you!'

'What's he doing to them?!' Max raged.

Monica coughed twice. 'He's strangling dad! He's killing him!'

That was it.

Time for this waiting around business to take a bloody hike.

Max retrieved The Cornerstone from the pedestal and threw it over to Borne. 'Hold it up Arma, with the cover open.'

Borne did as he was told without arguing. He knew a voice of command when he heard it.

'Max...' Emerelda said, standing between him and the book. 'What are you planning to do?'

'You said Venhaligan would kill me as I crossed over. You think he'll have much chance if I'm going at a hundred miles an hour?'

Emerelda's eyes went wide. 'That is *not* a good idea Max.'

'The Cornerstone won't let you!' Merelie agreed.

'Won't it? I think it's fairly obvious by now that The Cornerstone does what it bloody well wants. It either lets me through... or smears Borne and I against the wall when I hit it.'

Borne, veteran of a dozen battles and hardened to the point of being made of rock, swallowed hard.

'This isn't wise Max,' Jacob said, the last one to offer his objections.

'I don't care. My sister is tied up, my dad is dying and I don't know what's happening to my mother!' A hand shot out towards The Cornerstone. 'Now! Open up!'

The book's cover shot open again the instant the command left Max's mouth. He squared his shoulders, braced one leg in front of the other and started to build the kind of energy throughout his body that could have powered the national grid for a fortnight.

'Ready or not, here I come,' he whispered and shot forward like a bullet from a gun.

'By the Writer!' Borne snarled in fear as eleven stone of enraged Wordsmith came shooting towards him. He stood firm though, keeping The Cornerstone open in his hands.

The book, knowing what was good for it, screamed in a choral roar that shook the Library to its very foundations, and opened the pathway to Earth a split second before Max hit it at full tilt.

A vast percussive shockwave threw all of them to the floor as Max departed The Chapter Lands.

As the dust settled, Jacob Carvallen sat up and slowly shook his head back and forth. 'While I wish to see that murdering lunatic dealt the appropriate punishment, I can't help feeling that sending an angry Max Bloom to deal with him may be considered a disproportionate response,' he said, getting to his feet.

'I know one thing,' Emerelda told her brother. 'I'm glad I'm not over there. The mess is going to take weeks to clean up.'

-2-

There was no warning of Max Bloom's arrival.

One second Randal Venhaligan was throttling the life from Peter Bloom, the next the world became an explosion.

Max had every intention of going for Venhaligan the second he clapped eyes on him. What he had forgotten to take into account in his hasty exit from The Chapter Lands however, was the speed he would be travelling at when he reached the other side. Added to that was the fact that while The Cornerstone on The Chapter Lands side had been vertical, the other half of it on Earth was currently sat on the dining table between the two men, face up.

The practical upshot of this was that when Max came steaming into existence, he flew out of the book and immediately punched a hole right through the living room ceiling.

Then he punched a similar sized hole through Monica's bedroom ceiling.

Then the roof.

In fact, it took a good hundred or so feet for him to come to a halt, by which time he was floating high above Farefield, watching the debris blossom out below him and rain down onto the surrounding houses and gardens.

'Sod it,' Max said under his breath.

That was the problem with making grand entrances. They usually resulted in a high insurance claim.

Taking a deep breath, Max shot back towards the ground, through the holes he had made in his parent's house, and slammed down onto the dining room table. To his left he saw his father falling back against the patio doors. Below him was his unconscious mother. To his right was Randal Venhaligan, still dazed by Max's explosive entrance.

The patented finger of doom shot out. 'You!' Max said. 'I want a bloody word with you.'

Randal looked up, realised things were about to get terminally exciting and braced himself.

A wall of blistering Wordcraft hit him squarely between the eyes and sent him flying back across the living room, through the large bay window and out into the garden beyond.

Max jumped down off the table and went over to his father. 'Dad? Dad? Are you okay?'

Peter's eyes were like saucers. 'You're a Wordsmith,' he said.

Max gave him a dark look. 'No, I'm *the* Wordsmith. And when this is all over, you have a lot of explaining to do.'

Peter nodded. For the first time in his life he was quite in awe of his son... and not a little afraid of him too.

Max bent down and pulled his mother back into a sitting position. 'Mum? Are you still with us?'

Amanda Bloom looked at her son woozily. 'Max? Is that you?'

'Yeah mum, it's me.'

'Oh... oh good.' She blinked a few times, then her brow furrowed. 'You haven't gone and gotten a girl pregnant, have you?'

'What?'

Peter started to untie her. 'Don't worry son, she's just a bit overcome by everything that's happened. Is your sister okay?'

'Yes. Jacob and Emerelda can take care of her.'

'Jacob? Jacob Carvallen?'

'Yes. He's Chapter Lord now.'

Peter stopped and regarded his son more closely. 'You know about me then?'

'Pretty much dad.'

'I... I don't know what to say.'

'There will be plenty of time for that later, let's just help mum and get that son of a bitch back - *oh bloody hell!*'

Randal Venhaligan came flying back through the shattered bay window and straight at Max like an arrow. He slammed into him, sending them both flying back out through the rear patio doors, thus destroying the only side of the room left undamaged so far.

Their bodies cut an enormous furrow across the garden, spraying turf and dirt into the air. They both hit the compost heap, which was just about large enough to halt their headlong flight. A mixture of earth, dead plants and Batman gnome ruptured outwards.

Bat-gnome rocketed into the air, never to be seen again. Not by any members of the Bloom household anyway. It was discovered a week later by a small cow in a field eight miles away. The cow licked it for a few minutes before deciding that The Dark Knight didn't taste very nice and wandered off to look for some grass to eat instead.

Randal, although weakened by the various calamities that had beset him recently, was still powerful enough to give Max a run for his money. He straddled him, word shaped a ball of energy around one fist and started to repeatedly hammer the young Wordsmith about the head with it.

Luckily for Max, he was still enveloped in a protective barrier of Wordcraft, fuelled by his anger, and the blows only served to annoy him, rather than crush his skull.

He caught Randal's fist on its downwards trajectory and glowered up at the other man. 'Give it a rest, tossface,' he said and pushed upwards with all his strength.

Randal squawked in surprise as he flew a good forty feet into the air. By the time he was headed earthwards again, Max was standing up and waiting for him with one fist clenched like a goalkeeper waiting to smack the ball away from the goal line.

As Randal came within striking distance, Max launched a haymaker that connected with his enemy's midriff and sent him careering up through Monica's bedroom window.

'Get up from that dickhead,' Max muttered.

Unfortunately, get up he did about ten seconds later, coming to the shattered window and looking down at Max with an expression of utter malice.

Max groaned and prepared himself for another round.

Randal looked set to jump down and continue the fight, but his body, having been put through the wringer quite enough for one day, took matters into its own hands and told his brain to quit while it was behind. Randal's eyes unfocused and he fell back into the room, away from view.

Max sighed with relief, and walked back towards the house, trying in vain to wipe some of the mud off the front of his hoodie. He looked down to see that his Nike trainers were also covered in filth and ground his teeth.

From the shattered patio doors Max's parents emerged, holding one another up for support.

'Are you alright son?' Peter asked.

'Oh yes. I'm just dandy.' He waggled one foot. 'Have you seen these?' The pointy finger of doom came out. It was a little less severe than normal given the state his father was in, but it still carried the full weight of his displeasure. 'You're buying me a new pair of these dad.'

Amanda still looked highly confused. 'Can one of you please explain to me what's going on? Why have you blown up the house?'

Peter hugged her. 'It's okay sweetheart. Everything's going to be okay. I will explain everything to you.'

Max's eyebrow shot up. 'Really dad? Because I can't help feeling that explanations would have probably been a good idea long before now.'

Peter's eyebrow also shot up. Father mirrored son. 'I'm not the only one around here that's been keeping secrets Max.'

Amanda moaned and started to stagger back into the house. 'Where's Monica? Where's she gone? Where's my daughter!?' The hysterical note in her voice was getting louder. Now she was coming to her senses a bit, the full horror of what had gone on here today was starting to hit Max's mother hard.

'It's okay Amanda! Monica's fine!'

'Then where is she? I saw... I saw her read a book at the table. Then she disappeared.' Amanda bent down and picked The Cornerstone up from the corner of the room where it had come to rest. 'It was this book.'

Both Max and Peter suddenly started acting like Amanda had just picked up a live hand grenade. 'I think I'd better take that,' Peter said.

'No,' Max piped up in a firm voice. '*I'll* take it.' He went over to his mother and took the book from her nerveless fingers. 'Monica really is fine mum. The Cornerstone wouldn't have let anything happen to her.'

'What's a Cornerstone?'

Max held the book up. 'This is.'

'That's a book Max. How can it protect my daughter?!'

'Long... long, *long* story mum.'

Amanda broke down into tears. This was the first time Max had ever seen his mother cry like this. It was not a pleasant experience. He tried to put an arm around her to provide some comfort, but she pushed away.

'No! I want some answers Max! You and your friend have wrecked this house completely!'

'Friend?'

'Yes!' Amanda turned to look out of what was left of the living room's bay window. 'Look what you did!' Then she looked past the devastation to see the front garden full of concerned neighbours. One of them, a tall man in his late sixties, hesitantly stepped forward and looked through the ragged hole at the three of them.

'Are you alright Blooms? Only we all heard some loud noises and came out to see all this damage.'

'I've called the emergency services!' said a small woman from behind him.

Max exchanged looks with his father. The last thing they needed now was the police and fire brigade tramping all over the place.

'Everything's fine,' Peter told them. 'It was just... just a...'

'Gas explosion,' Max volunteered. 'A big, big gas explosion.'

'Yes!' Peter agreed. 'Very nasty. I'm sure the insurance claim will be huge!'

'Where is Monica?' Amanda asked the old man. 'Have you seen her Trevor?'

The old boy looked non-plussed. 'No Amanda, I'm sorry I haven't.'

Amanda looked at Max. 'Where's your sister Max?'

'I told you mum, she's safe,' Max replied, very carefully. His mother obviously wasn't quite right in the head thanks to all that had happened. This situation had to be treated with caution.

'Is she upstairs? I'll go look upstairs.' And with that Amanda turned on a heel and was off up the staircase before she could be stopped.

'Mum! Stop!' Max shouted after her.

'Venhaligan is still up there!' Peter said.

Both of them climbed the stairs after her. 'Don't worry about it!' Max called back down to his father as they reached the landing. 'I think that last punch stopped him good and proper. No way he could have recovered - '

'Don't come a step closer!!' Randal Venhaligan roared, his arm round Amanda Bloom's throat.

'Oh for crying out loud!' Max spat. 'Who is this bloke... bloody Wolverine?'

'Throw me The Cornerstone or I break her neck. Do it now!'

There was no time to argue. Max knew there was nothing more dangerous than a cornered animal. He couldn't risk arguing. He threw The Cornerstone over at Venhaligan. 'Now let her go!'

Randal smiled. 'Oh, you really are too trusting Max,' he said and tensed the muscles in his arm, ready to deliver the killing blow.

'No!!' Max and Peter cried in unison.

Before they could do anything, both men bowled over by a large black blur that barged past them, headed straight for Venhaligan and his hostage.

With a growl that could have signalled the end of days, Nugget the fat Labrador jumped into the air and clamped his huge jaws around Randal Venhaligan's arm. He immediately started to thrash his head back and forth, forcing Randal to release Amanda and stumble backwards into the bathroom.

'Nuggie!' they heard Charlie Pearce call up the stairs. 'You come back here right now!'

Nugget was having none of it. From the instant they'd turned into the street he'd known something was dreadfully wrong. Without thinking, he had bounded away from Charlie, up the garden path past the straggle of onlookers and into the house with barely a pause. He could smell the fear on Amanda Bloom from the living room and had launched himself up the stairs to deal with whatever it was that was hurting her.

Nugget pulled Venhaligan to the floor and ripped into the man's arm with his teeth. All the ghostly wolves that had been ashamed when Nugget had left the fox alone, now howled with ancient approval as he drew blood.

'Nuggie!?' Max exclaimed, unable to believe what he was seeing.

'Get off me!' Randal screamed and pushed Nugget as hard as he could against the toilet bowl. This took the wind out of the big dog, and he lost purchase on his quarry.

Venhaligan ripped The Cornerstone open, read the words on the page, and in the familiar detonation of silver light, fled back to The Chapter Lands, covered in blood and exhausted. He had vastly underestimated the entire Bloom family, and was paying for it in pain and humiliation.

Nugget saw the man disappearing into the book, as he had seen Max do so many times, and tried to follow. Sadly - or possibly luckily - for him, by the time he got there Randal was gone and the book was spent. Instead of following him across the void, Nugget head-butted The Cornerstone where it sat on the lino and gave himself a mild doggy concussion for his troubles.

'Nugget you silly dog! Come here,' Charlie said and went over to where his best friend was now sat back on his haunches, slightly cross-eyed and panting loudly.

Max gathered up The Cornerstone from the floor as Peter comforted Amanda. He opened the book and saw that the pages were blank. 'Oh bugger it,' he said in a voice of pure irritation.

'What's happened?' Peter asked.

'It's run out of bloody charge,' his son replied, flapping the book about a bit by way of explanation.

'Don't do that Max,' Charlie complained. 'It's no way to treat a book.'

'Dad? Why are you here?' Amanda said in a trembling voice.

Charlie contrived to look innocent. 'Oh, just happened to be walking past and saw all this commotion going on.'

'Just happened to be walking past?' his daughter said suspiciously.

'Yes. Just walking past...' Charlie repeated, knowing full well it sounded about as likely as the sun coming up purple tomorrow.

Amanda looked at her father's now guilty expression, then round to both her husband and son, who had exactly the same looks writ large across their own faces.

If Max Bloom's finger of doom was pointy and stern, then his mother's took it to levels of pointyness and sternosity that Max could never hope to match. 'I've had quite enough of this!' she snapped. 'You three are going to tell me *exactly* what the bloody hell is going on here! Starting with where Monica is!!'

The sound of police sirens cut through the air.

'I'm getting a tremendous sense of deja vu,' commented Charlie from where he sat on the edge of the bath.

Max nodded. 'Me too.'

Charlie pointed at The Cornerstone. 'That'll need charging if you're to follow that man back across the old dimensional void.'

'Yeah. I'd best get back to your house before we get bogged down with talking to the police.'

'I'm coming with you,' Peter said. 'I want to make sure Monica's alright.'

'Are you sure dad? I can check on her. It would mean you going back to The Chapter Lands.'

Peter grimaced. 'I know. But I can't rest until that madman is caught. I want to see it for myself. You never know, I might be able to reason with him.'

'Good luck with that,' Max said in a very doubtful voice.

'What the hell are you lot talking about?!' Amanda screeched. 'Chapter Lands?! Charging books?! Dimensional void?!'

Charlie stood up and went over to his daughter. 'There, there. I'll explain everything to you, daughter of mine. It'll all make sense.'

'Will it?' Max said incredulously.

They all heard the sound of boots crunching on broken glass coming from below them. 'Hello?' a strong male voice called up the stairs. 'Is anybody here?'

'That'll be the local constabulary then,' Charlie commented. 'I'm sure they'll be delighted to see me again.'

'Sorry Grandad,' Max said.

Charlie waved his grandson's apology away. 'No trouble Maxwell. I'll think of something to tell them. It's incredible how frequently gas explosions can happen when you need them to.'

'Good stuff.'

'Er... how exactly are we going to get away son?' Peter asked him.

Max grinned, put one hand against the bathroom window and winked as the glass burst outwards, showering the ruined garden below with even more debris. 'In style, dad. In style.' He grabbed his father by the arm, turned back to the window, drew in as much Wordcraft as he could manage from all the books in the surrounding area and shot them both out of the window and into the sky fast enough so that no-one in the street below saw them leave.

Amanda looked out of the now ruined bathroom window slack-jawed. 'Dad?' she said.

'Yes dear?'

'Did I just see my son and husband fly out of the window?'

'Yes my dear, I rather think you did.' He squeezed her shoulder. 'Don't worry, I was a little dumbfounded the first time I saw it too.'

Amanda patted Nuggie on the head as they listened to the sound of the emergency services cautiously coming up the stairs. 'This is going to take a long time to explain isn't it?' she remarked.

Charlie smiled. 'I should say so, my dear. You could probably write a book about it, to be honest.'

Nugget, ever the critic, rolled his eyes and farted.

-3-

'So you're my brother's girlfriend?' Monica asked as Merelie handed her a glass of water.

Merelie blushed. It was one thing to think of yourself as such, it was quite another for someone to say it so blatantly out loud. 'Yes, I am,' she replied, beaming from ear to ear. She tried to ignore the huffing sounds her father was making from where he stood over by The Cornerstone with Emerelda.

Monica looked around. 'And this, this is another world? Another planet?'

'Yes and no,' Merelie told her. 'It's the same planet, the same Earth. Just a different dimension.'

Monica pointed at the scuffed green book across the chamber from her. 'And that is how you cross between the two?'

Merelie smiled again. 'That's right.' She patted Monica's leg. 'You're a lot quicker on the uptake than your brother was.'

It was Monica's turn to smile, somewhat smugly. 'I've always been a lot smarter than him.' She looked at The Cornerstone closely over the rim of the glass. 'I knew he was up to something. That story he told us about getting a night job stacking shelves in Asda was a load of old rubbish.'

Merelie didn't understand what Max's little sister was talking about, but she could imagine what was going through Monica's mind right now. It wasn't every day you found out your older sibling was a powerful sorcerer who spent most of his time in another plane of reality - and was not in fact a feckless layabout with the career prospects and personal hygiene of a one-legged pig farmer.

'That man really hated my dad,' Monica then said, her expression darkening again. 'Who is he Merelie?'

'Someone very bad. Don't worry though, Max has dealt with far worse.' An unwelcome vision of Lucas Morodai and his demonic Dwellers flashed through her mind. '*Far* worse.'

'Do you think they'll be okay? Do you think they'll stop him?'

Merelie glanced over at The Cornerstone. 'I hope so. I truly do,' she said, taking Monica's hand in hers and squeezing it gently.

From where he leaned against the wall beside them, Borne let out a grunt of disgust. 'I've had it up to here with all this waiting around.'

Jacob glanced over at him. 'I share your frustrations Arma, but there is little we can do to alter the situation. If we cross over we may just make things worse. We have to trust that Max can subdue Venhaligan on his own.'

'He's not on his own. My dad is there too!' Monica told him, her voice full of fierce loyalty.

Jacob smiled. 'Indeed he is child. Two Blooms are no doubt better than one, I'd imagine.'

'Looks like we're about to find out how much better,' Emerelda said, noticing that The Cornerstone had started to glow once more.

'Prepare yourselves,' Jacob muttered, backing away.

Borne cracked his neck, slammed his fist into his other hand twice and spat on the floor. 'Consider me prepared.'

The Cornerstone's cover flipped open and disgorged a battered and bloody Randal Venhaligan in front of all of them.

'Looks like Earth didn't agree with you much,' Emerelda said to him as she began to word shape.

Randal held out his hand, which still dripped with blood from the ragged holes Nugget had put in both arm and coat sleeve. 'Stay back,' he warned them all.

'You're looking decidedly second hand Venhaligan,' Borne said. 'I don't think you've got enough in you to put up much of a fight.'

'Be quiet, you neanderthal!' Randal spat and gestured with one hand. Borne was thrown back against the stone wall behind him.

Emerelda struck out with Wordcraft of her own, but Randal parted the blow down the middle, sending it harmlessly to either side. 'I suggest you all stop trying to punch above your weight,' he snarled. 'One more move from any of you and I'll create a storm in this chamber so powerful it will kill all of us.'

'We have more than enough Wordcraft at our disposal to stop that from happening,' Jacob told him.

Randal looked at the Chapter Lord with contempt. 'Oh? Enough even to stop that pretty little thing over there from getting damaged?' He pointed one bloody finger at Monica. 'The rest of you may be able to protect yourselves from me, but I wouldn't like to bet on her chances if I chose to do something... *unpleasant*.'

'What do you want?' Emerelda asked.

'My League Book.'

'Not a chance.'

'I'm forming a sharp spear of Wordcraft in my mind as we speak, Carvallen. You want to bet you can block it before I fire it through the girl's skull?'

Merelie stepped in front of Monica. 'You'll have to go through me first.'

Randal chuckled. 'I didn't say which girl's skull, now did I?'

Jacob's eyes narrowed as he gauged the situation. Venhaligan was weakened, but still highly dangerous. They could probably take him in a combined effort, but they couldn't guarantee that the man would be subdued before hurting his daughter and Max's sister. The damage Venhaligan could do with just one word shape could be catastrophic.

'Borne, give him what he wants,' Jacob told the Arma.

'My Lord?'

'Do it Borne. But give him a League Book of our choosing. Not the one we took from his lackey at Venhallas.'

'Don't test me, Chapter Lord!' Randal said, eyes blazing.

'That is the deal Venhaligan. I am sick of the sight of you, but I also want to know exactly where you flee to so I can come find you at my leisure, when you don't have any children to threaten.'

Randal sighed. 'Very well Jacob. Hand me your book and let me leave this accursed place once and for all.'

Borne retrieved a League Book from a shelf on the other side of the round chamber. 'This one goes to a northern town called Shattingly, my Lord.'

Jacob smiled. 'A rather grey little place in the middle of nowhere. Very sparse population. It sounds ideal. Give it to him.'

Borne chucked the book at Randal who caught it clumsily.

Instead of throwing the cover open and vanishing, he put one hand on its underside and the other on top. He looked up at Jacob and smiled. 'You really are a fool, aren't you Carvallen? Haven't you learned from all this that I have a level of control over League Books you can't begin to understand?'

Blue light began to emanate from beneath Randal's hand. Slowly, the town's name disappeared from the League Book's cover. 'You see, reconfiguring a League Book isn't easy, but it is possible with enough skill and understanding of how they function.' He held up the book to show them the blank cover. 'I don't think I will be visiting the delightful town of Shattingly after all. In fact, I think I'll go wherever I damn well please!'

Now he did open the League Book, and with a cackle of triumph Randal Venhaligan was sucked into the blue light and away from the Great Library to a destination only he could know.

'Damn it all!' Jacob raged and retrieved the book from where it had fallen.

'You couldn't have known he had the ability to do that father,' Merelie said.

'Nevertheless... damn it all!'

Emerelda took the book from her enraged brother. 'So now he's gone again, and we have no idea where.'

'Perhaps the custodians could tell us where the League Book took him?' Merelie ventured.

'Only Garrowain has the ability to do that,' Jacob argued.

'Then it is just as well that Garrowain is awake again, my Lord,' said a wise old voice from the chamber's entrance.

They turned to see the head custodian standing in the doorway, leaning on young Bevens for support.

'Garrowain!' Merelie exclaimed happily.

'What have I missed?' the old man asked, looking directly at Monica Bloom with curiosity setting his eyes afire.

Max touched down in Charlie Pearce's back garden and immediately started walking towards the house, fishing his keys out of his pocket. He opened the back door, strode through the kitchen into the living room, and went over to the bookcase. Finding The Cornerstone's empty place, he slotted the book in and sat down in Charlie's ratty old armchair with a sigh.

His father came in behind him, flattening his hair down. 'Well, that was a mildly terrifying experience. I've never seen a Wordsmith with the ability to fly like that before.'

Max looked at him. 'There's never been a Wordsmith like me dad.'

Peter sat down opposite Max and put his head back against the sofa cushion. 'I think I could sleep for a week.'

'Trust me, by the time this is over, you'll want a solid month.'

Peter laughed and closed his eyes. This gave Max a chance to study his father more closely for a moment. 'So,' he said. 'Your real name is Petren Florren?'

Peter's eyes snapped open. 'It is. Though until today I hadn't heard the name in decades.'

Max looked back up at The Cornerstone. 'And here was me thinking Corny had chosen me at random. When all along it was just waiting for your son to walk into that library.'

'Is that what happened?'

'Oh yes. There I was minding my own business when I got sucked into another dimension and had to fight off a load of brain sucking monsters.' Max glowered at his father. 'At least I know who to blame for it now.'

Peter looked contrite. 'I'm sorry son. I never thought any of this would follow me here to this world. That's why I fled here through... Corny, as you call it.'

Max sat forward. 'What happened dad? What *really* happened all those years ago?'

Peter rubbed his face. 'I've tried to block it all out for so long, I doubt I could tell you the whole story.'

Max's eyes went wide as he remembered something. 'Not on your own, but maybe with a little help...' He stood up, retrieved The Cornerstone, and went over to sit next to his father.

'What are you doing?'

'Something Merelie did last year when we were waiting for Corny to charge in the Great Library. She used the book to show me her dreams. Her memories.'

'Isn't it too drained to do it right now?'

'Nah. It was something Merelie got Corny to do even when he was knackered out like now. I figure we could take a look at your memories, like we did with hers.' Max flipped The Cornerstone open. 'Put your hand here.'

Peter blanched. 'I don't know Max. That might not be a good idea. It'll dredge up a lot of stuff I don't know if I'm willing to face.'

'I *have* to know dad. I need all this to make some sense.' He offered his father a lopsided smile. 'Besides, if we encounter anything really nasty I generally just kick it between the legs and it goes away.'

Peter gave his son a look that suggested he was deeply worried for his offspring's sanity, but placed his open palm on The Cornerstone's page.

'Right Corny,' Max said, doing similar. 'I don't really know how Merelie did this, but I want you to show us dad's memories.' Max looked at his father. 'Maybe skip the really horrible stuff though, if you can.'

In response, The Cornerstone resolutely did bugger all.

Max sighed. 'I think he's being a bit temperamental.'

'You talk about it like it's alive.'

'He is. That's the first thing you have to understand if you want to get anywhere.' Max looked back down at the book. 'Look Corny, I know you've been bashed about a bit today and had to do loads of work, but I promise, when we get back home and all this is over, I'll have Garrowain give you a dust, and maybe even a nice bit of a cover wax to make you look really spiffy?'

Peter pulled down on one earlobe. 'This morning I was buying gnomes, and now I'm listening to my eldest child trying to bribe a magic book with a massage,' he said. 'There's every chance I've gone bonkers.'

Max rolled his eyes. 'You ought to spend a day in my shoes. You'd be praying for the blokes in white coats to come get you by lunchtime.'

The Cornerstone, apparently pleased with Max's offer, started to glow and writing started to appear across its pages. Max and Peter removed their hands and watched as the book filled with words.

'What's it doing?' Peter asked.

'Writing us a story,' Max told him.

Both Blooms looked down at the first line The Cornerstone had produced and began to read.

The first time my father and Xander Florren used The Cornerstone, I was there with my mother, watching excitedly as the book cover opened in a flash of silver brilliance...

'Hang on a minute,' Peter said. 'These aren't my memories.'

'No, it looks like Corny's got his own ideas on what to show us,' Max said as silver light enveloped them both. 'Brace yourself!'

-4-

The silver light died away and Max and Peter found themselves standing in a wide aisle of the Great Library.

It looked different to Max. He couldn't quite put his finger on why until he looked up and could not see the familiar thick grey mist hanging above his head.

Standing in front of them were two men both holding The Cornerstone - which was looking newer and a bit less scuffed up. Standing to one side was a man Max recognised as Garrowain, only with less wrinkles. On the other side of the two men was a strikingly beautiful woman and two young boys, one about the age of seven, the other barely four. Both were dark haired with serious expressions on their faces. The woman wore a white shirt, a tight black waistcoat and a long skirt in the darkest green imaginable. Her wealth of curly auburn hair was tied back with an elegant brooch.

'Can they see us?' Peter whispered.

Max stared at the ensemble and waved his hands around for a second. This elicited no response. 'Doesn't look like it,' he said loudly. 'This is a memory. None of them know we're here.'

'That's Viana,' Peter said, pointing to the woman.

'Right... so Corny hasn't brought us to one of your memories.' They both looked at the small boy staring up at his father. 'It's brought us to Randal's,' Max finished.

'Can't say I'm too bothered,' Peter said. 'Mine will be worse.'

Colter Venhaligan, dressed in the same dark green tone as his wife and stone-faced even at this young age addressed the small crowd assembled. 'Lord Carvallen has given Xander and I permission to travel to Earth, even if only for the briefest of periods.'

Xander Florren then spoke up in a somewhat reedy voice. 'It's a great honour for us both, and we look forward to reaching the other side, and learning more about the world that the Carvallen's preside over.' Florren was tall, thin, wearing a long pale green coat, and exhibited some features that Max saw in the mirror every time he looked into one.

Max looked round at his father. There were tears in his eyes. 'Dad?' he said softly.

'This is the first time I've seen him since...' he trailed off, unable to finish.

'Why aren't you here watching too?'

'My mother never liked us to be around Wordcraft too much. I think The Cornerstone actually scared her.'

Max thought back on everything the remarkable book had done since he had first encountered it. 'Fairly understandable,' he said.

'And so,' Colter Venhaligan continued, 'we venture to a place of magic and mystery, the likes of which few of us have seen before.'

Max did a bit of mental arithmetic in his head. Xander and Colter were about to visit Farefield in the seventies. He doubted they would discover much magic and mystery. Flared trousers and a lot of brown furniture perhaps, but definitely no magic.

'Farewell until we return!' Xander added.

Both men looked down at The Cornerstone, and disappeared in the usual silver display of light. Max idly wondered as they went, whether either would encounter any purple monsters on their way across the void.

'Daddy gone!' little Randal said, pointing a finger at where Garrowain was now reverentially placing The Cornerstone back in its slot on the shelf behind him.

Viana stroked the little boy's head lovingly. 'He has indeed my treasure, but he will return with gifts for you.'

Randal smiled and clapped his hands together.

'And will I get a gift too mother?' Marran Venhaligan asked.

Viana sniffed. 'We shall have to see, boy.'

Max's eyes narrowed. He prided himself on being a pretty good judge of character. Viana Venhaligan struck him as a right nasty piece of work and no mistake. She spoke with honey in her voice when addressing Randal, and nails when speaking to his older sibling.

Max gave poor Marran a sympathetic look.

'It was always like that,' Peter said. 'I remember she was quite awful to Marran.'

'Any ideas why?'

Peter shrugged. 'Look at them both. Marran is the spitting image of his father, Randal his mother. Maybe that had something to do with it.'

'Yeah... what an old witch.'

Peter's brow creased. 'You haven't seen the half of it.'

Silver light started to form around them again. 'Looks like we're done here,' Max observed, and they disappeared from the Library as Viana walked her two children away.

This time they were in a comfortable looking study. Smaller than Jacob Carvallen's, it was still very well appointed, featuring a wide ornate wooden desk, several expensive leather couches and walls covered in bookcases.

'Where are we now?' Max asked.

'No idea. I've never been here before.'

A door slammed open behind them and Colter Venhaligan stalked in, his wife trailing in his wake. Randal, now at least ten years old, was at her side again.

'He has no right to tell you to stop doing it Colter!' Viana spat as her husband sat down in a chair behind the desk. Viana stood on the other side, clutching Randal's hand. 'It is our right to plunder Earth for whatever prizes we desire!'

'The man thinks he rules my hand, damn him!' Colter agreed, slamming a fist on the table.

Viana drew herself up. 'What right does he have to prevent us enjoying a few trinkets? The visits to Earth are so rare, we should be allowed a few mementos!'

'Absolutely,' Colter said and opened a drawer in the desk. He brought out the Webley service revolver that Randal had shot Darel Cornelius with, and started to run a finger down the barrel, a look of undisguised delight on his face.

'No-one misses them,' Viana added. 'A few clothes here, the odd antique there... it should not be such an issue!'

'Xander is a fool,' Colter observed. 'He always sides with Carvallen. Neither sees the potential of what Earth has to offer us.' He stroked the gun again. 'What technologies it can provide us with to defeat our enemies in the other Chapter Lands.'

Max sighed. 'This is all starting to sound extremely familiar,' he said.

'What do you mean?' his father asked.

'Lucas Morodai wanted Earth for its resources as well. He was more about enslaving the population to use as a workforce, but the attitude was more or less the same.'

'Colter wanted to bring weapons over then. No wonder my father opposed him.'

'Yeah. And Viana sounded like she just wanted lots of pretty things to play with.'

Peter observed Colter's expression as he slowly pulled the trigger on an empty chamber. 'I think Colter felt much the same, you know.'

'If Xander won't come around, we may have to take steps,' Viana suggested to her husband, as she absently tousled Randal's hair. The boy didn't seem to mind.

Colter put the gun down. 'True. If he does not change his attitude towards Earth, we may have to engineer a fall from grace for him and the rest of his brood.'

'You can only do such a thing if you have the power, husband,' Viana reminded him.

Colter glowered at his wife. 'I am working on it, woman. The money I secured from the Carvallen treasury will allow me to score the trade agreements I need with the Morodai scum. And when I do, this family will rise higher than ever before. Xander will have to do as I tell him, or face the consequences.'

Max groaned. 'And there you have it. It always comes down to greed in the end.'

'And murder Max,' Peter added, unable to take his eyes off Viana as she continued to play with her child's hair.

Once again the silver light sprung up around them, signifying that The Cornerstone had showed them everything it wanted to, and they were spirited away once more.

———

This was a courtroom.

Much like the ones on Earth it had a high bench at one end, a dock in the centre, and a gallery of chairs behind, all made from a polished biege wood and embossed everywhere with the Carvallen crest.

Colter Venhaligan stood in the dock. A tall bald man of advanced age, who resembled Jacob Carvallen right down to his lack of hair and piercing blue eyes, sat in a high backed chair behind the bench. Xander Florren sat to one side of this man, along with three other men dressed in Wordsmith long coats.

Max looked around to see Viana in tears sat at the front of the gallery. One hand held Randal's, who sat quietly next to her, now a teenage boy. Marran was on her other side, a look of absolute hate on his face. The rest of the gallery was full of a variety of people, including one young man who bore a striking resemblance to Jacob Carvallen, only with a full head of hair.

'He looks better without it,' Max muttered.

'What?' Peter said.

'Nothing. This must be Venhaligan's trial.'

'Yeah. I'm here somewhere,' Peter told him and craned his neck. 'There, at the back with my mother.'

Max looked over and saw his grandmother for the first time. She had a soft pleasant face, wide brown eyes and raven black hair. Sat with her was a miniature Peter Bloom. 'You're picking your nose,' he pointed out.

'It's a trial Max. Not the most interesting environment for a young boy. Nose picking is something of an inevitability.' Peter was trying to sound light hearted, but Max could tell that seeing his mother was causing him great pain. There was a catch in his voice that was hard to listen to.

'Sounds like the case is being summed up,' Max said, to take the attention away from his grandmother.

'These crimes are extremely serious Venhaligan,' the elderly man said from his place in the high chair. 'If it weren't for Xander Florren's wit and ingenuity, your deceit would never have been uncovered.'

Max was somewhat dismayed to see that his paternal grandfather was sat there with a smug smile on his face. One that Max would very much like to have punched off. It indicated that while the Venhaligans had been the bad guys here, maybe things hadn't exactly been whiter than white on the Florren side of the equation either.

'Your words mean nothing to me Carvallen,' Colter said, chin out and chest puffed up. 'Speak your sentence and let us have done with this farce.'

'Very well,' the elder Carvallen said. 'Colter Venhaligan, you are sentenced to life imprisonment within the confines of the Chapter Gaol. You will be cut off from the word source, and your access to the books of our land is now forfeit.'

There was an audible gasp from the gallery. Max remembered just how important books were to the people of The Chapter Lands. To have them denied to you for the rest of your life must be punishment indeed.

Colter Venhaligan seemed to think so. Max could see the man's face drop in horror and his skin go as pale as snow.

Viana Venhaligan screamed from behind them and stood up. 'Curse you Carvallen! Curse you and your Florren lapdog for this injustice!' In a most unladylike manner, Viana spat on the floor directly in front of her. 'May the Writer erase you from the pages of this world,' she told the entire room.

Carvallen was having none of this. 'You will sit down and be quiet Viana, or I will lock you up next to your husband.' One of his eyebrows shot up. 'I fancy the prospect of leaving your sons with no parents at all is enough to make you hold your counsel?'

Viana immediately sat down. Her hand went to Randal's head and started to stroke his hair. The threat was well understood.

Carvallen turned back to Colter. 'Do you have any final words before the Chapter Guards take you away Venhaligan?'

The sentenced man drew himself up to his full height. 'I have no words for this jumped up court that do not speak of my contempt for it, and everyone here.' He fixed his eyes on Xander Florren. 'But I do wish my former ally the best of what remain of his days on this earth. May he - and his family - reflect on what has happened here today in the days and weeks to come.'

As threats go, Max thought this one was a bit roundabout, but Xander Florren understood its intent very well. He couldn't bring himself to look Colter in the eye. Venhaligan grunted in disgust. 'You cannot even look at the man you have doomed, can you Xander? A man of principle you may call yourself, but I think those principles have robbed you of your backbone.'

Max hated himself for thinking it, but he found himself agreeing with Randal's father. Xander Florren did not seem like a man of strong character - from the little Max had seen of him anyway.

'Chapter Guards, take this man away,' Carvallen ordered.

The clanking armoured soldiers did as they were bid, and as they carted Colter Venhaligan off to start a sentence that would end with a self inflicted knife wound across the throat, Max looked round to see what Randal's reaction to this was.

The boy was sitting contentedly as his mother twirled her hands in his hair. If he was distressed by his father being taken away, he certainly wasn't showing it.

Marran Venhaligan on the other hand looked ready to kill anyone he could get his hands on.

'What an awful day this was,' Peter said. 'Reliving it is very unpleasant.'

'Sorry dad,' Max apologised. 'I know this must be hard for you.'

Peter ran a hand across his brow. 'You have no idea son, no idea.'

Max placed a sympathetic hand on his father's shoulder as the silver light once again obscured his vision. He couldn't help feeling a little guilty for putting Peter through this, but Max was not the type to let something go until he was satisfied, even if it meant hurting the ones he loved. He sighed as he accepted this rather troubling aspect of his personality, and resolved to talk to Merelie about it once this business was settled.

From the safe environs of the courtroom, The Cornerstone now dumped them into a scene of utter chaos.

'Oh God no,' Peter said with a moan.

They stood in a long dark hallway full of choking smoke and dancing flames. The sounds of screaming could be heard coming from multiple directions.

'This is it, isn't it?' Max said in shock. 'This is the night of the fire.'

Peter leaned against a wall, not noticing that his hand went through the flames that charred the surface black. 'I don't think I can... this is too much Max. Too much.' Peter sank to his knees and put his hands over his face. When he brought them away again, they were wet with tears.

'Maybe you should stay here,' Max suggested, displaying wisdom beyond his years. 'I can go look for myself.'

His father didn't answer him directly. He just stared down the hallway towards a set of stairs at the end. 'I couldn't run fast enough,' he said, almost to himself. 'I couldn't run fast enough,' he repeated, as if lost in a trance.

From ahead of them a door banged open and Petren Florren, fourteen years old and about to become an orphan, came running out of the room and down the hallway. Max took off in pursuit, intent on seeing what the boy was running into.

Petren reached the staircase and bounded upwards two at a time. He was screaming for his mother and father as he went. Max followed, barely able to keep up.

The floor at the top of the staircase opened out onto a broad landing that to the left looked down into a large atrium two stories below, and to the right led to a grand set of double doors. Above his head Max could see a wide glass dome, similar in style to the one atop the Great Hall of Carvallen. Through it he could see a starry night above.

He looked back down to see Petren run towards the double doors, still calling for his mother and father.

Before he could reach them, they flew open, sending gouts of acrid black smoke out onto the landing. Through the smoke came Viana Venhaligan, trailing her youngest son Randal, who was coughing his guts up. The boy was covered in ash and wide eyed with terror. Viana dragged him along by one arm. Randal screamed as she yanked him even harder to get them both clear of the devastated room they'd just left.

'What have you done?!' Petren wailed.

Viana drew herself up imperiously. 'I have taken the revenge my husband promised boy! Look at what your parents brought down on themselves!!' She pointed one hand back into the room behind her. Petren ran towards it.

'No!' Max screamed, forgetting he was merely a ghost here. 'Don't go in there Petren! Don't go in there dad!' He ran after the boy, into the large master suite which was ablaze and thick with smoke.

There, on an enormous bed that burned like a bonfire, Max could just about make out the charred remains of two human bodies. He stumbled. 'Oh God,' he said, his voice breaking.

Petren Florren screamed, then screamed again.

A few terrible moments passed where both could not turn their gaze from the horror in front of them, then Petren started to stagger backwards out of the master bedroom, and into the clutches of Viana Venhaligan.

As Max followed, swearing with frustration that he could do nothing about what was happening in front of him, Viana grabbed Petren and threw him against the ornate wooden balustrade that ran around the outer edge of the landing. Such was the force with which she pushed him, Petren nearly went over the railing completely and down into the inferno that now ate the building out from under them.

'You saw them boy!? You saw how pretty I'd made them with fire?!' Viana screeched. It was obvious to Max that she had gone stark staring mad.

All Petren could do was collapse against the balustrade and cry his eyes out. Max felt his vision blurring with tears too as he looked back at the mad woman in front of him.

Viana lurched towards Petren and leaned against the balustrade beside him. Randal, still coughing and choking, fell to the floor and lapsed into unconsciousness, overcome by the smoke.

'So dies the last of my family!' Viana wailed, looking down at Randal. Her diagnosis was off though. Max could see the boy twitching and breathing quite clearly. 'All dead!' Viana continued. 'Both houses dead... drowned in blood and burned in fire!'

Viana threw her arms open and tilted her head back, her full weight against the wooden balustrade.

Max could see what was about to happen and leapt over to the woman, grabbing for one of her arms. His hand passed right through of course, but he was close enough to see the utter madness in Viana's eyes as she leaned further back and fell over the railing to her death.

Max watched as she plunged into the fires below, one of his hands still held out in a futile attempt to stop her suicide.

'Bloody hell,' he gasped and staggered back as she disappeared from sight.

Then he saw Petren stand up again and wipe a combination of tears, sweat and muck from his face. The boy came over to where Randal lay unconscious and looked down at him for a moment, as if deciding what to do.

Then he took both of Randal's arms and started to haul his body back towards the stairwell.

Max watched them go, and started to cry again as he did so. This boy, who had just seen an insane woman murder his parents, was still risking his own life to save her son. Max felt a huge burst of pride for his father overwhelm him.

To have done such a selfless thing, and to have carried the memory of this dreadful night around for so long...

Max could not take his eyes off the boy who would become his father until The Cornerstone's silver light enveloped him one final time, sending him back to the real world and away from the burning carcass of a house that was already starting to fall apart around him.

-5-

Max opened his eyes and saw his father on the floor in front of the couch, sat on his knees and still repeating the same words over and over. 'I couldn't run fast enough. I couldn't run fast enough.'

'Dad?' Max said gently.

Peter looked up at him. 'I couldn't run fast enough Max. Did you see? Did you see me? I couldn't run fast enough.'

'I know dad, I know.' Max put an arm around his father and helped him back onto the couch. Peter lapsed into silence.

'You didn't kill Viana Venhaligan,' Max said after a few moments. 'Randal lied.'

'He was unconscious. He didn't see what happened.'

'But he told me you killed her. That you pushed her into the fire.'

Peter shrugged. 'Easier for a boy who dotes on his mother to believe she was killed by another person, than to know she abandoned him when he needed her most.'

———

'Good grief,' Max said and exhaled.

The Cornerstone started to flash silver along its edge, indicating to Max that it was charged enough to send them back across the void to The Chapter Lands.

'Time to go,' Peter said looking down at the book.

Max thought about the ordeal his father had just been through, both the actual event and having to relive the whole thing again thanks to him. It was no wonder Peter Bloom wanted no part of The Chapter Lands anymore.

'Look dad, if you don't want to come, I can go alone. You don't have to.'

Peter smiled thinly. 'Yes I do Max. If only to see that Monica is okay.'

'Alright.'

Max opened The Cornerstone, took one last look around Charlie Pearce's living room and read the words on the page.

Max thought about the ordeal his father had just been through, both the actual event and having to relive the whole thing again thanks to him. It was no wonder Peter Bloom wanted no part of The Chapter Lands anymore.

'Look dad, if you don't want to come, I can go alone. You don't have to.'

Peter smiled thinly. 'Yes I do Max. If only to see that Monica is okay.'

'Alright.'

Max opened The Cornerstone, took one last look around Charlie Pearce's living room and read the words on the page.

'Daddy!' Monica cried as her father and brother materialised in front of them all. The stress of the whole day had reverted her temporarily to the little girl she once was.

Monica was up and flying over to wrap her hands around her father's neck before The Cornerstone could complete its transfer procedure.

'Don't I get one?' Max asked.

'Sod off bog breath,' Monica replied with a smile, but then did indeed give him a hug as well.

If one hug from someone you love isn't enough, then two will certainly do the trick. Merelie's arms encircled Max and by the strength in her grip, there was a chance she never intended to let go. 'Are you okay?' she asked, looking up into his tear stained face.

'Just about. Corny showed me what happened in the Florren house, when Viana killed my grandparents. It wasn't fun.'

'Oh Max,' Merelie said and hugged him even harder.

Jacob came over and held out his hand to Peter. 'It is good to see you again Petren. We all thought you were dead with the rest of your poor family.'

Peter took the hand. 'I wish I could say I was happy to be back Lord Carvallen. And please, my name is Peter now. I don't like to be called by that other name anymore.'

Jacob sighed. 'Understandable my friend.'

Max was surprised to feel slightly taken aback by this exchange. He never thought for one moment that his father would ever meet Merelie's. He'd never even considered the idea that they might already know each other if they ever did.

He was then taken even further aback when Garrowain came forward, still using Bevens for support, and introduced himself. 'A pleasure to meet you Peter,' the old man said, his voice strong and light.

'Garrowain?' Max said. 'Aren't you supposed to be in a coma somewhere?'

'I shall sleep when the opportunity arises young man,' the custodian replied. 'Right now I am needed here.' By way of explanation he held up the blank blue League Book.

Max's heart sank. 'He got away again, didn't he?'

'He did,' Emerelda said, coming forward. 'Jacob here will try to convince you it was his fault, but please do your best to ignore him.'

'Emerelda,' Jacob chided.

The ex librarian studied Peter for a moment. 'So, you're the one I have to blame for bringing this ruffian into my life then?' she said, pointing at Max.

Peter smiled. 'I am indeed. I'm very sorry.'

'Here, hang on a minute...' Max began.

'Oh calm down Max,' Emerelda told him. 'I'm just having some fun with your father.' She held out a hand for him to shake. 'Emerelda Carvallen. Pleased to meet you.'

Peter took her hand and kissed it. 'Charmed,' he said, smiling for the first time in quite a while.

Emerelda looked over at Max. 'Learn,' she said, in a pointed tone.

Merelie punched Max's arm and coughed. He took the hint. 'Er dad, this is Merelie. She's my... '

Friend? Girlfriend? Person I get up to shenanigans with, if I ever get the bloody opportunity?

'I'm his girlfriend,' Merelie said, avoiding her own father's level gaze. 'I'm very pleased to meet you Peter.' She detached herself from Max and gave him a hug. 'I'm so sorry for everything you've been through.'

Max could see Peter well up again and felt tears start to prick his eyes as well.

He held out both hands. 'Enough! This sentimental stuff is starting to get on my nerves.' He looked at Garrowain and the League Book. 'So where's Randal gone now then? I feel like hitting him in the face for a while and I need to know where he is.'

Garrowain opened the League Book. 'We do not know. This volume once went to a town in our northern province, but Venhaligan has altered it to lead somewhere else, and has managed to both keep the destination secret, and prevent us from following. His skill to reconfigure these books is beyond even my ability to counteract.'

'Bugger,' Max said.

'That pretty much sums it up,' Emerelda agreed.

Max thought for a second. 'Maybe there's something I can do?'

'What like?'

'Well, me and Corny have an understanding. Maybe I can get that thing to co-operate as well.'

Garrowain shook his head. 'I fear a League Book is not the same as The Cornerstone Max. They are simple tools, not blessed with the sentience of our remarkable friend over there.'

'Fair enough. It can't do any harm though, can it? Unless anyone has a better idea?' Max asked.

There was a collective shaking of heads.

Max clapped his hands together. 'Right then!' He took the League Book from Garrowain and looked at Merelie. 'Do you want to give me a hand? It's always been easier when you've helped me with this kind of thing.'

Merelie smiled. 'Of course.'

Max walked over to one of the empty plinths that circled the one The Cornerstone sat on, opened the League Book and propped it up. He placed a hand on the open page and Merelie did the same on the other. She closed her eyes and started to whisper quietly.

Garrowain silently came up behind them. 'I think the trick is to be calm, careful and precise with what you do, in order to get the book to tell you its secre - '

'Oi! League Book!' Max hollered. 'Where did that spiky haired pillock go? I want to smear his face across the nearest wall!'

Peter Bloom put his head in his hands. 'I do apologise,' he told the assembled crowd. 'He gets it from his mother.'

The League Book did nothing. Deliberately.

Merelie continued to whisper with her eyes closed, which wasn't easy with Max shouting right next to her.

'Right, you papery little git,' Max hissed when another few moments passed with no results. 'Don't say I didn't warn you!'

Max's hand thrust out towards The Cornerstone, which flew into it at his unspoken command. The book glowed silver happily through Max's fingers.

'I don't think that's a good idea,' Garrowain said, trying his best to remain calm.

Max smacked the League Book with The Cornerstone a couple of times to show it who was boss. 'WHERE' *smack!* 'DID' *smack!* 'HE' *smack!* 'GO?!' *smack, smack, smack.*

Garrowain threw his hands up in the air. 'Oh I give up!' he yelled and walked away.

Sadly for Garrowain's sanity, and everybody else's sense of propriety, the League Book started to blaze with blue light, as if finally scared into a response. It shuddered, squealed a bit, and slammed its cover shut in what felt like a snippy display of petulance.

Then, rather reluctantly, it wrote two words across its own cover in bold, capital letters:

HOUSE FLORREN

'Oh Writer,' Peter Bloom said under his breath.

Part Six

1

Merelie sighed and took her hand away. 'I don't know why it didn't occur to any of us sooner,' she said. 'Of course he'd go there.'

'It does seem rather fitting,' Jacob agreed.

Max stood back, eyeing the book suspiciously. 'Er, does anyone else think that was too easy?'

'Far too easy,' Borne said from the back of the room. 'It has trap written all over it.'

'Venhaligan has already sent us to the ruins of his own household, where he had men and a bomb waiting,' Emerelda remarked. 'It's no great leap to assume he'd do the same in the wreckage of your old house too Peter.'

'The man has had back-up plan after back-up plan,' Jacob agreed. 'He could quite easily have something waiting on the other side of that book, knowing we'd take the bait.'

Max didn't reply, but focused his gaze on the book's cover, deep in thought.

Peter came forward between Max and Merelie and picked the League Book up. 'He wants to finish it,' he said in a dull voice. 'He wants this over with.'

'You can't be sure of that,' Emerelda told him.

'None of you know Randal Venhaligan like I do. None of you know the family.' Peter thought of Colter and Viana both taking their lives, rather than live with the consequences of their actions. 'He's had nearly thirty years of misplaced hate consuming him from inside.' Peter looked at his son. 'This is his way of telling you to come put him out of his misery.'

Merelie stepped in front of Peter. 'You can't go Max. It'll be too dangerous. Your father might be right, but what if he's not?'

Max lifted his head and stared at the ceiling, puffed out his cheeks and closed his eyes. He thought back on what had happened in the last couple of days. It felt like years since Nugget's cold nose had woken him back at Charlie's house. He thought of poor Darel Cornelius dying in front of him from two gunshot wounds, and the sight of the bodies of his grandparents burning to a cinder on their bed.

He saw the rage in Randal Venhaligan's eyes, the insanity in the eyes of Randal's mother, and the greed in the eyes of his father.

It was the same look of avarice that Max had seen in the eyes of Lucas Morodai.

'They never stop, until *you stop them*,' he said to no-one in particular. Then he looked at Merelie. 'And right or wrong, I'm the only one with the power to do it.'

She shook her head. 'You don't always have to be the one who runs into the fight Max.'

'Yeah,' he said, taking her hand. 'I kind of am, gorgeous.' He held up The Cornerstone. 'You knew that the second I used this book for the first time.'

'You're not doing this alone Max,' Peter said. 'I'm coming with you. Maybe I can reason with Randal. Convince him of the truth.'

'He's way past believing anything you say dad. Besides, you need to look after Moanica and make sure she gets home.'

'Don't call me that Max!' Monica moaned, putting her hands on her hips in disgust.

'Borne and I will come with you,' Emerelda said. The Arma came forward as his name was called.

Max held up a hand. 'Nope. I won't have the rest of you in danger. Let's not forget, I'm the only one here with the power to rip trees out of mountains if I want.'

'A fair point,' Jacob agreed. 'Any of us would likely hinder you, rather than help.'

Merelie put her arms around him again. 'Are you really expecting me to stand here and watch you disappear into a League Book to go face a madman for the second time in a year?' she said, her voice wavering.

'Looks that way,' he replied, trying his hardest to give her a reassuring smile... and failing completely.

Max handed Garrowain The Cornerstone and turned to face the League Book.

'I probably don't need to tell you this,' Emerelda said, 'but I'm going to anyway. Be alert, be cautious, and if it looks like a trap, come back straight away.'

'Will do,' Max replied. He kissed Merelie gently on the lips, gave his father a grave look that was returned in kind, and flipped the League Book open.

He was immediately suffused in the familiar blue light display as the book started to transport him to the house where his grandparents had died. As he felt himself being sucked into the whirling maelstrom of bright light, he saw his father leap forward through the corner of one eye.

'Dad! No!' he cried, but it was too late. Peter Bloom was now also caught in the current of Wordcraft that was opening the conduit between both ends of the book.

With the cry of protest still on his lips Max felt himself catapulted forward, his father right alongside him.

2

They popped into existence standing on blackened, buckled flagstones and surrounded by charred walls.

Max looked up and it took him a few moments to realise that they were stood in the atrium he had seen in The Cornerstone back at his grandfather's house. Far above he could make out the few remaining stumps of the balustrade that Viana Venhaligan had thrown herself over. They looked disturbingly like rotten teeth.

The house was now a mere husk. Nearly everything had been destroyed, other than the thick stone the building had been made from, which had been firm enough to survive the onslaught of the flames.

Max looked at his father who was bent over double and gasping for air. 'That wasn't a good idea, dad. I can handle this alone.' He bent and picked up the League Book from where it lay on the flagstones in a thick layer of soot and dust. 'You should use this and go back.'

Peter shook his head. 'I'm staying. Randal should know the truth. I owe him that.'

'You don't owe him anything!' Max barked in frustration. 'He nearly killed you!'

'He deserves the truth,' Peter insisted. 'Don't argue with me son. I'm staying.'

Max recognised the tone of voice from the thousand or so times he'd heard it during a scolding, so he didn't push the matter any further. He tucked the League Book into his belt with a sigh and looked around again.

Max saw several hallways leading away from the blasted atrium. Most were choked with debris and rubble, so were impassable, but a couple seemed like they could be walked down without much trouble. Max guessed the layout of the two floors above was more or less the same.

They certainly couldn't be accessed from the main staircase. That was more or less gone. Max could see the remains of a couple of risers poking out from the first floor landing up to his right, but not much else.

He supposed he could always use Wordcraft to get them up there, but it might leave them vulnerable to a surprise attack and he didn't want to take any chances.

'No sign of Randal,' he pointed out. 'And a lot of places for him to be hiding.'

'Why hide at all though?' Peter wondered. 'Why not come out and get this over with?' There was a note of impatience in his father's voice that Max did not like one bit. It suggested a man not thinking clearly and likely to put himself in danger if he wasn't careful.

'I don't know. He's up to something though, you can be sure of that.' Max turned to face one of the clear corridors. 'What's down there?' he asked.

'The kitchens and the back stairs. They only go up to the first floor though.'

'Seems as good a way to go as any. Come on.'

'Maybe we should split up? Cover ground easier?'

Max shook his head. 'No way dad. I'm keeping you right where I can see you. If I let anything happen to you I'll have mum and Monica to answer to.'

Peter managed a smile. 'Okay. Lead the way then Wordsmith.'

Max rolled his eyes. 'I'm thinking of getting that put on a t-shirt. Do you reckon it'd make me look cool?'

'It could start a new fashion trend in The Chapter Lands. They could probably do with it, to be honest. They're all wearing the same old long coats they were when I left.'

'They could certainly do with opening up a Primark.' Max started towards the corridor. 'Come on, I'm feeling pretty exposed out here.'

The two Blooms walked down the long soot encrusted hallway and into the broad and ruined expanse of the kitchen. The devastation wrought by the fire continued in here. All the kitchen cabinets were burned to a cinder, but Max could see remnants of metal objects lying around, twisted out of shape by the heat of the flames. He could make out what was left of a sink, several pieces of cutlery and even a squat oven, leaning drunkenly over in one corner.

'Fire doesn't muck about when it gets going, does it?' he said in a quiet voice.

'No,' Peter replied and said nothing more.

'Looks like the staircase might be intact over there though,' Max said, looking across the empty room to a large opening in the far wall.

'It was stone as I remember. It should have held out.'

And indeed it had.

They both emerged onto the first floor, trying to walk as quietly as possible. Max was starting to get the feeling they were being watched. He was wide-eyed and alert for any signs of an ambush coming their way. So much so that without even thinking about it, he had wrapped himself in an aura of Wordcraft that extended out to encompass his father as well.

Peter felt the hair on his head start to crackle as the invisible power surrounded him. 'I've never known a Wordsmith able to put up a shield this strong over two people,' he remarked, somewhat in awe. 'You really are that powerful, aren't you?'

'Afraid so. It sounds great, but it does tend to make you a target for every nutcase who comes past,' Max moaned, moving across the blasted room they were now in and towards the main first floor landing.

Peter shook his head. 'Who'd have thought it? Me creating the most powerful Wordsmith in history. My mother would have been very proud.'

'It's probably just as well,' Max ruminated. 'I'm gonna fail most of my A Levels, so it's nice to have something to fall back on. I can fly through the air and rip a building apart... just don't ask me to write a two thousand word essay on the Industrial Revolution.'

They emerged out onto the first floor landing and looked around cautiously.

'He's doing this on bloody purpose,' Max said as they tip-toed across it, tensed for attack at any moment.

'I don't know. He was pretty banged up when he escaped,' Peter reminded him.

Max gave him a look. 'You think he's spark out somewhere and we're just going to run across him all unconscious and easy to capture?'

Peter shrugged. 'Maybe.'

'Pffft. My luck never works out like that around here dad. If there's one thing I can guarantee about my life in The Chapter Lands, it's that nothing ever happens without at least one explosion.'

'Fabulous.'

Max looked ahead and saw that the main staircase here had been blasted away by the fire as much as it had below. There didn't seem any clear way up to the second floor. Max was increasingly certain that if they were going to discover Randal Venhaligan, it would be there.

'Do we find another way up?' Peter asked. 'I'm completely fine with it if you'd rather not.'

Max couldn't blame his father for some reluctance. The second floor was where his life as Petren Florren effectively came to a terrible end. It was no wonder he didn't want to go up there again. 'I think we have to,' he told him, 'If we're going to find Venhaligan, we'll have to search everywhere.'

Peter rubbed his face with both hands. 'Okay. Then how do we do it?'

Max walked over to the edge of the balcony and looked up. 'I can use Wordcraft. We'll be quick about it. Come here and grab my shoulder.'

Peter did as his son had asked and immediately felt his feet lifting off the landing floor as his Wordsmith son propelled them upwards.

However, just as Max had predicted downstairs, this was the moment Randal Venhaligan launched his attack. He came, not from above, but below. As Max's feet came level with the second floor, he looked down to see Randal powering up towards him.

'Oh shit!' he cried as the tall, bloodied man slammed into them both.

Peter lost his grip on Max's shoulder and started to fall. He thrust out both arms and managed to arrest his headlong descent by grabbing a couple of the stunted ends of the balustrade where they poked out from the landing's edge. His breath was knocked out of him as his chest hit the edge of the landing, and he found himself dangling over the drop to the atrium floor below.

Max could do nothing to help his father as he was still being propelled upwards by Randal Venhaligan, right towards the glass dome that topped off the house.

In an ideal world - one that was slightly fairer to Max Bloom and didn't demand quite so many explosions - the glass would have long fallen in due to the ravages of both fire and time. This wasn't an ideal world though, and Max had to cross both arms above his head and let out a strangled cry as both men hit the still intact dome and burst into the blue sky above, sending a cascade of sharp glass back down into the remains of the house. Peter was lucky not to be skewered by a particularly large piece as he clambered breathlessly up onto the landing.

Randal's hands were around Max's throat and he screamed with rage as the two of them flew higher and higher in an arc that took them out over a large sprawl of overgrown gardens that surrounded the house. Randal was a bloodied mess, his face scarlet from the head wound inflicted by The Cornerstone, his clothes tattered and torn from the fight with Max that had destroyed the Bloom household.

All this had not quelled his anger though, and he lashed out now at Max, intent on killing the person responsible for his current state.

'All my plans in the dust!' he bellowed with rage. 'You have denied me my revenge, you little bastard!'

Max clawed at Randal's fingers, summoning a flow of Wordcraft to assist him. Pulling the bigger man's hands away he administered a head butt that probably hurt his forehead as much as it did Randal's. It seemed to do the trick though. Venhaligan's grip on Max was lost and he started to plummet earthwards, dazed by the blow. Max followed him down, watching his enemy plunge through a thicket of trees and hit the ground with a bone breaking collision.

Max hit the ground just beside him, his feet driving themselves a good foot into the earth with the force of his impact. He started towards where Randal lay, but before he could administer another blow, Venhaligan was up and flying at him again, grabbing him around the waist and sending them both back towards the house.

They smashed through the outer wall, sending chunks of debris in all directions. For the second time since he'd got here Max found himself in the blasted kitchen, this time flying backwards in a bear hug with a madman. They then both struck the far wall, which held up better than the first had. It stopped their headlong flight through the house with a sudden stop that would have killed anyone not wrapped in a cocoon of Wordcraft.

Max hit the deck and screamed with fury. 'Will you stop throwing me through bloody walls?!' he shouted and pulled at his torn black hoodie. 'Have you seen what you've done to this?! This is my favourite!'

Randal didn't seem to care what damage he'd done to Max's wardrobe and spun a lance of Wordcraft at him, intent on skewering him where he stood.

The Wordsmith from Earth was having none of it though. The past few hours had been trying - to say the least - and what little remained of his patience had just well and truly evaporated.

Max deflected the lance of power with a grunt, picked up the heavy squat oven from where it lay in the corner behind Randal and started to hit him repeatedly over the head with it, with much the same technique as he had employed on the League Book back in the Library.

'YOU!'

Clang!

'ARE!'

Clang!

'A!'

Clang!

'NOB HEAD!'

Clang!

The oven, having survived a fire and decades of entropy, finally gave up the fight and shattered into several pieces. Max threw away the large chunk he still held and regarded his fallen opponent.

If being punched, kicked, hit with a book and mauled by an irate Labrador isn't enough to put you out of action, then being smashed over the head with a large, stout oven certainly is.

Randal Venhaligan was out cold and twitching slightly.

Max cracked his neck and waggled the pointy finger. 'And this time, stay down!' he demanded, before stumbling out of the kitchen and back into the atrium.

Still muttering about the damage done to his favourite hooded top, Max powered his way back up to the second floor to see if his father was alright.

Peter was bruised and wheezed audibly. His jeans were ripped, and his once white shirt was now a dirty combination of grey and black smears, but all things considered he wasn't in that bad a shape as Max floated down next to where he lay on his back.

'How are things?' Peter said, looking up at his son.

Max poked a finger through a rip in his hoodie, then rubbed the back of his head where a lump had formed thanks to being thrown through the thick stone wall. 'I'd say fair to middling right now.'

'And Venhaligan?'

Max thought of the hammering he'd just given the man with an oven, and decided this was the perfect time for a pun. 'He's well and truly baked,' he uttered, with only the slightest trace of an Austrian accent.

Max then grimaced. It was an awful line to come out with. He was sure that with enough time and maybe a thesaurus he could come up with something much more clever.

That would have to wait for the time being though, as Peter was getting to his feet and looking towards the large opening that led to his parent's master suite.

'Dad...' Max began.

'I have to Max,' Peter said in a small voice, and walked over.

Max was struck with heavy deja vu. This was the second time he'd followed his father into this room, and both occasions had made his heart very heavy.

Thankfully, there was little left to remind them of what Viana Venhaligan had done in here. Fire may destroy everything in its path, but it also cleanses as it goes.

The blackened room was bare. The bed was gone and the bodies with it. The stone window frames were open to the elements, letting the wind blow through the barren space, stirring up the dirt that covered the floor.

Max walked further into the room, the wind caressing his face as he approached the window. It was extremely refreshing.

Peter did not cross the threshold. 'It seems like a dream most of the time,' he said. 'But if I close my eyes,' he did so, 'I can still feel the heat on my face and the smoke in my lungs.'

Max turned from the window. 'Then don't close your eyes dad. Keep them open and looking at the present. Let the past lie.'

Peter nodded, his eyes watery. He then gave his son a look Max was unable to decipher straight away. 'I'm very, *very* proud of you son,' Peter said with heartfelt pleasure.

Max was rather staggered by this. The idea that anyone from his family was particularly proud of him had never really occurred to him before. As far as he was concerned he was just happy when they weren't mad at him, and left things at that.

'Thanks dad,' he said, voice thick with emotion.

This was probably the moment to walk over for a hug.

The Blooms were not by and large a hugging family, so it promised to be quite awkward. This was an appropriate occasion to give it a go though, so Max started back towards his father.

Right at that moment Randal Venhaligan appeared in the doorway and grabbed Peter round the throat.

Max was indignant. 'Oh for crying out bloody flaming loud!' he yelled. 'I mean, come on! Seriously! I'm starting to feel like Sarah Connor at the end of the sodding Terminator.'

'Stay back!' Randal spat and dragged Peter out onto the landing and over to the edge. 'Try anything and I'll snap his neck.'

Max walked forward with his hands up. 'Come on Randal, give it up. Just let my dad go.'

'I don't think so Wordsmith! I will not be denied.' He put his mouth against Peter's ear. 'You knew it would come to this Petren. You knew I wouldn't rest until you were punished for my mother's murder.'

'He didn't kill your mother!' Max said in disgust. 'She threw herself off the balcony into the fire below.'

'Lies!' Randal hissed.

'It's true Randal,' Peter said breathlessly. 'You were unconscious. You didn't see what happened. *I did not kill her.*'

'No!' Randal screamed, shaking his head violently back and forth. 'You killed her. YOU KILLED HER. She would never leave me!'

'But she did Randal,' Max said in a calm tone. 'Petren isn't to blame. *You're* not to blame,' he told him, slowly closing the gap between the three of them as he did. 'It was your *mother*. She caused all of this. Why don't you let this end with her death? It doesn't have to end with more blood.'

Venhaligan's head slumped. His eyes darted back and forth. For the first time, Max could see the man moved by an emotion other than rage. Randal's eyes were glassy and there was a haunted look in them now.

Sympathy welled up from somewhere deep inside Max. This was a boy born into a family of greedy, back stabbing fools. He had been brought up by a mother who coddled him at every turn. How else was he supposed to react when that mother left him alone in a burning building to die?

Ironically, it was the very man he intended to kill here today that had been the one who had saved his life. These two should be best friends, not mortal enemies.

Max was struck for the first time in his life how the actions of a parent can irrevocably alter the lives of their children, for better or for worse. Max realised that the reason he had turned out to be one of the good guys was because he was the child of Petren Florren, who at the age of fourteen had saved the life of Randal Venhaligan, the son of his parent's killer.

Randal shook himself out of the trance and regarded Max with loathing. 'Don't try to trick me boy. I know what happened that night. My mother was pushed into the fire by Petren here.' He spoke to Peter again. 'You remember, don't you Petren? The flames? The heat?'

From below great gouts of flame burst into life, instantly filling the atrium as it had all those years ago. 'There, that should help you remember,' Randal whispered and backed up right to the edge of the landing.

'I never... I never wanted any of this Randal,' Peter gasped, clawing at the man's arm around his throat. 'It shouldn't end this way.'

'Yet it will, Petren. You die here and now.'

'No!' screamed Max, but it was too late. Randal tipped backwards in exactly the same way his mother had nearly thirty years ago. One arm still gripped Peter round the throat, and Max's father fell back with Venhaligan, eyes wide and full of fear.

Max lunged, the scream still on his lips. One arm grabbed his father's flailing hand as all three now tumbled out and over the landing, down towards the inferno raging below. He caught hold of Peter's hand, and at the same instant he unleashed a cataclysmic detonation of Wordcraft that sent a shock wave out in all directions. Randal Venhaligan's body buckled in mid air as it took the brunt of the blast, his death grip on Peter torn away by its power.

Max flailed with his other hand and found purchase as his father had earlier on one of the wooden stumps that was all that was left of the heavy wooden balustrade ringing the landing. His hand closed around it and his jaw tightened as he prepared to take the full weight of his father, who was holding on to his other arm for dear life.

Max screamed in pain as both arms were nearly wrenched out of their sockets as Peter's descent into the fire was abruptly halted.

Through the agony Max looked down at Randal Venhaligan.

The man's arms were now thrown out to either side, and a bellow of both rage and fear erupted from his mouth. The two images of mother and son falling to their doom superimposed themselves in Max's mind for an instant, before Randal was swallowed by the flames he had sparked into life with his Wordcraft.

Max felt, rather than heard, Randal's body hit the floor below. A great plume of flaming, twisting Wordcraft exploded up from the firestorm as it did, robbing the immediate air of all its oxygen, and extinguishing the flames almost instantly.

All that remained of Randal Venhaligan once the smoke had cleared was a charred body, laid out flat on top of the buckled, twisted flagstones.

Max and Peter hung in space, silently looking down at their fallen enemy and digesting what had just happened.

'Can you pull me up?' Peter then asked, turning his head to face his son.

'I don't think so,' Max replied and gasped in pain. 'My arms feel like they're about to fall off, and I've pretty much used up all my Wordcraft from the feel of things.'

'Try swinging me then. I can jump down to the first floor.'

'You sure?'

'We can't hang like this anymore.'

Max was forced to agree. He could feel the fingers of his other hand starting to slip and what was left of his energy reserves deserting him.

He began to swing Peter with all the strength he could still muster, and on the second time his father swung back over the lower balcony Max let go. Peter fell, landed a bit awkwardly, but was spared the far longer drop to the hard flagstones below where Randal Venhaligan's body now lay.

This relieved the weight on Max's arm and he was able, using what little remained of his stores of Wordcraft, to float himself back down to the first floor landing as well. His power gave out about two feet above the floor and he fell hard next to his father, twisting his ankle.

'Ow! Sod it!' he screeched and nearly fell over. His father was there for him though, catching him under one arm and keeping him from a rather ignoble tumble onto his rear end.

'Steady son, steady.'

'Thanks dad.'

Max then hobbled to the edge of the landing and looked down at Venhaligan's body. 'I suppose we'd better go and check Mr Crispy.'

'You think he could have survived *that*?' Peter asked dumbfounded.

'With this guy, I'm taking no chances,' his son replied and limped his way back towards the kitchen staircase.

There was no sign of movement from the burned body as they moved slowly across the atrium floor. Max knelt painfully down next to it and narrowed his eyes.

'Wait for it,' he said.

'I think you're giving the man too much credit Max, he's definitely dea - *Jesus Christ*!'

Randal Venhaligan emitted a long, laboured breath and was still once more.

'Told you,' Max said darkly. He studied the body for a while longer. 'I think that's it for now though. We'll have to take him back with us. I wouldn't trust this git to die here, and the last thing I want is him popping up in a few years all burned and horrible, but still looking for a fight.'

Max pulled the League Book from his belt and put it on the ground. He looked up at Peter. 'You want a last look around or anything?'

Peter's eyes did not leave his son's. 'No. I'm done with this place. Let's get out of here. Let's go home to our family.'

Max smiled with difficulty through the pain. 'I think that's the best thing I've heard anyone say all week.'

He flipped open the League Book. In a splash of bright blue light, father, son, and Mr Crispy, disappeared from the ruined hulk of House Florren, never to return.

-3-

Merelie was in Max's arms the second they reappeared in the Library.

Monica also gave Peter no time to readjust to the journey before throwing her arms around him and crying in that melodramatic way only teenage girls can truly accomplish.

Emerelda, Jacob and Garrowain all huddled round Randal Venhaligan and looked down at him. 'I gather putting across a reasoned and well thought out argument didn't work then?' Emerelda asked Max.

'Not really. Watch it though, he's still alive under all that crusty stuff.'

'Remarkable,' Jacob said. 'I'll have the Chapter Guards transport him to the infirmary, where he will be kept under armed guard... and very heavy sedation. Borne?'

The Arma stood to attention. 'I'll see to it my Lord,' he said and went to order his subordinates into action.

Garrowain bent down and placed one hand on Venhaligan's forehead. 'I would not trouble yourself too unduly my Lord,' the custodian said. 'This man's mind has been burned away. We have nothing to fear.'

'Good,' Jacob replied. 'That's the way I like my murderous lunatics. Mindless.'

Peter unhooked his daughter and went over to them. 'I'm so sorry,' he said, looking down at what was left of Randal Venhaligan. He lifted his head. 'So sorry to you all, I mean. If I hadn't fled all those years ago, if I had stayed and tried to sort things out between us...'

'He would still have hated you dad,' Max said. 'Your families... sorry, *our* families were cursed the second Xander and Colter went through The Cornerstone for the first time.'

Merelie went over to the green book where it sat on its pedestal. 'Maybe that's why it's done so much to help us. Against the Dwellers and now Venhaligan.'

'What do you mean?' Max said, joining her.

She ran a finger down its spine, causing it to flash silver along its edge. 'It felt guilty for setting them at odds with one another.'

Max's eyebrow shot up. 'Hmmm. Maybe,' he said. 'I'd like to think I get on with Corny better than any of you, and even I can't be sure what his motives are.'

This resulted in another longer flash of silver that encompassed the whole book for the briefest of moments. Max couldn't tell if it was agreeing with him, or warning him not to push it.

Several Chapter Guards clanked into the chamber, Borne leading them in. They picked up Randal Venhaligan's body with a gentleness that surprised Max and spirited him out of sight. Max expelled a relieved breath once they were gone and rubbed the back of his head again.

'Er, Garrowain,' he said to the old man, 'can you do the healing thing again? I appear to have twisted my ankle quite badly. And whacked my head. And nearly dislocated my shoulders. And been strangled. And... no, actually, I think that's about it.'

Garrowain sighed. 'I really should start charging you for this, my boy.' He smiled. 'Mind you, you've already saved me once today, so who am I to argue? Sit down in the chair and let's see what I can do.'

Max slumped into the seat gratefully.

As Garrowain got to work, Max looked at his father. 'Of course, this really isn't over yet dad. Our real problems haven't even started.'

'What do you mean?'

Max looked terrified. More terrified than he had when facing Randal Venhaligan, Lucas Morodai and the Dwellers from another dimension. 'We still have to explain all this to *mum*.'

The blood drained from Peter Bloom's face, and the enormity of the task still facing them hit him like a ton of bricks. He fell to his knees in horror. 'We're doomed,' he uttered solemnly and began to rock back and forth on his heels.

-4-

Actually, as it turned out, Amanda Bloom was too delighted to have her family back safe and sound to be angry with them. Well, to begin with anyway.

Also, Charlie had already spent a good long while explaining things to his daughter at the hospital, so she was fairly clued up about the whole saga before Max, Peter and Monica reappeared in Charlie's living room a few hours later.

Delight did rather give way to mind-bending terror a couple of days later as they persuaded her to use The Cornerstone, and travel back to The Chapter Lands with them. Jacob had offered them a luxury suite in the Chapter House to live in while their own house on Earth was being repaired. Peter had accepted graciously, which surprised Max a bit, given everything that had happened. It looked like Peter's attitude to The Chapter Lands had thawed somewhat. The family would still have to use The Cornerstone to jump back to Earth whenever they needed to, but at least they had a roof over their heads.

Charlie refused to come over though. 'I'm quite happy only ever seeing that book from this side, thank you Maxwell,' he told his grandson. 'As I've said before, I'm too old to be jumping around realities at my age. Besides, Nugget would never do it and I couldn't leave him behind, now could I?'

Which was fair enough.

So almost the entire Bloom family had crossed the dimensional void to be greeted on the other side by the entire Carvallen family, and over the next few days and weeks a strong bond began to develop between them. So much so, that by the time Peter, Monica and Amanda were due to leave for the final time about three months later, it was with some regret on both sides.

Both families walked into The Cornerstone's chamber and went over to where Garrowain stood with a broad smile on his face.

Despite the fact that several weeks had passed, it was still strange for Max to see his mother, father and sister standing with all the Carvallens under one roof.

'You will visit regularly, wont you?' Halia Carvallen said to Amanda. The two women had become virtually inseparable in the past few weeks, a fact that disturbed both Max and Merelie no end.

'Of course Halia! If nothing else, I must show you that recipe for fruitcake.'

Max groaned. The only practical use for Amanda Bloom's fruitcake was as the foundations for a large building. Unless Halia was considering an extension to the Chapter House she was likely to get a nasty surprise in the not too distant future, as well as the need for emergency dental work.

Jacob shook Peter's hand. 'It was good to have you around Bloom. I will have to come and see your collection of gnomes at some point.'

Max groaned again. This was getting worse by the minute.

'That would be wonderful Jacob. I think you'll enjoy them a great deal.'

Max leant towards Merelie. 'You think we can get Corny to conjure up some more Dwellers? I think I'd prefer that to our families acting like this.'

Merelie giggled, then her expression grew sly. 'At least we won't have to worry about introductions at the wedding,' she said.

Max Bloom died right there and then on the spot.

...well, he didn't, but there was every chance he wished he had. 'W - w - w - wedding?' he spluttered.

Merelie kissed his cheek. 'We'll talk later.' Then she whispered in his ear. 'When there will also be shenanigans.'

Max instantly forgot about weddings - which of course had been Merelie's intention. For the time being anyway.

Amanda gave her son a hug, as did Monica. Since finding out her brother was an incredibly powerful sorcerer from another dimension, she had decided that she actually liked him a lot more than she thought she did. This probably had something to do with her obsession with the Harry Potter books, but Max didn't mind being compared to a skinny weed in spectacles if it meant she didn't call him bog breath anymore.

Then Peter Bloom gave his son a hug. It was something they did more often these days.

'Thank you Max,' Peter said. 'Thank you for everything you've done. And thank you for forgiving me.'

'No need to thank me dad,' Max replied, his voice cracking a little. 'You're my dad and... I love you.' This was the first time he'd ever said that out loud to his father.

It wouldn't be the last.

The three Blooms went and stood next to Garrowain and The Cornerstone.

'You and Merelie will be around for Sunday roast, won't you Max?' his mother asked. 'I want to give that new cooker a good try out.'

'Will do mum,' Max replied with a smile on his face.

'Who would like to read the words, and send yourselves home?' Garrowain asked.

'I'll do it!' Monica exclaimed.

Max was surprised to see The Cornerstone glow gently for a moment with its usual silver luminescence.

'What does that mean?' Monica turned and asked him.

'It means it likes you,' Max replied.

'You might not be the only Wordsmith around here with the surname Bloom, Max,' Emerelda said with a grin on her face. Then she winked at Monica. 'Remember the things we practised my dear,' she said to the girl.

'I will Emmy!' Monica said excitedly.

Max's mouth dropped open as he realised what was going on. 'Hang on a bloody minute... ' he said, but Monica had already turned back to The Cornerstone and was reading the last few moments of their lives.

The Cornerstone, knowing this was a rather special occasion, burst into life with the sound of a million choral voices raised to the heavens in a breath-taking harmony.

As the three Blooms were engulfed in its silver light, the chorus approached the highest note it could - a gigantic, soaring sound full of triumph, happiness and hope for the future.

All in all The Cornerstone considered this to have been a good day's work.

Many years ago, two families had been ripped apart by hate and greed, but now two families had been brought together by love and trust, with Max Bloom the powerful link between them.

As happy endings go, it wasn't a bad one at all.

The End

173

...almost.

The pain was constant.

The agony unending.

From the moment Randal Venhaligan had fallen into the flames, his world had become a hellish torment he could not escape from.

His body was broken, his flesh scorched and melted beyond all recognition, but his mind still raged behind his charred and blinded eyes.

For longer than he could fathom he had been a lifeless prisoner in this bed - unmoving, unseeing.

But Garrowain had been wrong. What he had taken for a mind lost, was simply a mind overwhelmed by constant suffering, constant fear, constant *fire*.

And now, all Randal Venhaligan wanted was the end.

For death to finally take him.

His revenge had been denied him, but he no longer cared. Now all he desired was the peace of eternal sleep, and escape from the burning that went on day in, day out.

One dark and cold night in the Chapter House infirmary, while Max Bloom slept in Merelie Carvallen's arms following the kinds of shenanigans that middle aged British housewives write bestselling books about, a figure appeared to Randal Venhaligan in his mind's eye, cutting through the clouds of pain and flame that wracked him, providing sweet, sweet relief from the never-ending agony.

'Who are you?' he spoke silently as the figure coalesced into substance.

'I am a friend,' Lucas Morodai said, his eyes boiling with purple smoke. 'A friend who has come to set you to a *most* important task.'

'Anything,' Randal breathed. 'I will do anything if you keep the pain away.'

Morodai came closer. 'Excellent. Then awake Randal Venhaligan. Awake, and let us send Max Bloom, his loved ones, and every soul in these Chapter Lands to their deaths.'

With a smile on his charred and twisted face, Randal Venhaligan's eyes flew open and he saw the world for the first time in what felt like aeons.

Then he began to laugh, loud and strong, as thick, purple smoke started to boil and spin from both eyes...

About the author:

Nick Spalding is an author who, try as he might, can't seem to write anything serious. He's worked in the communications industry his entire life, mainly in media and marketing. As talking rubbish for a living can get tiresome (for anyone other than a politician), he thought he'd have a crack at writing comedy fiction - with an agreeable level of success so far, it has to be said. Nick lives in the South of England with his fiancée. He is approaching his forties with the kind of dread usually associated with a trip to the gallows, suffers from the occasional bout of insomnia, and still thinks Batman is cool.

Nick Spalding is one of the top ten bestselling authors in eBook format in 2012.

You can find out more about Nick by following him on **Twitter** or by reading his blog **Spalding's Racket.**

Printed in Great Britain
by Amazon